All the Pretty Little Collies

Dorothy Bodoin

A Wings ePress, Inc.
Cozy Mystery Novel

ings
ress, Inc.

Wings ePress, Inc.

Edited by: Jeanne Smith
Copy Edited by: Lynn Hanson
Executive Editor: Jeanne Smith
Cover Artist: Trisha FitzGerald-Jung

All rights reserved

Wings ePress Books
www.wingsepress.com

Copyright © 2019 by Dorothy Bodoin
ISBN-13: 978-1-61309-618-5
ISBN-10: 1-61309-618-6

Published In the United States Of America

Wings ePress Inc.
3000 N. Rock Road
Newton, KS 67114

What They Are Saying About
All the Pretty Little Collies

All the Pretty Little Collies is the twenty-eighth installment in Dorothy Bodoin's Foxglove Corners Mystery Series. Filled with surprises, twists, and turns, it is another winner that will keep you riveted until the last page.

The book begins with Jennet Ferguson, an amateur sleuth/ teacher, visiting a friend's horse ranch to take her turn caring for her friend's collies. The dogs discover a slab of raw meat tossed into the grass. Alarmed, Jennet manages to grab the meat before the dogs touch it. Worried, she has it tested by her deputy sheriff husband and discovers that it's been poisoned. Who could be trying to kill dogs in Foxglove Corners?

Heightening the suspense, Jennet learns that her friend, Annica, has seen a ghost, a young girl picking wild flowers on the site where a pink Victorian house once stood. Intrigued, she investigates the phenomenon.

As if that isn't enough to keep Jennet busy, she learns that Minta Maynard, owner of a prize-winning blue merle show dog named Sparkle, is receiving threatening messages in her mailbox. If Minta continues to show Sparkle, the collie will be harmed.

Readers will be perched on the edge of their chairs wondering how these storylines will be resolved. I highly recommend this new addition to the Foxglove Corners Mystery Series.

It is exciting to note that the collie on the cover of this new book is the author's own blue merle collie, Fantasy's Bell Bottom Blue—Layla.

—Suzanne M. Hurley
Author of *The Christmas Rose*,
The Dream Smasher and many others.

Dedication

To Roseann Cyngier, who kindly transported my blue merle collie, Layla, from Ohio to my home in Michigan, a friend bringing me another best friend.

* * *

One

The collies saw it first...a thick chunk of meat, red and glistening against the green grass that grew on Sue Appleton's horse ranch. It was impossible to miss seeing it or hearing the buzz of flies in the afternoon silence.

"Icy! Scarlet! Get away from that! Now!"

The dogs, noses to their disgusting find, didn't look up. Icy's tail was wagging.

I broke into a run. I had to reach them in time.

I did. At least I hoped I was in time and they hadn't taken a bite of the meat. How long had it been lying in the grass, an irresistible temptation to an ever-hungry canine? Had Scarlet or Icy passed the initial investigation stage? A drop of drool hung from Icy's mouth.

I swatted the flies away.

What if the meat were poisoned? Certainly it might be spoiled, depending on how long it had been exposed to the hot May sun.

Ignoring my disgust, I reached for it. Scarlet, bred and raised at the renowned Silverhedge Collie Kennel—in other words, not my dog—gave a warning growl while Icy, seeing his prize snatched away, raised his lips to expose sharp, white teeth.

Collies, deprived of a coveted treat, lose all resemblance to the gentle Lassie.

"You two—in the house!" I turned away from the angry dogs to search the meadow that separated Sue's ranch house from the woods.

I should see five more collies running through the grass and wildflowers. I saw two, Echo and the blue merle, Bluebell. Where were Tara, Reddy, and Quincy?

I called them and rolled up my sleeves, conscious of the increasing heat. I'd volunteered to take care of Sue's collies in her brief absence, sharing the responsibility with Emma Brock and Ronda Leigh, fellow members of the Lakeville Collie Rescue League, well aware of how much time and effort would be involved. I hadn't counted on suspicious meat or recalcitrant collies, though.

I waited. Bluebell and Echo were already at the back door. Presently Scarlet appeared. She sniffed the ground, her mouth still wet from the dripping meat. Quincy dashed up to Scarlet, his favorite, and executed an endearing play bow while Reddy looked on. But play time was over.

Holding the dripping roast away from my green linen dress, I led the way to the house, counting collies to be sure I had all seven.

In Sue's kitchen I found a plastic bag large enough for the meat, then dropped it inside and pulled the slider shut. That done, I washed my hands thoroughly, passed out treats, and filled water bowls. I was done. Emma would take the last shift. Which reminded me...I had to warn her.

Hastily I wrote a note telling her about the meat and cautioning her to be on the lookout for anything that didn't belong on the property when she let the collies outside.

Now I was done.

~ * ~

Jonquil Lane is one of the most beautiful roads in the little town of Foxglove Corners. In the spring, yellow jonquils, daffodils, and tulips bloom along its winding verge, providing bright contrast for the last two houses on the lane: my green Victorian farmhouse with its gable-bracketed stained glass windows and the grand yellow Victorian in its surround of old-fashioned flower gardens.

My husband, Crane, was home from his long patrol of the roads and by-roads of Foxglove Corners. I parked behind his Jeep and listened to the raucous welcome-home barking of my own collie brood. They were gathered in the kitchen on the other side of the door, ready to engulf me in wagging tails, waving paws, and cold noses.

Candy, my chief mischief maker, licked her chops. She had spied the plastic bag in my hand. Misty, the white collie, was close behind her. Halley and Star, the matrons of the pack, waited patiently to be acknowledged along with the others, timid Sky, Gemmy, and Raven.

Yes, I had seven collies of my own.

Crane stood at the sink, drying a wet mug. He hadn't changed out of his uniform yet, but that was all right. He looked handsome, tall and impressive in his tan deputy sheriff's uniform with its shining badge and his gun still strapped to his waist.

His gaze fell on the plastic bag, and a gleam found its way to his frosty gray eyes. "What do you have there, Jennet? Dinner?"

"Hardly."

"Good. It doesn't look very appealing."

I stashed the meat on the counter as far back as possible. "It might have been poisoned," I said and told him about finding it on Sue's property and whisking it away from Icy and Scarlet.

"I'll have it tested," he said.

"And if it was poisoned, we have a problem, too. Unless someone is targeting Sue."

He frowned. "It's best to be on the safe side. There must be a special place in hell for a person who'd set out poison for a dog."

"I'll have to let Camille know."

Camille was my good friend and aunt by marriage who lived across the lane in the yellow Victorian with her husband, Gilbert. She had two dogs and took care of our brood while I taught English at Marston High School and Crane patrolled the roads.

"What's really for dinner, honey?" Crane asked. "I skipped lunch."

"I wish you wouldn't do that."

"I didn't have time."

"We can finish the stew," I said, creating a menu as I went along. "I'll make biscuits and a salad. We have half a lemon meringue pie left."

"Great. I'll go shower."

I hoped I'd be able to eat. The memory of that hunk of beef rotting in the sun was as vivid in my mind as it had been lying on the lush green grass.

What if Sue's precious collies had torn into it before I reached them? Suppose they died and on my watch?

It didn't happen. Don't think about it.

Thankful that the stew was cooked and I didn't have to deal with raw meat, I brought the flour out of the cupboard. Candy placed her paws daintily on the counter, nudging the canister with her long nose, poised to catch whatever tidbit might fall to the floor.

"Candy, down!" I said.

She struck the canister with her paw. Just in case I hadn't understood her hint.

The collies could be so silly at times. They were like children, needing constant watching. I would do anything in my power to protect them.

~ * ~

After dinner I crossed the lane to tell Camille about my experience. We sat in her blue and white country kitchen with Twister, the Belgian shepherd, and Holly, the black collie, who had to make sure we were only having tea and not one of Camille's homemade muffins or coffeecakes.

The last rays of the sun struck the collection of cobalt glasses on the windowsill and turned Camille's honey-blonde hair to silver. She was the first friend I'd made in Foxglove Corners, and we'd sorted through many a problem in this room.

"That's terrible," she said. "Our dogs love beef. They can't resist it, even raw. Why once they stole a pot roast from the counter before I had a chance to serve it. They ate every bit, even the potatoes and carrots."

She smiled at the remembrance, the pride evident in her voice. This was typical of the kind of stories we all tell about our dogs, each one trying to outdo the other.

"I hope the dognappers aren't back," she added.

A band of dastardly dog thieves had descended on us during my first winter in Foxglove Corners, ultimately posing a threat to people as well as their pets. They were cunning and without scruples. Our safe little corner of Michigan wouldn't be safe any longer if their kind had returned.

"This may be an isolated incident," I said.

"You wouldn't think Sue Appleton would have any enemies. She's done so much good in the county. Look at all the collies she's rescued."

The president of our Rescue League, Sue led a relatively quiet life on her horse ranch, giving riding lessons to a group of young equestrians and caring for her dogs. I couldn't imagine Sue with an enemy either. But one never knew. Perhaps the owner of a collie she'd rescued resented her interference.

That seemed unlikely. People who surrender their pets aren't likely to look back.

"This may be an isolated incident," I said. "Whoever left that meat where animals could find it could be a demented sadist working alone."

A dog thief, on the other hand, might drop a piece of meat laced with a tranquilizer and stand by waiting to scoop up the unfortunate dog who took the bait. I hadn't seen anyone loitering near the horse ranch.

Camille refilled our cups and rested her hand on Holly's head. "Let me know if the meat turns out to be poisoned."

"I will, as soon as Crane has it tested."

"In the meantime, we'll have to beware of every foreign thing in our environment."

"That's all we can do," I said.

Two

I stood in my classroom at Marston High School trying to outwit spring fever. I was the teacher, after all, the leader of this rowdy group of juniors whose interest in American literature ranged from mild to nonexistent.

What if the view taunted us with shades of green and the warm May weather conjured images of sand, lakes, and ice cream cones? All the windows were open, and the spring breeze had the power of a siren's song. But I should be able to resist it.

Collies running on the beach at Sagramore Lake, a chocolate ice cream sugar cone...

I was the one appointed to push distraction out the window and generate enthusiasm for Ray Bradbury, a revered science-fiction writer who, one would think, spoke their language. The story was *A Sound of Thunder,* which they had supposedly read for homework. I had been explaining the butterfly effect in simple terms even though 'chaos theory' was light years beyond their capability.

Rachelle raised hand. "I don't understand how crushing a little old butterfly could keep the dinosaurs from dying out," she said.

She wore a deep blue tank top, a garment at the top of Principal Grimsley's banned list, but I wasn't about to send her to the office for that infraction. I wished I were wearing one myself instead of the navy polka dot midi-dress that fell above my ankle.

Before I could answer, Harold shouted, "It's just a story, Rachelle."

"You'll run into the butterfly effect in literature over and over again," I said. "Who likes to read science-fiction?"

About a dozen hands went up. That, of course, required a modicum of effort.

"How about time travel?" I asked.

"Like *Back to the Future*?" Rachelle appeared to be interested in the discussion, but I noticed the compact on her desk. Before long, she would be touching up her lipstick.

Still, I was happy she was familiar with that charming classic. "What if Marty McFly's parents hadn't fallen in love and gotten married?" I asked.

"Marty wouldn't have been born," Rachelle said. "Even though he was. See? It's confusing."

"That's why he was careful not to change the future. The butterfly effect."

"I get it!" Harold announced.

"Hey—deer! Guys, look!"

I didn't know who had spoken, but suddenly a third of the class rushed to the window. A deer had emerged from the wooded acreage behind the building, property owned by the school district.

Major distraction. I couldn't push this one out the window.

The rumors were true, then. We all knew that a herd of deer had moved into the woods, but I'd never seen one. Students were forbidden to trespass in the woods under pain of suspension. The more daring among them ignored the rule.

"Aw, isn't he cute?" Gail gushed.

Someone else said, "It's Bambi!"

"Hey, do you think he's hungry?"

As if frightened by human voices, the deer turned tail and disappeared into the darkness of the trees.

"Excitement's over," I said, as students returned to their seats with marked reluctance.

How could time travel and Ray Bradbury outshine a deer sighting? *Your job is to see that they do.*

"Who knows what an anachronism is?" I asked. Who can find...?"

The bell rang, cutting me off in mid-sentence. I hadn't noticed the time, which was a rarity in this class where the hour hand often seemed to move backward.

My class exited in a cacophony of noise and shouting.

Distraction had won today, but there was always tomorrow.

~ * ~

Because our lunch period was only twenty minutes long, with five minutes tacked onto each end for travel time to and from the cafeteria, my good friend and fellow English teacher, Leonora, and I often ate in her classroom or mine.

As soon as weather permitted, though, we took our lunches outside to the courtyard where only teachers could dine amidst spring flowers, ornamental trees, and the fountain maintained by the Bio-ecology Club. Even a prosaic sandwich tastes better when eaten out of doors.

Because we took turns driving the hour-long distance from Foxglove Corners to Oakpoint, I'd already apprised Leonora of the chunk of beef at Sue's horse ranch. By now I was convinced it had been poisoned. Still concerned, I brought it up again.

Leonora, who had two collies, preferred to look on the bright side. "Maybe someone just lost track of her groceries."

She pushed back a strand of long blonde hair and unwrapped her sandwich. Lunch meat on pumpernickel bread. Someone else's lunch always looked better than mine.

"I think there's more to it than that," I said. "If a roast somehow fell off the back of a truck, wouldn't it still be in the wrapper?"

"Not if a creature had gotten to it."

"Then he abandoned it?" I asked. "Not likely."

I continued to torment myself with a variety of 'what if's.' Suppose I hadn't noticed the meat. Minutes earlier I'd been tossing a Frisbee for Tara, who hadn't mastered the concept of retrieve. If we'd continued the game, I wouldn't have wandered over to the corral to visit Sue's horse, Sunshine. Scarlet or Icy would have gobbled up the meat.

I'd called Emma Brock early this morning to check on the dogs. They were all right, and she hadn't seen anything untoward around the ranch. I could relax. That is, until the bell called us back to the stuffy building for our afternoon classes.

Leonora took a packet out of her brown bag. "Have a brownie," she said.

~ * ~

On the way home, Leonora decided it was too nice an evening to chain ourselves to a stove. I was easily led astray. Usually I prided myself on serving Crane hearty dinners every day, but my husband was remarkably easy to please. When I substituted restaurant take-out dinners for homecooked ones, he never raised an objection.

Of course not just any restaurant food would do. We always frequented Clovers, a charming little eatery in a wooded section of Crispian Road where the owner, Mary Jeanne, provided good old-fashioned comfort food and the most delectable baked goods in Foxglove Corners.

We agreed to stop at Clovers. I had an ulterior motive. My friend and sometime partner-in-detection, Annica, combined her waitress job with English classes at Oakland University. I knew she'd be working this afternoon; and there she was, filling the dessert carousel with a variety of pies and cakes, all cut in generous slices. Now I'd have to bring home dessert, too.

She looked up and smiled, which set her earrings jingling. They were clusters of orange shells to complement her red-gold hair and orange dress. She looked the same as ever, pretty and radiant, but something was wrong. A certain sparkle was missing from her eyes. Annica without her sparkle was practically unrecognizable.

We'd arrived well before the dinner hour, which meant she would have time to chat with us while Marcy, her fellow waitress, waited on customers.

She set the last cake onto the tier. "Is this another no-cook night?"

Leonora blushed. A relative newlywed, she still felt a twinge of guilt about serving a restaurant dinner to her husband, Jake, a twinge that didn't stop her from doing it.

"This is the first time I've been here this week," I said. "I'm dog sitting for Sue Appleton for a few days. It doesn't leave me any time to cook."

"I can recommend the ham dinner with asparagus and yams," Annica said. "I just had it for lunch."

As she led us to a booth that offered a view of the Crispian woods with their shades of bright new green, I prepared to segue into my tale of poisoned meat. Annica motioned to Marcy, her fellow waitress, and joined us.

"Marcy will bring us tea and apple pie," she said. "I have something to tell you."

Something? Not good, I thought. She didn't look particularly happy. I hoped nothing had gone awry in her relationship with Brent Fowler. Annica was enamored of Brent, Foxglove Corner's premier entrepreneur, fox hunter, and perennial bachelor. In a sense, they were perfect for each other, in spite of a certain age difference and level of experience.

But that was their business.

"What happened?" I asked.

"Yesterday I saw a ghost in the wildflower field," she said.

Three

For a moment no one spoke. Then Leonora said, "But Jennet is the one who sees ghosts."

Annica's voice held the slightest trace of pride. "Well, yesterday, *I* was the one who did."

In a sense I wasn't surprised at her revelation. The wildflower field was located on Huron Court, a road on which the unwary traveler could suddenly find himself in a different season and catapulted into the past or future. The wildflowers flourished on the site of a pink Victorian house that had burned to the ground. Shortly after the fire, Brent and Annica had cleared the area of rubble, added topsoil, and planted thousands of seeds.

However tempting the prospect of viewing the fruits of their labor, I had resolved never to set foot on that bedeviled road again. I had to content myself with pictures taken by my friends.

"What exactly did you see?" I asked.

Before Annica could answer, Marcy appeared with our tea and apple pie. "Enjoy the pie. It's still warm. Take your time, Annica," she added and left to wait on her next customer.

When she was out of earshot, Annica said, "I didn't tell Mary Jeanne or Marcy. They'd think I was crazy."

I broke off a piece of apple pie with my fork. Annica lowered her voice, and I leaned forward, unwilling to miss a single word of her story.

"Since the weather warmed up, I've been driving out to the wildflower field," she said. "Everything is so colorful and lush. The wild violets came back. They're as gorgeous as ever."

They had bloomed during the first season, although neither Brent nor Annica had planted them. That, however, was another story.

"Yesterday I took my camera," she said. "I saw a girl in a white dress picking flowers. She already had a handful of them. Her face was turned away from me, and her hair fell almost to her waist. It was dark brown.

"I yelled at her to stop. We don't want strangers tramping through the field and stealing our flowers. That's Brent's private property. He even put up a 'No Trespassing' sign."

"Did she stop?" Leonora asked.

"No, she didn't even look my way. It's like she hadn't heard me. So I yelled again, but she just kept adding to her bouquet. I decided to confront her, to demand that she leave, when a thick white fog came out of nowhere."

Mist and fog were common on Huron Court. As they usually went along with ghostly apparitions, I thought I knew what was coming next.

"It was the strangest fog," she said. "It seemed to settle just around her, nowhere else, and it thickened. Then it dissipated. Just like that!" Annica snapped her fingers. "The girl was gone."

Leonora shuddered and held her hands around the hot mug. "I'd have been terrified. What did you do then?"

"What could I do? I took my pictures and went on to class."

"Are you sure she wasn't still there, hiding behind a tall plant?" I asked.

"I thought of that. She wasn't."

"And you didn't imagine it?" That was Leonora.

"I saw her as clearly as I see you," Annica said. "Only from a distance. But I know what I saw."

"Could she have left the field under the cover of the mist?" I asked.

"I don't see how. And it wasn't a natural mist. It didn't last that long."

"A white dress in a white fog," Leonora murmured. "It'd be easy to mistake what you saw."

Annica ignored her. "Ever since that happened, it's all I can think about."

"I assume you told Brent," I said.

"Sure. He wants to see her, too."

Annica glanced at her pie. She hadn't touched it. But she took a sip of tea, staring toward the door where an incoming customer had set off the clover wind chimes' delicate music.

"I don't understand why she appeared," Annica said. "Just to pick flowers? What was she going to do with them?"

"Don't ghosts sometimes linger on earth to take care of unfinished business?" Leonora asked.

"Sometimes," I said.

"Then the ghost's business was to pick flowers?"

This sounded incredibly frivolous, but then so did the entire conversation. Except we were in Foxglove Corners, where natives spoke freely about the denizens of the world beyond.

"She could also be reliving a scene from her life," I said. "A happy one or a traumatic experience, like her death."

After a moment, Annica said, "At first I wondered if I was looking at the spirit of Violet Randall."

That was possible. Violet had lived in the pink Victorian and after her death was believed to walk on Huron Road with her collie. Was believed to? I had seen her myself, albeit from afar.

"I never saw Violet," Annica said.

I smiled at Annica's claiming the ghost in the wildflower garden as her own. Obviously she wasn't frightened. Not at this point. Not like Leonora.

"You and Brent did such a fantastic job turning that burnt-out acre into a garden that even the ghosts are coming to see it," I said.

She smiled. "We did well, didn't we? I'm going back every chance I get. I want to see her again. Jennet, will you help me understand why she returned to earth or maybe never left it."

I set my tea cup down with more emphasis than necessary. Annica knew about my vow to stay away from Huron Court. She had also experienced its power but had no qualms about returning to the site.

"I don't know what I can do," I said. "You know I can't go to the— the source."

"Yes, but I thought you could help me find out who she is."

I thought about Annica's request. Until recent years, the pink Victorian had stood on the land where the wildflowers now grew. Had the ghost girl once visited Violet in her home? Or had she come from another part of Foxglove Corners, lured by the vibrant flowers as any living person would be?

She could have come from anywhere. From any time.

"Tell me what you want to me do, and I'll do it," I said. "As long as I don't have to drive or walk on Huron Court."

She nodded. "Thanks. Let me think about it for a little while."

~ * ~

The gentle breeze that had blown in Oakpoint turned into a robust wind in Foxglove Corners. It whipped the trees into a frenzy and stripped petals from the tulips and fragile daffodils that grew along the lane.

I parked in the driveway and walked toward the barking of my collies, glancing as I did at the weeping cherry tree Crane had planted last spring. Its pale pink blossoms were a poignant reminder of the fleeting nature of spring and of another spirit, a dog who had come back to Foxglove Corners to look for his family, only to find them gone.

The apparition had proved to be a forewarning of danger for me. To issue a warning of impending death could be another reason for a spirit to visit the earth.

That possibility had obviously not occurred to Annica. It hadn't occurred to me until now; and in truth, what Annica had seen, a girl dressed in white gathering wildflowers, seemed too mild, too peaceful, to be a warning of coming disaster.

Now if she had seen a black-clad crone with a scythe cutting her way through the wildflowers, that would be different. That would be ominous.

I was glad I'd only thought of it now. Annica was intelligent. Sooner or later she would figure it out for herself. Let her enjoy her first ghost sighting and not worry about dire events to come.

Four

The roast was laced with arsenic.

Even though I'd expected positive test results, hearing the news still shocked me. Now I could only hope the tossing of tainted meat on Sue's ranch was a random act rather than the work of a sick individual who would likely strike again.

Once more I resolved to keep an eye on my seven collies, especially Candy, who would eat anything in her path.

At this inopportune time, Raven showed signs of wanting to live outside in her dog house again. While recovering from a broken leg, she had been content to stay inside during the day and sleep with the other dogs at night. Suddenly the small house Crane had built in imitation of our Victorian farmhouse was the only place she wanted to be.

"She can't stay outside," I said to Crane. "Especially now, with a poisoner on the loose."

Crane agreed with me. "She's going to object."

"We'll have to retrain her, then."

"It's for your own good," I said to Raven, who must have sensed that we were talking about her. She lay her head in my lap and gazed at me. I wished I could make her understand why running free was now forbidden. I would have to steel myself to listen to her whining. It would be like having a new puppy in the house.

How long would it take before she was used to the new regime?

All I could do was pray it would be soon.

~ * ~

By the time Brent Fowler called to invite himself to dinner, which was unusual as he preferred to drop in unannounced, I had gotten over my aversion to working with raw meat. Both Crane and Brent loved beef. I'd taken a standing rib roast out of the freezer to defrost and put it in the oven as soon as I came home.

Brent never arrived at our house empty handed. He always brought flowers or wine for us or, sometimes, candy. He remembered the dogs with treats from Pluto's Gourmet Pet Shop. Tonight's offerings were a spring bouquet and small tarts baked especially for canines. They were filled with venison.

He liked nothing better than to feed the dogs himself. Needless to say, the collies adored him.

Brent was a handsome man with dark red hair the shade of a certain maple leaf in autumn, complemented by a light jacket of his favorite color, forest green. With his lord-of-the-manor air and characteristic bonhomie, he was the personification of everything that was wonderful about Foxglove Corners—the woods, the lakes, the ponds, and the hunt mentality.

Treats dispensed, wine poured, and roast checked on, we repaired to the living room to wait for dinner to finish cooking. Brent sat in the rocker and patted his knee, which was Misty's invitation to leap into his lap. Sky, normally timid but not with Brent, lay at his feet as devoted as if she belonged to him.

"Did Annica tell you about the ghost?" he asked.

"She told Leonora and me, and I told Crane," I said.

"What do you make of it?"

I didn't know how to answer him. Finally I said, "I believe her, of course. A ghost is exactly what you'd expect to find in a field on Huron Court."

"I think she saw the spirit of Violet Randall. It's a sign that Violet approves of what we did on the land."

"I'm sure she does," I said.

"I want to see her too, but all I've seen there are flowers. It's funny. After Annica told me about the ghost, I took a walk through the field. When we planted it, we left rows, but some of the vines have covered them. Anyway, Annica claims the ghost picked a ton of flowers. I didn't see any empty spaces."

I thought about that. "Those flowers are probably growing so close together you wouldn't miss them."

"Maybe that's it," he conceded.

"She told me the ghost had a handful of them."

"I guess you have to be there at the right time to see Annica's ghost," Crane said.

Brent grinned. "Yeah. Twelve o'clock midnight on Halloween."

"Annica saw her in the daytime, and it's May," I reminded him.

"It freaked her out," Brent said.

"Really? I didn't get that impression."

Now that I thought about it, though, I recalled Annica's diminished sparkle and her request that I help her identify the apparition.

"She wants me to try to find out who she was— in life," I said.

"How the Sam Hill are you going to do that?"

"I have no idea.

No sooner had I said that, though, than I thought of my friend, Lucy Hazen. Lucy wrote horror novels for teenagers, and she possessed an impressive knowledge of the supernatural, as well as certain unique talents. The future often revealed itself to Lucy, either in the patterns formed by tea leaves in plain white cups or in premonitions which were often vague but nonetheless helpful.

"I'm going to ask Lucy's advice," I said.

Brent nodded. "I should have thought of that. Tell me again, Jennet. Why won't you go near Huron Court?"

"I'm afraid. After the last time, I don't want to take a chance on being lost in time again. Once was enough."

"It happened to Annica and me, too," he said. "But we went right back. Got right back on the horse, as they say."

I reached over to touch Crane's arm. "I won't risk losing everything that matters to me."

"Take the sheriff with you," Brent said lightly. "If you don't come back, I'll adopt your dogs."

After our recent rescue of the lost Silverhedge collies, Brent already had a full house of collies, along with his gigantic guard dog, Napoleon.

"It's good to know you'll step in and raise our brood if anything happens to us," Crane said.

I had a feeling he wasn't talking about our being swept out of our time, but about everyday calamities such as diseases and accidents. Such as his being shot in the line of duty, which had happened once before.

The subject matter cast a pall on our evening. Talk of the supernatural and future tragedy can have that effect on a conversation. I needed to get away for a moment.

"I know you guys are hungry," I said. "I'll see if the roast is done."

Roast? Tail wagging, Candy jumped up and followed me into the kitchen.

I peered into the oven. It was perfect. Not too well done but certainly sufficiently cooked. I had never eaten rare meat and certainly wasn't going to start now.

~ * ~

After dinner, Brent mentioned Lucy Hazen again. One of Lucy's novels, *Devilwish*, had been made into a movie, filmed mostly in Foxglove Corners. It was scheduled to premiere in Lakeville in July. Several of us planned to attend the premier as a group to support her.

"Lucy thought about having a party after the show," Brent said. "But I talked her out of it. We're going to celebrate *Devilwish* with a nice dinner at the Hunt Club Inn. This way she won't have to do anything but enjoy the evening. Can you be with us, Sheriff?"

"I'll try."

"It'll be something to look forward to," I said.

A happy event. For one day we could leave the specter of a poisoner and a strange new ghost behind.

While Brent began to talk about the latest exploits of the Hunt Club, I thought about what dress I'd wear and what jewelry. The Hunt Club Inn was *the* place to go in Foxglove Corners. I wanted everything about the night to be perfect.

Five

The next day after school, I visited Sue at her horse farm. Emma had already told her about the poisoned meat, but Sue wanted to hear the story again from me. She came out to the car to meet me, followed by her seven collies, who were prancing around her feet in their race to welcome their visitor.

As we walked to the house, a brisk spring wind blew Sue's strawberry blonde hair in her face. She brushed it back with her hand furiously as if it had launched an attack on her.

"Let's get out of this infernal wind," she said, calling her dogs to heel. We took refuge inside the house in the family room. Sue had started a fire in her wood burning stove, even though it was spring.

"I can never thank you enough, Jennet, for being there and being alert," she said. "I could have lost all of them."

"I'm glad I saw it in time."

"Tell me everything," she said. "I want to hear every last detail."

She sat on the edge of her rocking chair with Scarlet and Tara at her feet. Bluebell and Icy lay close to me, while the other dogs formed a half circle around the stove.

"I was playing Frisbee with the dogs," I said.

When I'd finished the story, Sue said, "Look. I'm shaking." She closed one hand around the other. "Just the thought of a chunk of poisoned meat anywhere near my babies..."

I knew how she felt. Last night I'd dreamed of steaks scattered in our flower beds. Easy for human eyes to miss, but a dog could detect their presence in moments. Candy, my chief chow hound, was the first to gobble up a steak. The first to die. I saw her body clearly, still and silent, her essence drained out of her.

I didn't see the poisoner but heard a fiendish, unnatural laughter.

In the dream, I was frozen, as immobile as a stone statue. One by one the collies found the steaks and devoured them. I woke with tears in my eyes.

It's only a dream, I told myself. *A nasty nightmare. I won't let it happen.*

"We have to find out who did this," Sue said. "He has to be punished."

Again someone was giving me a task without an easy answer. Not that I didn't agree with Sue. I'd like nothing better than to see the wretch pining away in a prison cell. But first he'd have to be caught, then tried, then sentenced.

"I don't know how we can find him," I said. "All we can do is make sure it doesn't happen again. That means constant vigilance."

"An end to our free and easy way of life. I'll never again just open the door and let the dogs out without watching them. But it's worth it to keep our collies safe."

She revealed a seldom seen vengeful streak. "I'd like to feed whoever did this a strychnine burger. See how *he* likes it."

Hell hath no fury like a woman whose dogs have been threatened or hurt.

"I'm going to make us some tea," she said. "There's something I need to talk to you about. Oddly, it sort of ties in with what happened."

"Another case of poisoned meat?" I asked.

"Not exactly, but close. I'll be right back."

While Sue brewed the tea, I took advantage of the rare opportunity to rest for a few minutes without having to do anything except admire

Sue's beautiful collies: Icy, Bluebell, Echo, and the Silverhedge dogs we'd all worked together to rescue.

She came back with the teapot and two tall mugs on a tray.

"I heard about this just before I went away," she said. "You'll remember I've often spoken about our collie network."

"Your secret society," I said. "You never talk about the members."

"That's the best way to know what's going on in our part of Michigan. Behind the scenes, so to speak. It's how I knew about that awful woman's plan to euthanize the Silverhedge collies in time for us to rescue them."

I knew about the network's existence and didn't mind not being in the loop as Sue was always willing to share relevant collie-related information with me.

"There's a young woman in Oakpoint, Minta Maynard. She has a young blue merle collie, Sparkle. Every time Minta shows Sparkle, she beats the competition."

"That doesn't sound like a problem."

"Here's where the problem comes in," Sue said. "Somebody must be jealous of Sparkle's wins. Last month Minta received a message warning her about the dangers of letting a dog compete in shows. Specifically, it mentioned the possibility of exposure to canine flu."

"That's true," I said. "But people will never stop entering their dogs in shows, and what does it have to do with poisoned meat?"

"A few weeks ago, she received a second warning, telling her to withdraw her dog from all future competitions. Both messages were printed and dropped in her mail box."

"That sounds like it came from a fellow competitor," I said. "And it's illegal for a citizen to use a mailbox for personal messages."

"I advised her to list everyone who had a collie competing against Sparkle."

"That would be a long list," I said.

"Minta has a few ideas about who might be behind the threats. She needs help, though."

In the ensuing pause, I could imagine what was coming next. I took a long sip of tea— fortifying tea— and waited.

"That's where you come in," Sue said.

"What can I do?

"Help Minta find out who's sending these messages. She's desperate."

"Has she withdrawn Sparkle from shows?" I asked.

"She has, but showing a fine collie like Sparkle has always been her dream. It's hard to give up a dream."

I understood that, but how much harder it would be to see a cherished dog murdered by an individual who wanted to eliminated the competition. Anyone like Sue whose collie had come close to death would understand that.

As for Minta Maynard, if I were in her place, I'd give up my dream without a backward glance. Even though the messages were a bit strange and vague.

"I already have a lot on my plate," I said. "Trying to track down the person who left the poisoned meat where your dogs could find it, and Annica..."

There I stopped. At present the ghost in the wildflower field was Annica's story to tell. She might not want it known.

"I might be able to help you with Minta," Sue said. "I probably know some of the people she associated with at the shows. But I don't have your talent for solving mysteries."

Sue was well aware of the benefits of flattery. I, however, didn't want to overextend myself, and I feared that might happen. Still, I was curious.

"Do you think there's a connection between the poisoned meat and the messages?" I asked.

Sue sought the solace of Icy's stove-warmed fur. It helped her to focus; I understood that.

"That occurred to me, but Sparkle is a show dog. My collies— yours too— are rescues."

"But no less loved."

"No, of course not. Sparkle stands in the way of a competitor's ambition. Wasn't there some talk of poisonings connected with Westminister a long time ago?"

"I think so," I said. "I can't remember any details. I guess I can talk to Minta."

"She lives in Oakpoint where your school is. I told her you were the best."

"I didn't realize you knew her."

"We've met. How would it be if I invited her out to the farm some day after school this week? She could fill in the background."

"As long as you understand I can't promise results," I said, "but okay. Give me a call when she'll be here."

~ * ~

At home I cooked dinner for my husband who would be home soon and took care of my collies. Tomorrow I'd be back in Oakpoint giving my students the English skills necessary to navigate the world. And tomorrow I'd be grappling with three puzzling matters.

It seemed I couldn't escape my reputation for solving mysteries and helping dogs in peril. Often the two went together.

Well, Sue and I and our like-minded friends were the Lakeville Collie Rescue League. We were dedicated to protecting our own collies from a sadistic poisoner and stopping a threatening bully in his tracks, whatever was necessary in a certain circumstance.

But, when had the sport of showing dogs, which should be fun for owner and dog alike, become infiltrated with evil? What happened to good sportsmanship?

The answer was simple: it had been replaced by an all-encompassing devotion to Self. All that matters is what *I* want. Proof that my dog is better than your dog. And if the so-called sportsman had to resort to cruelty, so be it.

I didn't want my world to be like that. Therefore, I couldn't *not* help Minta Maynard.

Six

The next day after school, after tending to my dogs and making sure the area around the house was free of dangerous substances, I drove to Sue's horse ranch. I'd been thinking about Minta Maynard's dilemma off and on all day. In her place, I would stop showing Sparkle immediately, but I'd still want to know who had threatened my dogs.

The guilty party might decide to harm Sparkle, no matter what Minta did.

I had gone over and over the gist of the messages Minta had received. While they weren't as blatant as meat laced with poison, they were still worrying.

Minta was sitting on the porch with Sue surrounded by collies, a pretty young woman in light blue denim whose dark brown hair fell to her shoulders. Her smile was friendly, and, I sensed, genuine. We collie lovers have a way of recognizing one another and form an instant bond.

She clasped my hand in a warm grip. "Sue has been telling me about your exploits, Jennet," she said. "I'd be so grateful if you would help me."

I could imagine that conversation. Sue embellishing every one of my adventures even those that were already sufficiently harrowing.

Minta had probably been convinced I'd be able to solve her problem even before meeting me.

How to redirect her focus?

"We're the Lakeville Collie Rescue League," I said. "We all work together. Take Scarlet."

I called her, and she happily bounded up the stairs to me. Collies never forget.

"Scarlet was trapped in an untenable situation," I said. "She landed in Collie Heaven."

Minta laughed softly. "I can see that."

"The other collies are rescues. They all have their stories."

They were on or near the porch with us— Icy, Bluebell, and Echo who'd been living on the ranch when the Silverhedge collies joined them. The blue merle, Blue, rescued with them, had found a loving home in Maple Creek as did Wonder, who'd had a litter of puppies.

"Sit down, Jennet." Sue slid a light wicker chair toward me, then poured iced tea into a tall glass and added an orange slice. "And drink up. Help yourself to the sugar." She handed me a silver teaspoon whose long handle was perfect for stirring sugar into iced tea or swirling ice cubes.

"The weather is so weird," she said. "I had a fire yesterday. Today I'm roasting."

"It's cool here on the porch."

Some years we took a giant step into summer with only a few days of spring weather, going from light jackets to sleeveless blouses in twenty-four hours. But I wasn't about to complain. Our winter had been long and hard, and after long hours of being confined to a school, it was heaven— yes, people heaven— to sit back and see blue sky, green grass, and beautiful collies.

"I was hoping to meet your Sparkle," I said.

"I left her at home where she'll be safe, but here's our picture."

It lay on the wicker table, Minta smiling proudly, her arm around a stunning blue merle whose name was perfect for her. The collie's eyes, her gorgeously marked coat, every hair—it all sparkled.

"I've been paranoid since the messages came," Minta said. "If somebody wants to harm a dog, he's going to find a way to do it."

"Even if you don't enter Sparkle in a show—which is what the note writer wants?"

"The threat was made. It's out there."

Rather it was in her purse, leather with denim trim to match her skirt. She handed me two pieces of paper. Apparently Sue hadn't gotten the messages exactly right. The first said:

Canine flu has been spreading rapidly from one dog to another. You can't count on your dog remaining healthy if you take her to a show.

The second was a bit more specific:

If you don't want trouble, keep your dog out of the shows.

"They're not exactly death threats but they're ominous," I said, "and strange."

But what the writer said was true.

"That's what I thought, and I'm afraid there'll be more to come."

"Wouldn't it be smart to heed the sender's advice?" I said.

"Sparkle's first owner wanted me to take her as far as she could go. I promised to do that. I *want* to do that. I won't give in to a bully."

I suspected Sue hadn't given me all the details. Well, Minta would. If I were going to help her, I'd need every fact available—and a hearty dose of good luck. At the moment I had no idea how to proceed.

"I take it you didn't raise Sparkle from a puppy," I said.

"No, but I've had her for six months. She belonged to a neighbor of mine, Nessa Whitman, who passed away last winter. We lived on the same street and got to be friends when she was walking Sparkle. Here's something I didn't tell you, Sue. Nessa left ninety thousand dollars to Sparkle for her care and entry fees for shows."

I set the ice in the glass spinning with my tall silver spoon. Had Minta just handed me a major clue? It seemed so.

"If Sparkle were to meet with an accident, where would the money go?" I asked.

"To me, but believe me, I don't want it for myself. I have a great teaching job lined up for the fall."

"And, if you'll forgive me for being nosy, you don't have any student loans to repay?"

She blushed. "I was lucky. I had scholarships all the way. I'm counting on having many happy years with Sparkle," she added.

"We were just about to go over Minta's suspect list," Sue said.

Minta drew a small notebook out of her purse. "My first suspect is Jeff Whitman, Nessa's nephew. He thinks he's entitled to his aunt's money. He expected to inherit it."

Apparently there was much more to the story. I leaned forward, eager to hear it.

"Did she give him any reason to think he'd inherit the money?" I asked.

"It's all in his head. He was her only relative, but Sparkle was her love. Jeff has been living in California ever since he graduated from college. He came back for the funeral, but now he's staying on...for a vacation, he says."

Without rushing to respond, I considered.

"My first impression was that the messages came from a competitor. Does Jeff Whitman show collies?"

She shook her head. "He doesn't even have a dog."

"Then why would he care whether you show Sparkle or not?"

She shrugged. "Maybe he figured if something happened to Sparkle, he'd get the money."

"Doesn't he know it's coming to you?"

"That I don't know. I didn't tell him. But where else would it go?"

She turned a page in the small notebook. "I wrote down the names of some of the people I see at the shows. They're friendly on the surface, but no one ever says a nice word about your collie."

That was typical of a certain type of competitor. It was as if he believed that a compliment directed to another collie would subtract a point from his own dog. Talk about poor sportsmanship. That was one of the reasons I never wanted to get on the show ring merry-go-round with my first collie, Halley, the only one of my brood I'd purchased.

Minta handed the notebook to me. She'd written about thirty names. Thirty suspects? This might turn into a bigger project than I'd first thought.

"Where do we start?" I asked.

"There's a show next weekend. I'm entering Sparkle. I thought you could go with me and see if anyone acts suspicious."

"Are you certain you want to do that?" I asked. "You realize you're using Sparkle as bait."

"I won't take my eyes of her. Not for a second. She'll be perfectly safe."

"If you say so."

I thought it odd, though, that Minta had left Sparkle at home where she'd be safe, yet she was doing exactly what the message writer had warned her she shouldn't do.

I glanced at Sue. She was stirring her iced tea slowly and frowning. Quite likely she was remembering the poisoned meat left in an area she'd considered perfectly safe. In my view, a dog's life was too precious to risk in this manner. 'Perfectly safe' didn't exist.

"I have a younger cousin, Randi," Minta said quickly. "We'll both watch Sparkle, and I'll keep track of anyone who starts a conversation with me, no matter what it's about."

She had a plan, albeit one fraught with danger. She didn't really need my help. Except she wanted moral support and felt I would be able to discover the identity of the threatener.

The few facts she'd given me had piqued my curiosity. Then, too, I wanted to do my part to keep Sparkle safe, even though, in spite of my passion for collies, attending dog shows wasn't on my list of favorite activities.

"Tell me where the show is and the time," I said. "I'll be there."

Seven

We saw the wildflower field in the morning sunlight under a clear blue sky. Traces of mist lingered over the waves of color, but no one would ever describe the area as haunted or even mysterious. It was simply lovely and unexpected.

A plant with lacy green leaves and pink flowers had entwined itself around the base of Brent's 'No Trespassing' sign. The way it was growing, it would soon hide his message.

I was so entranced by the vibrant color shining through the many shades of green that I almost forgot I was standing on Huron Court, the accursed road that had a fragile hold on time. But Crane was at my side. I could never forget that. Foremost Deputy Sheriff of Foxglove Corners, armed and alert, he wouldn't let me slip away into another century or dimension.

If I had the slightest hint that was about to happen, I would grab his hand and take him with me.

"I remember the pink Victorian the way it was when I first saw it," I said. "I was walking up Huron Court and heard a dog barking..." So long ago.

The elegant house had burned to the ground, leaving an unsightly mess behind. Brent had bought the acreage and with Annica's help planted wildflowers, turning this section of the road into a genuine showplace.

"I don't see a ghost," I said. "I wonder if Annica saw that tall white flower and let her imagination run away with her."

I pointed to a flowering plant that towered over its neighbors. It looked like Queen Anne's Lace that had been drenched with Miracle-Gro—and sunlight and soft spring rains.

"Is that what you think, honey?"

I reconsidered, realizing I was being unfair to Annica. She had never doubted one of my otherworldly sightings. Nobody had.

"Well, no," I said. "Annica isn't the type to look at a white flower and see a girl gathering a bouquet."

But she had seen fog. White fog.

"There's no ghost here today," Crane said. "It didn't know we were coming."

I could scarcely believe we were here. It was Saturday, a typical weekend day for me, a work day for Crane.

Before leaving for his patrol this morning, he'd said, "I'll come by at noon and go with you to Brent's garden."

I was surprised and happy that he'd remembered and added a visit to the wildflower field to his schedule.

"Now that I'm here, I'd like to see the violets," I said.

They were a genuine curiosity. Neither Annica nor Brent had planted them. Still they'd grown and reseeded themselves, a deep purple flower that resembled an African violet, only larger. None of us had been able to identify it.

"I'm going to check out Annica's ghost," Crane said.

I looked at him, not understanding at first.

"The white flower," he added.

A sensation rippled through me. Anxiety? Something more potent?

"Shouldn't we stay together?" I could hear my tremulous voice with the note—very faint—of apprehension in it.

"We *are* together."

I couldn't argue with that.

"Brent and Annica left rows so people could walk through the flowers," I said. "But it's hard to see where they are."

"The plants are too close together."

"Or growing too..." I thought of Jack's beanstalk, considered describing them as 'unnatural,' and settled for, "They're too lush."

Crane bent and pushed a wandering stalk out of the way. "Here's a path. Do you have your phone?"

I nodded.

"So do I. Let's take plenty of pictures."

A good idea. I doubted we'd come this way again.

~ * ~

Violet Randall, who had lived in the pink Victorian with her family, had been murdered on Huron Court. Afterward, or so it was said, she walked on the road with her collie.

I had seen her a long time ago, so long that sometimes I thought I'd seen a part of the moving fog disappearing around a curve. The fuzziness of the memory was the result of my effort to push Huron Court out of my mind.

I couldn't remember who first suggested that the strange flower no one remembered choosing had been planted by Violet (in spirit form) where her house once stood. It made sense, though.

I found the violets with ease. They were cornflower blue, tall, and full, nestled together. They were certainly eye-catching but not exactly as Annica had described them. She'd said they were darker, more purple than blue.

I reached down to touch a petal. Not to pick it. Never. That would be a sacrilege. I just wanted to feel it. The violet was like sun-touched velvet beneath my fingers. It would look so pretty in a vase on my table...

I straightened up, dismayed. Had I almost broken its stem with my fingernail? What was I thinking?

Move on, I told myself. *There's more to see in the field than Violet's plant.*

As my eyes swept the area, my heart skipped a beat. Where was Crane? I couldn't see him.

Panic moved in. Blind, painful panic. Had I been catapulted into another time, held in thrall by the magic violet? Leaving Crane behind in the here-and-now?

The sensation of loss, of being flung out of my rightful place in the universe passed as quickly as it had appeared.

I saw him. He was where he'd said he would be, at the white flower he called Annica's ghost. He must have knelt down, only temporarily out of sight, to examine something on the ground. An insect, maybe, or a small creature.

I lost no time in joining him, unmindful of tramping down wandering stalks. Not until I reached him did my heartbeat resume its normal pattern.

I wouldn't tell him about my moment of panic. It was too minor, a quick-moving blip on the screen, too insignificant to mention.

"Did you take a picture of the violets?" he asked.

I patted the deep pocket of my denim skirt. The phone was still there. I hadn't lost it in my dash through the field. In truth, I'd forgotten about picture taking.

"They're a lighter shade of blue," I said.

"These aren't the same as the ones Brent saw last summer."

"No. They're their descendants."

He had something in his hand, something that glistened in the sun.

"What did you find?" I asked.

"A watch with a pearl band," he said. "Three rows of pearls. I thought it was a bracelet. It doesn't look like it's been here long."

"It's pretty. Someone was trespassing in the field and lost it."

"Who? Annica's ghost?"

His eyes gleamed with humor. I smiled and pointed out the obvious.

"Ghosts don't need to tell time. No, I'm thinking of a real woman who couldn't resist picking flowers."

"Brent can put up all the signs he wants," Crane said. "He'll never be able to keep people out of the field."

I took the watch from his hand and brushed a speck of dirt from the pearls. "Whoever lost it will want it back."

"Probably. It was only by luck I spotted it. I almost stepped on it."

We would probably never know who had lost the watch. And if Crane left it in the field, no one would be likely to find it.

"I'll keep it for now." I slipped the watch into my pocket along with the phone. "Actually, I'll keep it for always."

It felt heavier than I thought it would be, and I felt suddenly uncomfortable. It had grown increasingly warmer. The sun beat down relentlessly on my head and bare arms. I should have worn a hat and a blouse with long sleeves. I blotted away the moisture at my throat and between my breasts with a tissue.

It wasn't only the heat.

"It feels like rain," Crane said, scanning the sky.

"It feels threatening."

"How do you figure?"

I couldn't explain it. As far as we knew, the wildflower field didn't have a resident ghost. That is, we hadn't seen evidence of one today. But there was something...It had insinuated itself into the heat and the heavy fragrance of flowers.

Something was here, and it wasn't pleasant or comforting.

Eight

A rumble of thunder followed us as we drove away from the wildflower field. We were still on Huron Court, and that feeling of hovering strangeness rode with me. It could still happen. In the blink of an eye, the season could change and we'd in the midst of a snow squall. When we emerged, it would be winter. Then *where* would we be?

In the future? 2038?

Together, I thought.

Crane slowed and steered the Jeep around a curve. Was that a light mist forming above the road, just ahead of us? I sat forward in the seat, closer to the window, and looked again. No, it wasn't the infamous mist. Only haze.

"I'm glad we checked out the field," he said. "Nothing happened. I don't think it will again. But..."

I interrupted him. "I know. I won't make it a habit of visiting this particular part of Foxglove Corners."

"I was going to say, you know Annica will be coming back here, maybe every day, hoping to see the ghost again. She'll want your help."

"I already said I'd try to find out who this flower ghost was in life."

"How are you going to do that?" he asked.

"Heaven knows. I don't." I sighed. "Everyone wants my help."

"You're too nice," he said and quickly added, "Don't change."

We were leaving Huron Court at last and, thank heavens, without incident. The road seemed longer and lonelier today, which was odd because I was with Crane. Sagramore Lake came into sight, an expanse of pure blue shimmering under the sun.

My heart lifted at the thought of long walks with the collies on the beach, with the touch of lake spray, and the chance of meeting my young friends, Molly and Jennifer, walking their dog. The girls fancied themselves junior Nancy Drews. If they knew about the ghost in the wildflower field, they'd be pestering me to let them 'in on' the mystery. But I cared for them and didn't want them anywhere near Huron Court.

Crane turned on Jonquil Lane. Its border of yellow and gold flowers still looked fresh and bright. For a few more weeks, I hoped.

"If you can stay a while, I'll make you lunch," I said.

He glanced at his watch. "Great. I've been hungry for roast beef sandwiches."

I smiled. That was all I had on hand for sandwich making.

"Thanks for going with me to Huron Court. Now maybe I'll stop fussing that everyone's seen Brent's flowers except me."

He pulled into our driveway. Before he parked behind my Ford Focus, the collies began their traditional welcome home. I laid my hand on his knee. "I want you to know, you're an A number one husband."

He gaze fell on my arm. "Why shouldn't I be?" he asked. "I have an A number one wife. By the way, that watch looks good on your arm, honey."

"Thanks. I think so, too."

I opened the door and stepped outside just as the rain began, water warmed by the sun as it fell. The earth would soon feel fresh and new.

~ * ~

On weekends, the hands of the clock always run a little faster, especially in the spring with the end of school in sight and summer vacation beckoning from the wings. Or so it seems.

After Crane left for his patrol, I cleaned house and walked the dogs; and on Sunday I rested. All too soon the alarm clock went off on Monday morning. The weekend was over.

It was going to be another hot day. Wishing I could wear a sundress to school—impossible, of course, but I could wish—I settled for a green polka dot knit with a V neck and added a string of pearls and my new watch. Yes, I'd begun to think of it as mine.

I should post a 'Found' notice on the bulletin board at Blackbourne's Grocers. Maybe I would; it was only right. But something else was right. The watch felt as if it had always belonged to me, fitting lightly and comfortably on my wrist.

I received a compliment in my first hour World Lit class, amidst a barrage of complaints about how hot and stuffy the room was. As if I were in control of the thermostat.

"I like your bracelet, Mrs. Ferguson," Brenda said. "Is it new?"

"Thank you, and yes. It's a watch."

I wore it so that the three rows of pearls were visible. The watch underneath wouldn't be seen unless I held my arm a certain way.

"She touched it. "It has a glow."

I smiled but also felt a bit uncomfortable with a student's hand on my watch. We were about to start an Edgar Allan Poe story, rather heavy reading for a hot spring morning, but it should hold their interest.

"Lots of schools are letting out early because of the heat," Rusty said.

"Wouldn't that be nice if ours did?"

Uh oh. Principal Grimsley wouldn't approve of that remark.

"If the heat reaches a dangerous level, I'm sure we'll be dismissed early, too," I said quickly.

"Can I get a drink of water?" Marcia asked.

"May I," I corrected. "No, not till the bell rings."

"Then there'll be a long line," she wailed.

"Let's start reading," I said.

Was this only the first class of the day? I stole a surreptitious look at the clock. Eight fifteen. The time Grimsley usually began his walk of the halls.

My next two classes were lethargic. Then came the rowdy fourth, American Literature. They were all here, all thirty-three of them, which was unusual. I expected at least a half dozen of them to have signed out...secret destination, the Ice Cream Twirl.

In this class the students were older and the selections more challenging. I collected the previous day's homework and began a short lecture on Archibald MacLeish's *Epistle to Be Left in the Earth*.

I'd written examples of Images and Symbols on the board and was about to call their attention to them when one of the girls screamed. Vivien? She was standing, swiping angrily at the front of her white sweater which was soaked with water.

"He hit me!" she screeched. "Ron! He has a water balloon."

Devices shooting water were at the top of Grimsley's Forbidden list. That included the mini water balloons that were so popular with the younger set this spring. Possession would cause the perpetrator three detentions. For use, the penalty was suspension. At our last teachers' meeting, Grimsley had called for a zero tolerance policy.

"Send him to the office," Vivien demanded.

"Ron," I said. "Hand it over."

"Hand what over? It wasn't me."

"Whatever you have," I said.

I walked to his desk, stood over him, and held my hand out to receive the forbidden object. He didn't move.

"I didn't do nothing," he insisted.

A blast of water hit me from behind, spreading rapidly downward. An orange balloon lay on the floor, deflated and sad.

I turned to survey the students sitting behind me. All boys. All wearing angelic expressions, their textbooks open. Lovely. How was I going to win this one? I didn't know.

Keep cool.

"Read the poem silently," I said. "You have five minutes."

I returned to the front of the room and stood at the podium, amazed that I'd managed this feat without acquiring another burst of water. From my new vantage point, I could watch the entire class, in particular the boys sitting in the suspicious area of the room.

No one moved. No one appeared to be concealing an illegal water weapon. No one appeared to be reading the poem either. The general feeling was the episode was unfinished.

"Aren't you going to *do* anything, Mrs. Ferguson?" Vivien demanded.

"I'll wait for the villain to trap himself," I said.

"Huh?" asked Brenda.

"Until he fires again," someone said.

"I'm all wet," Vivien pointed out. "You have to let me go to the restroom."

Her complaint met with a giggle.

"It'll dry eventually," I said.

I glared at Ron and, for good measure, the boys, one of whom had targeted me.

"This is a poem that should be read aloud," I said and, as I didn't want to take my eyes off the class, I asked for a volunteer reader. Ron raised his hand.

This class had gotten off to a slow start. It must be time for lunch. Turning my arm around, I quickly consulted my new watch. It was eight o'clock.

Nine

Eight o'clock? No, it couldn't be.

I looked again. Yes, it could. According to my new watch. In boring or stressful situations, I often asked myself this question: Is time moving backward? Especially when a class refused to come to order and a dozen distractions prevented me from teaching my lesson.

Today, for instance, in the midst of the water wars.

I looked again, hoping I was mistaken. No, it was two minutes to eight.

At eight o'clock I'd been taking attendance in World Lit class. At that time I was still more or less calm and collected and relatively cool. It only took a few minutes with the fourth period, *aka* the class from hell, for me to start unraveling.

All right. Easy explanation. This was an old watch that needed to be wound— even though it looked new. I hadn't examined the battery, being more interested in the three rows of glowing pearls.

"He did it again! Give him detentions!"

That was Vivien, screeching again. Drops of water glistened on her face. Blue eye shadow ran down under her eyes. She tossed the remains of what had been a yellow balloon at Ron. He wiped his face and retaliated, calling her a rude name. More blue smudges under Vivien's eyes.

"That is *enough!*" I announced, reaching for the disciplinary referrals. "To the office, both of you."

"He started it," Vivien whined. "It isn't fair. Can't you protect yourself in this class?"

"The principal has banned all water devices from Marston High School," I said. "You can ask him about protection."

"I'll do that."

I made out the referrals as quickly as possible. Thankfully no one took advantage of my preoccupation to douse his neighbor with water.

Vivien gathered her books and stomped out, closely followed by Ron. I heard another water-induced scream in the hall.

Exasperated, I glanced at my watch. The time was ten to eight.

~ * ~

"That's funny," Leonora said at lunch.

We had the bench and a peaceful corner of the courtyard to ourselves. It was hot, and the splash of water from the fountain had soothed my frayed nerves. That is until Leonora's comment and the laugh she didn't even try to suppress.

"What? My getting drenched with a water gun?"

"Better than getting shot with a real one." She gasped and said, "I'm sorry, Jen."

So was I. Inadvertently she had reminded me of one of the worst days of my life, when a student had opened fire in my classroom.

"I meant your watch," she said. "It's funny that the hand moves backward. Only you would find a haunted watch."

"Crane found it."

"In a haunted field. You should have kept your promise to yourself to stay away from Huron Court."

When she was talking, I consulted my watch. It was seven-forty. On an average weekday I'd be in the front office, collecting my mail. The first bell wouldn't have rung yet.

"I wasn't looking for the watch. It found me."

"And you're wearing it."

"The battery is dead," I said.

And immediately realized that whatever glitch governed the watch, it couldn't be a dead battery. The hour hand had moved. Only in the wrong direction.

I readjusted the watch so that the three rows of pearls were on top of my wrist. I felt suddenly...What? Defiant?

"I'm going to keep wearing it," I said. "I love it."

"Luckily you have a clock in the room to keep you on track."

Leonora unwrapped her sandwich. "Just think, if time *did* move backward, in a few hours, I could be eating breakfast instead of lunch. Chocolate doughnuts instead of chicken salad on white."

It wasn't like Leonora to succumb to fancy. I went along with her.

"In a few days, Crane and I would be in the wildflower field. A storm would be brewing. If time moved backward."

Leonora hummed the theme from the Twilight Zone. "Back and back and back in time to your wedding day. To when we lived in Oakpoint. Before the tornado."

A wandering breeze flung a spray of fountain water at me. In the cloying heat, it felt infinitely better than water from a gun spreading down the back of my dress.

"Eventually you'd be back to your childhood," Leonora said. "Back to your birth. Then...Do you remember that story, *The Incredible Shrinking Man?*"

"Stop," I said. "That's creepy. You're not usually so fanciful."

"I got carried away. Have a lemonade."

On the way to the cafeteria she'd stopped at the teachers' lounge for two lemonades.

I held the bottle in my hands for a few minutes, reveling in the cold plastic. "Thanks. This is just what I need."

I'd made a sandwich with the last of the roast beef, and it was a bit dry.

"Check your watch," Leonora said.

I did. "It's seven-thirty. Maybe I won't keep wearing it. No matter what time the watch has, I have two more classes. I hope they'll be free of water in every form."

"I'll bet Vivien and Ron wanted to get suspended. They might have planned that whole episode."

"Maybe. They're both average students, not particularly worried about their grades."

"They're probably en route to the beach," she said.

"Well, it's springtime at Marston High School," I said.

We finished our lunch and listened to the water splashing in the fountain and occasionally on our arms. The soothing effect of falling water is miraculous.

I was ready to take on my two remaining classes and my conference hour.

The bell rang.

"Back to work." Leonora drained the bottle. "My Jake makes the best lemonade. You'll have to try it. Keep dodging water," she added.

I nodded. "Those mini balloons are hard to detect. They could be tucked away in backpacks or purses."

Grimsley would say we had to be extra vigilant from now on. There was no sense antagonizing the boss on one of the last days of the school year.

~ * ~

Time moved on. Real time. I sat alone in my quiet room, thinking. Not doing any schoolwork or planning.

My watch continued to run, no doubt the only timepiece in the world whose hands moved backward.

There's a simple explanation, I told myself. *There must be. Whoever assembled the watch did something wrong.*

Maybe its previous owner had left it in the wildflower field deliberately, no longer wanting to deal with its eccentricity, not knowing how else to dispose of it.

Except in a haunted field.

But...How did she know a ghost haunted the acres?

She had seen her, a girl in white gathering flowers, then dissolving in the midst of a thick white fog.

That explanation was possible but didn't address the backward movement of the watch.

While it was true that a person could slip into another time when traveling on Huron Court, the watch obviously didn't have similar powers. I'd remained firmly anchored in the proper day in the month of May as had those around me. There was no benefit to be had by *not* wearing it.

I'd simply think of it as a bracelet and hope no one ever showed up to claim it for her own.

Ten

"This," Minta said, "is Sparkle."

Pride shone in her eyes. She was privileged to own a rare treasure and was well aware of it.

The blue merle was a treasure indeed with a thick silvery coat, flashy markings, and eyes like...I searched my mental thesaurus. Like sparkling gemstones.

Good grief. Couldn't I do better than that?

Like sapphires, perhaps, but she didn't have that charming blue eye often seen in merles. Still, dark eyes can sparkle; and it seemed as if every hair in her coat had been tipped by a benevolent sun ray. Silver-blue, deep black marling, touches of sable, and a ruff and tail tip of snow white.

Bright Oak Summer's Sparkle. Whoever had given Sparkle her name had chosen wisely.

"You are so beautiful," I told her, laying my hand on her head. Her fur was soft and warm, like a length of velvet left out in the sun.

She wagged her tail. I had no doubt she knew exactly what I'd said, having heard it countless times before.

"She has a beautiful personality, too," Minta said.

I wasn't so sure about Minta's decision to bring Sparkle to the club's Spring Specialty, though.

"Aren't you afraid something will happen to her?" I asked.

Minta tightened her grip on Sparkle's lead. "How could it? She isn't competing with any other dogs, and my cousin, Randi, came with me. We'll watch her every minute."

But where was Randi now?

I also had a companion. Annica, aware of the developing mystery, had elected to set aside a portion of her day off from Clovers to accompany me to the show. Her frown told me that Minta's answer didn't set well with her.

"Even so," I said. "Anything can happen."

Like a gunshot in a crowded venue.

Horrified, I turned away from that thought.

I wouldn't have brought one of my dogs to a place where an ill-wisher might be lurking in the crowd. The show was packed with collie fanciers assembled to engage in their favorite sport. Weather was the least of their concerns. Certainly they didn't appear to worry about traveling germs. Only placements and points.

"Did you receive any more threats?" I asked.

"Well, yes. One." Glancing down at Sparkle, Minta took a slip of paper out of her jeans pocket. "I found it in my mail box yesterday." She read aloud:

Catching flu isn't the only danger to a dog in a show situation. If you want to keep Sparkle safe, keep her home.

A dog show situation? What odd phrasing. Why not just 'a dog show?'

"And that doesn't scare you?" Annica asked.

"It sort of does, but it isn't exactly a threat."

"It's from someone who knows your dog's name," I pointed out. "Someone you may consider a friend."

"But anyone could know that. Sparkle has been shown before. She's won before. As a puppy she was featured in *Collie Parade*."

And Sparkle was distinctive. Easily recognizable. She was, in fact, the only blue merle at the show. The others were a mix of sables and tricolors.

I looked around, once again touching Sparkle as if that could ensure her safety. Everyone in my view looked normal and innocuous, all absorbed in preparing a dog for its moment in the spotlight.

The girl with her single blonde braid hummed as she put the finishing touches on her sable and white collie. The lady who had set up next to her placed a throw over the top of a crate to give the barking dog within a sense of security, and in a far corner, a woman who had brought four puppies to the show, obviously in the hope of selling them, struggled to keep them together.

I looked in the other direction. A tall, heavy set young woman in pink denim jeans led a stunning tricolor across the grounds. Twin boys, towheads in *I Love Lassie* tee-shirts, ran somewhere, cans of pop in their hands. A girl gazed admiringly at a frisky ginger-colored puppy.

And a woman in a long lemon yellow dress glided toward us. She wore an enormous straw hat decorated with buttercups and trailing lace ribbons. Strands of chestnut hair had escaped from an elegant low bun. Did she think she was at an English tea party or a royal wedding?

"There's Jacelyn," Minta said. "Now where did Randi go?"

The lady in yellow waved and made her way across the field, ribbons flying in the wind.

I couldn't stop staring at her. Her red lips had a touch of sunlit gloss, and yellow eye shadow emphasized the gold flecks in her darkly outlined hazel eyes. The ring on her finger was a large ruby or a red stone. She was an attractive woman, but, unfortunately, overdone.

"Good morning, Minta," she said. "How's Blueberry Muffin today?"

She gave Sparkle a quick pat on the head. I noted that the merle's tail didn't move.

"She's fine," Minta said. "But don't call her Blueberry Muffin. That isn't her name." She added, "Sparkle doesn't realize she's not going in the ring today."

"What a pity! She'd sweep the competition under the rug. Did you see that black scarecrow Abby Ryson's showing? What a..."

"Shh," Minta said. "Someone'll hear you."

"So what if they do? It's true." She turned to Sparkle. "Blueberry Cupcake. I could just eat you all up."

Minta started to say something but closed her lips tightly. Still, she didn't bother to conceal her exasperation, and Sparkle glanced at Jacelyn. I thought I detected a look of disdain in her dark eyes. I must have imagined it. She couldn't possibly have understood what Jacelyn had said.

The woman in yellow was oblivious.

Minta said, "Jennet and Annica are visiting from Foxglove Corners. They're fellow collie lovers. Girls, I'd like you meet Jacelyn Holloway."

Jacelyn gave me a sunny smile. "Are you two ladies showing today?"

"We're observers," I said.

"I have a collie, Angel, I may want to show," Annica said. "I'd like to see how it's done."

"Did you see Randi?" Minta asked.

Jacelyn indicated the area outside the grounds. "She's getting a hot dog." She reached for Sparkle's leash. "What about it, Blueberry Crumble? Shall we check out the competition?"

Sparkle didn't react. Why should she? Her name wasn't Blueberry Muffin or Cupcake or Crumble.

Minta held on to the leash. "Call her Sparkle," she said.

They went ahead, whispering together. They were an interesting contrast—Jacelyn, who couldn't have looked fancier and Minta in skin-tight blue jeans and an ice-blue top, chosen, no doubt, to match Sparkle's coat. As they walked away, Sparkle looked back at us, over her shoulder.

"How rude," Annica said. "Do you think they're talking about us?"

"Probably about someone else's dog."

"It's too bad Sparkle has to sit this one out," Annica said. "If I were the judge, I'd give her all the ribbons."

I smiled at the picture her image created. A cloak made of blue ribbons for a blue collie. "I just hope she'll be safe."

I hoped, too, that Minta didn't assume it would be safe to enter Sparkle in the next show if nothing untoward happened today.

~ * ~

I stood at the exhibitors' ring already tiring, wishing I'd thought to bring a lawn chair and wondering why I had come to the show when I could be doing almost anything else.

Oh, yes. As a favor to Minta. To see if anyone took a suspicious interest in Sparkle. So far, although Sparkle had received more than her share of compliments, no one appeared to have an ulterior motive for admiring her.

I was happy walking and playing with my collies and willing to take on the hard work involved in rescue. For exhibition, however, I had a short attention span. Once I'd seen and exclaimed over the competing collies, I was ready to leave. I'd already chosen my own winners.

I took a deep breath of hot, stuffy air filled with the mingled odors of wet dog and shampoo, along with a hundred other scents. Perfume, hot dogs, popcorn, and, oddly, tar. The noise level was giving me a headache. There was too much barking, too much talking, too much of everything crammed into the outdoor space.

I longed to go home and breathe in sweet, fresh country air.

Annica, however, was entranced. "I'm going to show Angel. She's prettier than any collie here. Except Sparkle," she added.

Sparkle had taken advantage of her chance to rest. She lay beside Minta, paws crossed, eyes half closed.

"There's a lot of work involved in showing dogs," I reminded her. "And it's expensive and time consuming. Also, you'll need to train Angel. See how gracefully those dogs in the ring move? They've been through conformation classes."

"We can do that."

"They have to be groomed to perfection, too," I said. "You can't leave wads or tangles in their coats."

"I wouldn't do that. I'd have her professionally groomed."

Minta's cousin, Randi, had found us. She was a slim girl with long pale yellow hair, younger than Minta but bearing a slight resemblance to her. Like Minta, she wore tight jeans and a light blue top with an unsightly mustard spill on her sleeve.

"I was a junior handler," Randi said. "If you're serious about showing your collie, I can show you the ropes. Or even handle her, if you like."

Annica backtracked as I knew she would. "Well, I have classes at OU," she said, "and I work part-time. But someday..." She trailed off.

"Call me when you're ready." Randi pulled a card out of her purse and thrust it at Annica.

Minta's whisper almost got lost in the cacophony of sound that assailed us. "He's here. Don't look."

"Who?" I asked.

"Jeff Whitman, the hopeful heir, and he brought a dog with him. Now what's this about?"

Eleven

"What a babe!" Randi's hand strayed to the mustard stain on her sleeve.

"Hush. He saw us."

The man who threaded his way through the moving crowd was tall and muscular, blond and tanned. He might have been a Viking strayed from a Hollywood movie set, an exceptionally handsome one with the requisite rugged features. His dog was in a state of high excitement, lunging at everyone they passed.

He had a winning smile that might have said, 'I know I'm irresistible, but I'm also unattainable. So back off.'

Really, Jennet, what man says that?

This one.

"Jessie, sit," he said and included us all in a smile that captured the warmth of the sun.

Randi moved a little closer to him. "Hi, I'm Miranda."

He sent a fleeting smile her way. "I don't know everyone here, Minta."

What could Minta do but make the introductions, which she did with a decided lack of grace.

Jeff reached out to pat Sparkle on the head. "And this must be the famous blue girl, Sparkle," he said.

Fool! Didn't he know that when you approach an unknown dog you should offer your hand for her to sniff and not just touch her? Lucky for him, Sparkle was laid back. She wagged her tail half-heartedly.

"I wouldn't say she's famous," Minta said.

"How many dogs inherit nearly twenty grand? My aunt must have been out of her mind."

Minta bristled. "She was as sane as you or I. Sparkle gave her love and companionship. What did you give her?"

"We were family," he said.

"When did you see last see your aunt?"

He dodged her question.

Minta's words fairly dripped with ice. I wished she could have tempered her responses. It's never wise to let your enemy divine your true feelings. *If* Jeff Whitman was the enemy. That hadn't been established.

"Do you live in Oakpoint, Mr. Whitman?" Jacelyn asked.

"Nope. I'm just here on vacation." He paused, remembering something important. "That is to say, I came to Michigan for my aunt's funeral. I'm in no hurry to go back."

"Back to where?" she wanted to know.

"The great state of California."

"Did you bring your dog with you?" Randi asked.

Jeff looked blank for an instant as if he had forgotten the lively sable who danced giddily around on the other end of the leash.

"Oh, Jessie. She belongs to my girlfriend. I thought since this was a collie show, I'd bring a collie."

His girlfriend? One he'd acquired recently or a girl he'd left behind? It didn't matter except I wondered what kind of woman would hand her dog over to a man, whatever he was to her.

I realized this could all be innocent, and it was only natural for Jeff to be disappointed when an expected inheritance went to someone else. Especially if that someone was a dog. But would he stoop to sending secret warning messages to Minta?

I wasn't ready to believe he was the villain in this scenario.

My pesky inner voice bounced back to life. *Why? Because he's blond and handsome?*

I didn't listen to it.

"Look, Minta," Jeff said. "How about we have dinner some night soon? I have no quarrel with you. You were a good friend to my aunt. She said so in her letters."

Minta gazed out toward the ring where a stunning dark mahogany collie had just been singled out by the judge.

Jeff was handing her a golden opportunity to gather information. I sent Minta a silent message: *Say yes.*

"I don't think so," Minta said. "I'm pretty busy these days." She pulled Sparkle closer to her, looping the leash around her hand.

"Too busy to eat dinner?"

She hesitated and faint color stole into her cheeks. "Sometimes, yes."

He shrugged, holding on to his sunny smile. "Call me if you change your mind. You have my number."

He bestowed a general smile on our little group and led Jessie away.

"Minta!" Randi said. "Did you seriously turn down a date with him?"

"I don't like the man."

Jacelyn said, "What's not to like?"

I assumed Minta hadn't told her friend about the warnings and her suspicions. Maybe Randi didn't know either, and obviously Jeff didn't. What must he make of Minta's coldness?

"All I can say is I wish he'd asked me," Randi said.

"Me, too," Jacelyn echoed.

"You're too young for him." Minta smiled. "Miranda."

In the ring, the mahogany sable had bested her competition. Her handler looked radiant, and I was happy. The collie, Autumn Breeze, had been my choice.

"I guess I'll call it a day," Minta said. "Are you ready, Randi?"

"I guess."

"I'll stay a little longer," Jacelyn said.

I glanced at Annica. "We should go, too. We have a long drive. Okay?"

"Sure, if everybody's leaving," she said.

Everybody but Jacelyn.

We parted, and Minta invited us to meet her at the next show. "I may enter Sparkle," she said. "We may be making mountains out of molehills."

Her apprehension about the warnings seemed to have diminished, which was what I'd been afraid would happen.

~ * ~

Annica and I stopped for a late lunch at a quaint tearoom in Oakpoint before beginning the long drive to Foxglove Corners. After ordering turkey sandwiches, iced tea, and strawberry tarts, we reviewed our day at the dog show. I relaxed and felt my energy level rising.

"The next time, I'm going to bring a lawn chair," I said. "That was way too long to stand."

"You sound like you're seventy."

"I just don't like standing. Would you like to stand during a whole movie?"

"Apples and oranges," she said.

"But I'm glad I went. I never get tired of looking at collies."

Our waitress brought tall glasses of iced tea. I unwrapped my straw and gave the ice chips a swirl.

"I've been meaning to tell you," Annica said. "That's a pretty bracelet. The pearls look real."

I'd intended to find the right time to tell Annica about the watch, when we wouldn't be distracted by possible ne'er-do-wells at the dog show. Subsequently I'd forgotten I was wearing it. Well, now the time was right.

"It's a watch, and it comes with a story," I said. "Crane found it in the wildflower field."

"*Our* field? What were you doing there?"

Her possessiveness made me feel like an interloper.

"Looking for your ghost," I said. "We didn't see her, but Crane discovered this watch. He almost stepped on it."

I extended my hand, letting her touch the pearls, saving the best for last.

"The girl in the white dress lost it," she said.

"Maybe. But it couldn't have just slipped off her wrist. It's one of those 'one-size-fits-all' bracelets."

I reminded myself that I was talking about a spirit's wrist.

"How did she lose it then?"

"I don't know."

"Well, I do. She left it in the field as a sign."

"A sign of what?"

"That she was there."

That didn't make sense, but instead of letting the discussion ramble on in this vein, I came to the heart of the matter.

"The watch has one distinctive characteristic," I said. "It runs, but the hands move in the wrong direction. Backwards."

"Watches and clocks don't do that."

"What time do you have?" I asked.

"It's one-thirty."

"My watch tells me it's nine o'clock. Look." I showed her the time.

"It stopped at nine. You need a new battery."

You'd think Annica would be more accepting of my explanation since the watch had come from the haunted field.

"We're still waiting for our food," I said. "It'll take about an hour for us to eat."

"I'm not following you."

I turned the bracelet around so that the three rows of pearls showed, the watch hidden on the other side of my arm.

"We'll check the time again when we're done," I said. "If you insist on proof."

Twelve

I scooped up the last strawberry and surveyed the dessert plate. Empty. Every dollop of whipped cream, every crumb of graham crust... gone.

"These tarts are too small," Annica said. "I could eat another one."

"I may bake a strawberry pie tomorrow," I said.

"Or take a Clovers pie home. Our fillings are better."

Our waitress had left the bill on the table. Annica reached for her shoulder bag.

"My treat," I said, pulling out my wallet. "Shall we check the time?"

I turned the watch around so she could see the hands clearly. "It's forty-nine minutes earlier than it was when we started our lunch."

"Cool," she said. "Seeing is believing. You must have the only watch in the world that goes backward." Her eyes lit up as they always did when she detected a new mystery on the horizon. "Do you think it's some sort of time travel device?"

Anyone overhearing her question would have been taken aback, but it wasn't so strange to those of us who lived in Foxglove Corners. After all, Crane had found the watch in the wildflower field on Huron

Court where, in the blink of an eye, a strange and powerful force could whisk the traveler into the past or future.

"I'm sure it isn't," I said. "I've been wearing it every day, and I've stayed firmly rooted in the twenty-first century."

"Just think," Annica said. "You put the watch on and—zoom!—you're in the Roaring Twenties with a denim maxi skirt and no long beads. How would you get back?"

"Take the watch off?"

"You do. Nothing happens."

"Then we're in nightmare time," I said.

"But, seriously, aren't you afraid?" she asked. "It used to be that you wouldn't even go near Huron Court."

"No," I said. "Would *you* be afraid?"

"You bet. I love my life. I don't want to leave it."

"Then why are you risking it by driving on Huron Road every day?"

"I don't think history will repeat itself," she said.

I counted out dollars and change to cover the bill and added a tip.

"There's more to Brent's property than meets the eye," Annica said. "Like the violets we never planted. Then the ghost in white helping herself to our flowers. Now a weird watch. Three strange things."

"They aren't necessarily connected," I pointed out.

"But they could be."

"If that's the case," I said, "I wonder what will come next."

~ * ~

On the way home, Annica mentioned Jeff Whitman. "I wonder if he's the one who's sending the threats to Minta."

"She thinks so," I said. "He heads her suspect list."

"He seems so nice."

"It could be a cover. Time will tell. I find it odd that he'd bring a collie to the show when he wasn't entering her."

"Why? Minta brought Sparkle."

"Supposedly he's in town for a little while. How does he acquire both a girlfriend and a dog in that time?"

"He's a man of mystery." Annica hid a yawn behind hands manicured with cobalt blue nail polish.

"I'm tired. You'd think I'd worked my shift and attended a class already, and it's only—three o'clock by my watch."

"We'll be home soon," I said.

In truth we'd just entered the freeway. Annica closed her eyes, and my thoughts drifted to Minta's suspects.

If Jeff's intention was to get rid of Sparkle, how could he be sure his aunt's money would come to him? Did he know Minta would inherit if anything were to happen to Sparkle?

If so, he'd have no reason to eliminate the blue merle.

I needed to take a look at Minta's other suspects, mostly the people who regularly brought their collies to the shows, even though that wasn't the best way to solve her mystery.

Then what was?

Wait, I told myself. *See if Minta receives other messages.*

They had been printed and dropped illegally in her mailbox. Wouldn't Sparkle bark when a stranger approached? My collies did, and our mailbox was some distance from the house. Perhaps Minta could install a camera.

The exit loomed ahead, the scenery on either side of the freeway swimming in haze. The day was warm and breezy, and several hours of light remained. I could do whatever I pleased until it was time to make dinner. Anxious to be home, I left the freeway and drove a little faster, watching for roaming wildlife and pets.

What had been happening in Foxglove Corners in our absence?

~ * ~

Play Doh.

"I found this disgusting glob near the corral," Sue said. "It's Play Doh."

She passed a small crudely fashioned statue to me, then pushed back a strand of strawberry blonde hair that had blown into her face. "It looks like a dog."

"Or any creature with four legs and a tail."

"I found a whole package of the stuff, spilled out of its wrapper," she added. "Just lying there, waiting for one of the dogs to notice it."

"Where was it?" I asked.

"Near the little figure. They were together."

"If a dog ingests Play Doh, he can die," I said.

"Almost certainly. It's a variation of the poisoned meat theme. It would be a horrible death."

I gave her back the little figure. "Here. Throw it away where the dogs won't find it." I paused as a horrid thought worked its way into my mind. "Are you sure none of the collies ate any of it?"

"No one is showing signs of distress. I found it early this morning, and I'll swear it wasn't there last night."

But she looked worried. With so much land, it was a challenge to make sure all was well on every acre. And what about the horses? Could they possibly be the target?

Not likely, if the Play Doh was left outside the corral.

"When is it going to end?" Sue asked.

When one of the dogs is dead.

I hadn't said that aloud. Had I?

"I reported it to the police," Sue said. "They know about the poisoned meat, too, thanks to you. I don't know what they can do. It's up to us to stop it. But how?"

"By not relaxing our vigilance. Not for a single minute. Other than that, I don't know, unless we catch the person who's doing it."

I remembered then. Sue didn't know about our day at the dog show, only about the warnings Minta had received.

"I met Jeff Whitman today. He's the man Minta considers her top suspect," I said. "In my view he has no motivation to harm your collies. He's from California. How would he even know they existed?"

"It's somebody else, then. I hate, absolutely hate, not knowing who's doing this."

As for myself, I felt ill with worry for Icy and Bluebell and our Silverhedge rescues who should be out of harm's way. My own dogs weren't any safer. Nor were Camille's Holly and her Belgian shepherd, Twister.

"Where are the dogs now?" I asked.

"In the house. On this beautiful day. I'm afraid..."

She hadn't seen the poisoned meat, I recalled. I'd told her about it. But the play doh was her own discovery, and it was new and terrifying.

"We're dealing with a maniac," she said. "A sadist. I'm going to call an emergency meeting of the League. We can brainstorm and find out if anyone else has come across dangerous substances on their property."

"I have a friend at the *Banner*," I said. "Jill Lodge. She may be willing to write a story about the situation. You may find out you're not alone."

That was a plan, then. I was surprised I hadn't thought of contacting Jill before. If people knew what was happening on Sue's horse farms, they'd be up in arms. That was what we wanted.

Thirteen

Whenever I found myself grappling with an out-of-this-world problem, I turned to Lucy Hazen. To be sure, the girl in white was Annica's apparition, but, in a sense, it was also mine; and I didn't know how to solve it.

I moved the bracelet-watch around on my wrist until I saw the clock face clearly. I had changed the battery, not expecting the hands to begin moving in the right direction. They didn't disappoint me.

I had worn the watch for a week and not once experienced the sickening feeling of slipping out of my proper time. And the season remained unchanged, the same string of warm spring days we'd been having since before Crane and I had visited the wildflower field.

It hasn't happened yet. It's not going to happen.

Still, it was strange and a part of the wildflower field scene, but I had no sense of urgency. I could wait until summer vacation and enjoy a long leisurely afternoon with Lucy and Sky. Annica, however, wanted to consult Lucy soon. The sooner the better.

I stopped at Clovers for take-out dinners and saw a strawberry pie in the dessert carousel. A luscious confection topped with meringue and a large red strawberry. It had a graham cracker crust and Annica's assurance that it was ten times better than the tarts we'd had at the tea room in Oakpoint.

I'd promised Crane a strawberry pie for tonight's dessert. Now I wouldn't have to bake one.

"I'll take it," I said.

"You're in luck. It's the last one until tomorrow."

Annica moved in a soft jingle of silver bell earrings. Ironically she had dressed to match the pie, in a red maxi dress trimmed with white. A neatly lettered sign in the carousel announced the celebration of Strawberry Week.

She showed me to a small table. "Do you think Lucy would mind a visit from us tomorrow?" she asked.

"She'll be delighted.

Lucy worked at home, writing her novels on her own schedule. She always welcomed company.

"Would you call her and set it up?"

"Sure. For after school."

Annica pulled out a chair, then, remembering she was a waitress, produced her order pad.

"What can I get for you?"

I didn't have to stop and think. "Two ham dinners and the pie to go; tea for here."

After a hectic school day, I always liked to wind down with a cup of tea. I'd probably have another one at home.

"Tell me why you suddenly need to see Lucy," I said. "What happened?"

"The apparition is changing. This morning I heard a dog barking in the wildflower field."

"A dog barking in the country," I said. "That's hardly unusual and certainly not ghostly."

"Think about it while I get your order together."

I did. Briefly. It still seemed ordinary. We were surrounded by dogs in Foxglove Corners. Consequently, barking was as common as the wind's shriek or moan. Sometimes annoying. Never frightening.

In record time, Annica placed my take-out boxes on the corner of the table, along with a cup of tea and joined me.

"Well?" she asked.

"You heard a dog barking. How does that change the apparition?"

"It's becoming more complete, although I didn't see the girl in white this time."

"Why couldn't you have heard a real dog?"

"I didn't see one. Not anywhere. I called out to her. She didn't come, but I still heard her barking."

It seemed that Annica had made up her mind. She had heard a ghost dog, a logical companion for her flower-gathering spirit.

I took a sip of tea, a quick sip as it was too hot to drink without burning my lips and throat.

"Let me try to explain this better," Annica said. "The barking sounded like it was coming from far away. At the same time it didn't. Or…" She frowned. "It sounded like it had been run through one of those machines that distort sound."

"In other words, barking that originated in another dimension."

"Yeah. That was my first thought. It didn't sound natural, and I never saw the dog."

"Okay, I understand, but what do you want Lucy to do?"

"She knows all about ghosts. She can read our tea leaves or have one of her premonitions."

I tried to conceal my smile but was too late. She'd seen it.

"It doesn't work like that, Annica. Lucy doesn't have premonitions on demand, but she can certainly read our tea leaves."

"Do you think she will?"

"Of course. Maybe she can tell you if your romance is going in the right direction."

"It is," she said quickly, but just as I couldn't avoid smiling, she couldn't control her blush.

"I just want to know why I see the ghost, whoever she is," Annica said. "I need to know what she wants with me. You haven't found out who she used to be when she was alive."

That reminded me. The impossible task.

"I haven't had time with school and Minta's warnings and the Play Doh Sue found on her ranch. Besides I have no idea how to start."

"What Play Doh?" she asked.

I told her. She leaned back in her chair. Under her vibrant, glowing makeup her face seemed pale.

"But isn't Play Doh poisonous for dogs? The salt or something?"

"It is. First, poisoned meat. Now Play Doh."

"I'm sorry, Jennet," she said. "Naturally the dogs' safety comes first. I didn't mean to imply you were falling down on the job."

"What job? I'm not a detective." Abruptly I reined in my indignation. "That is, I haven't done anything yet, but I will."

"Maybe Lucy knows who the ghost is."

"I'll give her a call tonight," I said. "I'm sure she'll want to help, but be prepared. She may not be able to. Remember what they say about heaven."

"What's that?"

"Heaven helps those who help themselves."

"I'm trying. I stop at the field every morning to see if the ghost is there. It can't hurt to have someone with Lucy's talents on board."

"Not at all," I said.

~ * ~

Dark Gables sat far back from Spruce Road, protected by a small forest of evergreens that bordered the well-shaded driveway. You couldn't see the house until you were within a few yards of it. Then the gables came into view: dark, graceful shapes rising up to a cloudy sky.

"What a perfect place for a horror writer," Annica said. "It's like some of the houses in her books."

I nodded. "It's nice and spooky."

Lucy's blue merle, Sky, stood on the porch barking a welcome. Lucy, all in black, was never far from Sky, even though she had trained the collie to stay close to the house. Although she owned several acres, she was glad she'd done that after hearing about Sue's experience with the deadly substances.

"Come in," Lucy said, holding the door open. "How lovely to see you two."

Sky circled us, tail wagging, in a blatant bid for attention. I ruffled her fur, and Annica asked her to shake hands. Sky didn't often have company to entertain. She made the most of our visit.

"We have another ghost, Lucy," Annica said. "This one is all mine."

"My goodness," Lucy said.

"She materialized in the field that Brent and I planted with wildflower seeds," she added. "Where the pink Victorian used to be."

"On Huron Court? That explains it."

Lucy led the way to the back of the house where an all-season sunroom offered a view of woods and a fountain. We sat at the white wicker coffee table, and Sky leaped up to sit in the space between us.

"Tell me all about it while I make tea," Lucy said.

I glanced at Annica. My marvelous watch was part of the story, but rather than confuse the issue, I'd let Annica talk about the manifestation first.

"I thought she was a real person stealing our flowers," Annica said. "Then I saw the fog—"

While the water boiled, she told her story, which didn't need embellishment to capture Lucy's attention.

Lucy nodded. "I can't say that I'm surprised. That's haunted ground."

"I've been a little concerned," Annica said. "A spirit in white gathering flowers. Could this be a forewarning of my death?"

Fourteen

I had no idea that Annica was thinking of the appearance of the ghost as a foreshadowing of her death. I thought her daily visits to the wildflower field were inspired by curiosity and excitement at having her own supernatural experience.

Lucy was surprised, too. "A girl in white gathering flowers doesn't suggest a funeral to me. I think of renewal. Tranquility and springtime joy."

"Are you sure?"

The relief in Annica's voice saddened me. As her friend, I should have known she was troubled.

"We can never be sure what the future holds, but I don't see any dark clouds over your head."

"That's good, then."

"Very good. When I look at you, I see radiance...the kind that can't be easily extinguished."

"What do you think the apparition means then?" she asked.

"You'll have to wait and see what happens in your life. If an event connects with the sighting."

The tea kettle's shrill brought us back to the here-and-now. Sky stirred, nose pointed toward the kitchen.

"Let's see what the tea leaves say." Lucy rose. "I should have a package of cookies in the cupboard—if I didn't eat them all. They're chocolate chip walnut and even better than homemade."

Annica wrapped her arms around the collie's neck. "Did you hear that, Sky? I'm going to live."

"Of course you are," I said. "Think of everything you have to live for."

She smiled. "Angel, graduation… love."

"All good things. Now if you were to hear tolling bells, it'd be different."

"Found them," Lucy said. She set a plate of cookies on the coffee table and gave Sky a treat of her own, a jumbo biscuit. "I'll make the tea."

~ * ~

I've lost track of the cups of tea I'd had in Lucy's sunroom. She had a collection of hand-painted teacups, but for readings she used plain white cups, as any inside decoration could distort the patterns created by the leaves.

I knew the ritual by heart. After drinking the tea, drain the excess liquid into the saucer and turn the cup toward you three times while making a wish.

Whether I believed what Lucy told me was a different story. In the beginning I was skeptical. Then I became aware of Lucy's unique talents. Sometimes she misinterpreted an image, but often she was able to warn me of impending danger. I couldn't possibly think of Lucy's tea leaf reading as a mere parlor game.

We drank our tea and ate the cookies, which were every bit as good as Lucy had claimed.

Finally Annica handed the cup to Lucy and looked at her, eyes bright with anticipation.

After a long moment, Lucy said, "I see your wish, and here you are standing at a two-forked road." She pointed to a thin, light leaf. "It's imperative that you take the right one."

I repressed a shiver. That road sounded like Huron Court. Annica had no qualms about traveling on it. She did so every day en route to the wildflower field.

"How will I know which fork to take?" she asked.

"You'll have to wait. There'll be a sign. All you have to do is read it correctly."

"A literal sign?"

"The other kind. You'll have to be very observant."

"What happens if I take the wrong fork?"

"There'll be a different outcome."

Lucy was often vague, but that was part of the fun. I imagined Annica's life was full of choices.

"Your current project will be a success," she added.

"My Emily Bronte paper! Oh, I hope so."

"It could be. That's all I see today, Annica. I'll be happy to read your tea leaves anytime."

Lucy turned to me. "Jennet? Are you ready?"

I gave her my cup and fidgeted as she seemed to take longer than usual to interpret the patterns of the leaves.

"This is strange," she said. "I see the same two-forked road in your cup, Jennet."

"Maybe Annica and I will be together."

"That would explain it. I also see danger for you. That's nothing new. And you have an enemy."

"Oh, no. Not another one."

For someone who lived a quiet life, I seem to have acquired a whole parade of people who wished to harm me. Well, I knew of one. The shadowy person who dropped poisoned meat and Play Doh where a dog could find it. He might be my enemy, but I intended to be his.

"I see your wish," Lucy added. "Your home life is stable. I don't see that female deputy sheriff who has her eye on Crane."

She meant Veronica Quent, whose attempts to attract Crane had been the source of past grief for me. I hoped she had grown tired of her game.

"That's all, Jennet. You have a good cup today."

"If you consider an enemy and danger good," I said.

"Well that's part of life. The danger, anyway."

"Now," I said. "Let me tell you about my watch."

I turned it around, showing Lucy the clock face.

"I noticed it," Lucy said. "But I thought it was a bracelet. It's lovely, like everything you wear. Is it another gift from Crane?"

"In a way. He found it in the wildflower field."

"It looks expensive. Couldn't you find the owner?"

I hesitated, remembering that I'd never posted a 'Found' notice on Blackbourne's bulletin board.

"Not yet," I said. "In the meantime I'm wearing it. And that's not all. The hands run backward." I showed her the time, which was almost four hours before we'd arrived at Dark Gables. I held my arm still while the hour hand moved— in the wrong direction.

"That is most unusual. What do you think causes this...er... aberration?"

"I haven't figured that out."

"I think my ghost lost it,"Annica said.

"Based on what?"

Annica shrugged. "It's a strange watch found near Huron Court where the pink Victorian was, before the fire. It makes perfect sense to me."

"Oh, yes," Lucy said. "Time travel. May I see it, Jennet?"

She reached for the watch, and the large gold charms on her bracelet jangled. She looked at it intently.

"As far as I can tell, it's just a watch," she said. "It *is* a mystery how it ended up in the field." She glanced at Annica. "I don't think your ghost wore it."

"Why does time go backward, though?" I asked.

"It doesn't. Not really. Have you taken the watch to a jeweler or clock person?"

"No, but that's a good idea."

"I think it's just a very pretty watch with an odd quirk," she said. "But why take chances? If I were you, I wouldn't wear it."

"That's good advice," I murmured.

But would I take it? I didn't think so.

Fifteen

After leaving Dark Gables, I considered Lucy's advice about the watch. Was I taking a risk by wearing it? I honestly didn't believe so, if that risk involved a blink-of-an-eye trip to another time.

Nothing of that nature had happened. Time travel was reserved for people who walked or drove on Huron Court when the season changed without fanfare, where spring blossoms drifting through the air turned to flying snowflakes. Where a strange power wrapped the earth in an instant freeze.

Crane and I had already taken on the risk by visiting the wildflower field and lived to tell the tale. In our proper time.

Besides, I liked to look down at my arm and see the pearls. They had a mesmerizing glow in sunlight, moonlight, and lamplight. Wherever I was.

I *did* feel guilty about keeping the watch from its owner, though. The next time I went to Blackbourne's Grocers, I resolved to pin a 'Found' notice on their bulletin board—and hope no one came forward to claim it. Until then I would wear the watch, but as a bracelet. It complemented every dress in my wardrobe.

The next day after school, I parked in my usual spot and for some reason glanced toward the weeping cherry tree, all green now, its blossoms blown away in the wind, then at the custom doghouse Crane had built for Raven before she moved permanently into the house.

There was something in front of the dog house that shouldn't be there. Alarmed, I walked over to investigate. Five pork chops lay on a sheet of thick white paper. A cloud of nasty flies buzzed on and above them.

My heart skipped a beat. Then another.

Were they poisoned? I couldn't tell. Although who tosses expensive meat from the side of the lane so close to a dog house that it might as well be inside?

If I hadn't looked at the cherry tree and the dog house, I wouldn't have seen the chops, and that knowledge made me feel faint.

You would have seen it when you took the dogs out, I told myself.

And what if the meat had been hidden inside the dog house? Just to be safe, I walked over and peered inside. It was empty.

My collies were in the kitchen barking at the door. Camille would have let them out around two o'clock. Maybe I didn't have to worry. Still, I had no way of knowing how long the pork chops had lain in my yard.

I shooed the flies away and took a closer look at them, five chops in a package large enough for six. A knife or some sharp implement had made two slashes in the wrapping. I hoped no woodland creature had seized a rare opportunity to steal a substantial meal. The coyotes were always scrounging for food.

I wrapped the offending chops back in their paper and took the package into the house, holding them well out of reach of leaping collies.

"No," I said. "Baaad."

I put them out of sight. Crane would have them tested, but I already knew what the result would be.

The vile poisoner had come to Jonquil Lane.

Misty shoved her nose into my hand. I hurried to the sink to wash off any scent of meat that might still cling to my hands. They were shaking. The danger had come too close to home. Now more than ever I needed my cup of after-school tea, and I had to call Camille and tell her what I'd found.

~ * ~

Sue's meeting of the Collie Rescue League was scheduled for that day. Crane was bringing home a pizza. Hurriedly I made a salad and drove to the horse ranch. I couldn't wait to tell my friends about the pork chops.

Icy and Bluebell stood in the hall greeting me with polite barking through the half-opened door. I found the Silverhedge dogs in the family room, enjoying pats and compliments from the half dozen or so League members. There should have been twenty, but it was always difficult to convince people to attend a meeting on a lovely spring afternoon. I was late.

I took an oatmeal cookie from Sue's makeshift buffet and settled myself in a chair. During a lull in the proceedings, I told the group about the pork chops. "I left a message at the *Banner* for Jill Lodge," I said. "We need to publicize this outrage. Maybe someone noticed a stranger lurking around or an unknown substance in their yard. At least, people will be warned."

Ronda Leigh brushed imaginary crumbs from her light pink sweater. I noticed she wore a medallion with a picture of her tricolor collie, Starla, in a silver heart frame.

"Sorry to interrupt you, Jennet, but she already did. Didn't you see the article?"

"I guess not."

"It was in yesterday's paper. The Lakeville Police Department reported three cases of attempted dog poisonings during the past two weeks."

A cold panic squeezed my heart. Three times the poisoner had struck. Add Sue's and my experience and we had five attempts to kill dogs in one of the worst ways imaginable. Between Sue's brood and mine, that amounted to fourteen collies.

For some reason I recalled Misty thrusting her nose into my hand yesterday, lured by the enticing scent of meat. My collies trusted me to protect them. Some dogs like Candy would eat anything, always hungry no matter how well fed they were.

I left my cookie in my lap, wrapped in its napkin. I didn't think I could swallow a bite.

"What are we going to do?" Emma Brock asked.

"Keep watching," Sue said. "Before I let my dogs roam free, I walk over every inch of my property. I don't let them run in the woods. Well, I never did. They're full of ticks and snakes."

"Yes," I said. "I used to love hiking in the woods. Now I just look on them as scenery."

Emma rose and walked around Scarlet to refill her coffee cup. "I think we all agree. We have to catch this person. The question is how."

"We're open to any and all ideas," Sue said. "Ronda, tell us what you did."

"I've invested in a surveillance camera. If anyone comes near my house, I'll have his picture."

"But you won't have *him*," Mattie said. She was an elderly lady, a long-time member who leaned toward pessimism.

"Everybody hates a dog poisoner," Emma pointed out. "If his picture appears on the front page of the *Banner*, someone ought to recognize him."

"Remember, this person could be a woman," Mattie added.

"He wants to destroy something beautiful," Ronda said.

I agreed. "Beautiful and good, God's gift to man."

"And to women." Ronda's smile was the first of the meeting. "In the meantime, maybe we can figure out his—or her—motivation."

Several people began to talk at once.

"He doesn't need one. He's simply evil."

"He hates dogs."

"...a sadist..."

"He likes to see living things suffer."

Sue said, "Or all of the above. According to the article, none of the dogs died, but for one of them, it was a close call."

I broke off a tiny piece of my cookie and tasted it. I was going to be okay; the ill feeling had passed. Renewed determination took its place.

So far it appeared that we were holding our own, but how soon before the poisoner outwitted one of us? A moment of distraction, a chunk of meat hidden from human eyes in the weeds but still retaining its smell, a temptation impossible for a canine to resist. A horrible, painful death.

We couldn't let that happen.

"Vigilance is the watchword," I said.

~ * ~

Vigilance was also the watchword at Marston High School. The seniors had graduated, but five days remained until the end of the school year, two of them set aside for final exams for the underclassmen. As might have been anticipated, mini water balloons had soared in popularity.

The next day, Principal Grimsley shortened first hour and called a special meeting to remind us to "keep a tight lid" on student misbehavior.

I listened, knowing exactly what he was going to say.

How were we to do that? We were professionals, weren't we? He relied on us to keep control in our classrooms. He'd hired an extra hall monitor and wanted every teacher to stand in the hall between classes. (While chaos erupted inside the room.)

"Over in the middle school, a kid brought a water pistol to class," he said. "A water pistol but it looked like a real gun. That's cause for expulsion these days. I don't want that to happen here."

I had an unbidden flashback to the terrible time when one of my students had opened fire in my classroom. That moment of violence had cost a boy his life. Its effect on me and other class members had been long-lasting.

I forced my mind back to the meeting.

Coach Adam Barrett never hesitated to speak out at a meeting. "Hey, Chief, a little water feels good when it's ninety-two degrees."

Grimsley glared at him. "This isn't a joking matter, Barrett."

But the sports department, sharing a table, disagreed, giving Adam the laughter he craved. Not everyone stood up to Grimsley and emerged from the encounter unscathed.

"We have five days left," Grimsley reminded us, as if anyone could be unaware of the date. "I want them to go smoothly."

I sympathized with the concept of zero tolerance, but after all, a toy was a toy, especially if it looked like one, with plastic parts and gaudy colors.

The bell rang. By the time my first hour students made their way to class, the period would be sadly decimated. I wouldn't be able to accomplish what I'd planned. We gathered our books and picked up one of Grimsley's printed guides for proper behavior.

"Watch out for water guns," Leonora said as we set out for our classrooms.

"Mini-balloons," I corrected.

"Anything that dispenses water."

Sixteen

Coach Barrett had the right idea. On a muggy June day when the temperature passes ninety degrees, a little water is welcome, no matter that it arrives via an illegal water pistol. Even with final exams breathing down their necks, all my students could think of was water.

I couldn't sign endless passes and still teach my class. Ignoring my own thirst, I pictured Grimsley rounding the corner in time to see Rachelle or Andy at the water fountain, those two being the boldest and thirstiest members of my rowdy fourth period class.

So I made myself unpopular and continued to deny the requests. The heat rose, and my carefully prepared review fell by the wayside. I tried to revive it.

"Who can define local color?" I asked.

Andy left his seat and sauntered to the front of the room, brandishing a slip of paper as if it were a weapon.

"Can I get a drink?" he asked.

"It's almost time for the bell," I said.

"But I need a drink now. I have a sore throat."

Oh, yes, Marston was experiencing an epidemic of sore throats.

"You can watch me," he said.

The fountain was across the hall, almost opposite from the classroom door. Less than a dozen steps there, a dozen back. I'd heard variations of the directions all morning.

They could fill up their water balloons at the fountain, although in his tight jeans and denim shirt, Andy could hardly have concealed so much as a pencil, to say nothing of an illegal toy. I was certain he didn't have a sore throat, and I wasn't taking a chance on incurring Grimsley's wrath.

"Please," he said, an annoying whine creeping into his voice.

"Please go back to your seat," I said.

He waited a full minute to obey me, then crumpled the pass, tossed it into the basket, slumped into his desk, and sulked. There's something ludicrous about a teenager sulking.

"Now, local color. Can anyone define the term for me?"

Linda raised her hand. "Local color is—um—lots of description."

We were on the right track.

"Can anyone add to that or give me an example?" I asked. "It'll be on the exam."

Silence. I wrote a title on the board: *The Luck of Roaring Camp*. "Bret Harte. Does this ring any bells?

As if on cue, the bell rang to end the hour and send my lethargic class streaming out of the room. As soon as the last one left, I grabbed my lunch from the desk drawer and hurried to the door, anxious to reach the relative cool of the courtyard. Suddenly my foot slipped in a puddle of water.

It must have leaked from a water balloon. But no one had been drenched; no one had screeched. Still the evidence pooled on the floor.

Thank heavens a student hadn't slipped and fallen in the mad dash to the cafeteria. I pulled the mop out of the closet and dried the whole area. There. Evidence gone.

I'd missed something crucial on the very day Grimsley had cautioned us to be extra aware. I had to do better.

~ * ~

I met Leonora in the courtyard where the splash of water in the fountain and the shade provided a respite from stuffy rooms and noise. It was her turn to bring the lemonade. I opened my bottle and took a long, long drink. Bliss. Pure bliss.

"It's too hot to keep the kids interested," Leonora said. "It's too hot for *me*."

She looked crisp and cool in mint green, a perfect color for a blonde. "I'm longing for a shower and my A/C."

"If you're not in a hurry to get home after school, could we stop at Blackbourne's?" I asked.

"Good idea. I'll buy a gallon of ice cream."

"I'm going to buy strawberries and see if I can make a better pie than Mary Jeanne," I said. "And I need to pin a 'Found' notice on their bulletin board."

"For the watch?" she asked.

"Yes." I touched my watch lovingly. Not surprisingly, the pearls were warm in the heat of the day. So was my arm.

"I don't think you'll find the owner," Leonora said. "She'd have to admit she lost it trespassing on private property."

"Annica thinks it belongs to the ghost."

Leonora laughed. "In that case, you can look forward to keeping it."

"All I wrote was that I found a watch on Huron Court. Whoever tries to claim it will have to describe it—three rows of pearls—and tell me exactly where she lost it."

"That sounds like you found a watch in the road."

"That could have happened, and some creature carried it into the wildflower field."

"You're making sure you get to keep it, aren't you?"

"I guess I am."

"Did you write anything about the hands running backward?" she asked.

"Of course not. I don't want the manager to think the notice is a joke."

"Well, good luck," Leonora said. "It *is* a pretty watch."

Quickly I unwrapped my sandwich. The minute hands on all the clocks in the building were flying by. Flying forward.

Posting the notice was a nod to basic honesty, a quality I'd always assumed I possessed, but I didn't think anyone would claim the watch. I wouldn't have to give it up. Ever.

~ * ~

Minta Maynard surprised me on Saturday morning by driving to Foxglove Corners with Sparkle in the front passenger's seat. I was strolling through the planted area around the house, my eyes focused on the ground, ready to whisk any suspicious substance out of sight before Halley or Sky smelled it.

Halley ran up to the car, barking, obviously aware of the collie inside, while Sky stayed at my side.

"You can bring her out," I said. "My dogs won't hurt her."

The pretty blue collie looked at Halley and Sky and lay down in the back seat. Minta swung her jeans-clad legs out of the car. "Sparkle?"

"Come, Sparkle," I said. "Meet Sky, your mirror image."

But Sky had disappeared behind the side of the house.

Meeting another collie who looked like her didn't impress Sparkle, but a treat from my pocket caught her interest. I held it in front of her nose, assuming Minta didn't object as she had plied Sparkle with treats at the show.

"My neighbor, Camille, bakes them for the dogs," I said.

"She loves treats," Minta assured me.

Sparkle jumped down onto the grass, and every hair in her coat shimmered, the ends touched with fire.

While Sparkle ate the cookie daintily, Minta said, "I received another message yesterday. This one was even worse. Here, I'll let you read it." She took a paper from her shoulder bag.

I saw you and Sparkle at the show last weekend. Why are you choosing to ignore my warnings? The show ring is a dangerous place for your collie. Do you <u>want</u> to lose her?

Even worse? I folded it again and gave it back to her.

"He doesn't beat around the bush, does he?" Minta said.

"He says he saw you and Sparkle. Did you see him?"

"Sure. We all did. He asked me to have dinner with him."

"You don't think Whitman wrote this, do you?"

"Who else?"

"Let's go inside," I said. Aware of the dogs barking in the house, I added, "Don't be alarmed. They're noisy but harmless."

Sparkle didn't seem convinced. She sat, but Minta tugged gently on the leash and the two followed me into the kitchen. As soon as my collies greeted their guest and settled down again, I said, "Whitman doesn't have to say he saw you at the show. You know that. This is someone else you weren't aware of."

"No one paid any particular attention to us," she said. "It's creepy to think of someone spying on me and Sparkle."

"Waiting to make his move before he does something," I added. "I wonder how many times he's going to warn you."

She nodded. "Me, too. This is the fourth message, and every time he drops it in my mailbox. I talked to the police."

"What do they say?

"They can't help unless he does something to harm Sparkle or me."

"A familiar story. By then it'll be too late."

"I'm at my wit's end," she said. "I've decided not to take Sparkle to any more shows."

I hoped she wouldn't change her mind.

"I think we'd better take another look at your suspect list," I said.

Seventeen

I arranged slices of blueberry bread on a paper plate, poured iced tea—and thought about an aspect of Minta's problem that we hadn't yet addressed.

Suppose Minta agreed to stop showing Sparkle and still the message writer wasn't satisfied. Suppose his last message would be something like this:

You didn't heed my warnings. Now it's too late. Say goodbye to Sparkle.

The memory of the pork chops was as fresh and terrible in my mind as it had been when I'd discovered them. Could two people have targeted our collies for a similar fate? Or, could it possibly be the same person?

Minta had told me what she knew of the exhibitors she saw most often at shows. There were the ones she greeted in passing and others with whom she'd shared conversations, lunches, and dinners.

"They all seem so nice," she said as she closed her notebook. "Take Aura Lindsay. She always asks me about Sparkle's health. Could that be suspicious? Aura is a vet tech," she added.

"Does she have a collie to show?"

"Yes, she has Spice, a pretty tri-factored sable. Spice beat Sparkle twice."

In my opinion Aura was definitely a candidate for the suspect list.

"We'll keep an eye on her." I transferred the refreshments to a tray. "Shall we sit on the porch? It'll be cooler."

In warm weather, the porch was my favorite place to entertain company. The air had a fresh, sweet scent, and breezes set the flowers and leaves in motion. The scenery was soothing, with Jonquil Lane still in bloom, although on the way out and the gardens of the yellow Victorian splashing color across the landscape.

The collies came out with us and lay close together. Minta held on to Sparkle's lead.

"Aura has long red hair," she said. "Do you remember seeing a redhead who wears sunglasses like a headband?"

I didn't.

"I wondered why she was concerned about Sparkle's health," she added. "Now that I think about it, it's odd."

"I assume she doesn't know about Sparkle's inheritance," I said.

"Jeff is the only one who knows."

"Then she's just making conversation?"

"Possibly."

"What if this isn't about eliminating the competition?" I said. "Maybe we're dealing with a person who wants to frighten you in slow stages and ultimately kill your dog?"

I told her about the pork chops. "I don't know for sure if they were poisoned. My husband will find out. My guess is they are."

"But why would a dog hater zero in on me?" she asked. "I've never hurt anybody."

"Who knows? Because Sparkle is so beautiful? Because you're happy? Just because Sparkle is a dog? Why do crazy people do anything?"

"I'm uncomfortable around anyone who is even a little bit unbalanced," she said.

"So am I."

I refrained from telling her that in the past I had dealt with a few genuine lunatics. My sweet Sky's tormentor, for example.

The dogs spied a deer in the woods across the lane and started barking. By the time Candy sprang to her feet, pursuit on her mind, the creature had disappeared into the dark of the woods.

"Candy," I said. "Down. It's gone."

"Imagine seeing a deer so close," Minta said. "I wished I lived in the country."

"You could."

"It would be too far from the job I've accepted."

"That's a consideration," I said, thinking about the long commute to Oakpoint.

Minta said, "What we were talking about...I'm not saying you're wrong, but I still believe it's Jeff. So does my boyfriend, Gavin. He thinks it's about the money."

This was the first time Minta had mentioned a boyfriend. Could he be another suspect?

"How long have you known him?" I asked.

"We met in April," she said. "It's nice to have someone to go places with. But we're not serious. Gavin isn't a dog lover."

"He doesn't like Sparkle?"

"Mostly he ignores her. Gavin thinks dogs are okay in their place, and that place isn't inside the house. Otherwise, he's a fine boyfriend."

Not 'I love him.' Thank heavens for that. Their relationship might not last if he didn't share Minta's love for collies.

Sparkle was more important to Minta than Gavin was. Wouldn't any man, sane or unbalanced, resent that? I added him to the suspect list. All the way to the top, in fact.

"Would you and Annica be able to meet me at the next show on the seventh?" Minta asked. "I'll introduce you to Aura, if she's there, and maybe we'll see someone to add to the list."

I agreed, although I wasn't enthusiastic about attending another dog show, even though it was probably the best place for us to find other suspects.

~ * ~

I didn't expect to receive any responses to my "Found" notice. The call on my cell phone, coming as it did while I was cleaning the kitchen after dinner, startled me.

"Is this the number for the watch?" The voice was feminine and tinny, reminding me of a cartoon character.

"It is," I said. "Did you lose one?"

"Yeah I did. On Huron Court."

Instinctively I touched the rows of pearls.

"Can you describe it?" I asked.

"Well, it's a watch. What more can I say? It has a silver band and keeps good time if you remember to wind it. My grandma gave it to me."

Silver? I breathed more easily. Still I asked, "How did you lose it?"

"It must have slipped off my wrist when I was walking on Huron Court. I could give you a small reward. Say five dollars. Can I have it back?"

"Uh, no," I said. "That doesn't describe the watch I found."

With no further word, Tinny Voice ended the call. It had unnerved me, not because I'd grown used to wearing the watch every day and didn't want to part with it, but...

But what?

I couldn't figure it out. I'd expected to receive at least one response to my notice. Well, this had been the first, and it was obviously false. Ordinarily people didn't lose a watch on a country road. An earring, maybe.

I heard Lucy's voice as clearly as if she were here in the kitchen with me. 'If I were you, I wouldn't wear that watch, Jennet."

She hadn't given me a reason, and I couldn't think of one.

With a sigh, I stacked the dishes in the cupboard. In all likelihood, this was the only call I'd receive. The next time I went to Blackbourne's, I would take the notice down. I told myself that I didn't want my phone number out there for everyone to see and didn't need to deal with an unknown person who wanted a free watch.

~ * ~

The next day after school, Leonora and I stopped at Blackbourne's Grocers. Leonora bought another gallon of ice cream—Fudge Royal this time—and I bought two more quarts of strawberries.

"Are you going to bake another pie?" Leonora asked.

"The last one wasn't sweet enough," I said.

"Did Crane complain?"

"He never does. I did. Now I'm going to take that notice down and we can be on our way. Unless you want to buy take-out dinners at Clovers."

"What a good idea," she said. "It's been too hot to cook. I thought about pizza, but let's see what Clovers has."

I wheeled our cart over to the bulletin board and scanned the broad white expanse looking for my notice. Papers of all sizes and colors covered every inch of the board.

Taylor Tree Trimming...Grass cutting, light weeding...Pet Sitting—All Breeds...Puppy Lost on Sacramore Lake Road...*As You Like It* at Oakpoint Park...

"My notice isn't here," I said.

"Good. You don't have to remove it."

"But where did it go? Who took it?" I looked on the floor but didn't see anything remotely resembling my index card. I felt a tinge of unwarranted panic.

"It got lost in the shuffle," Leonora said.

Then I realized that the caller with the tinny voice must have taken it off the board instead of copying my phone number, which meant there was no mystery and no problem. Except one person out there had my phone number.

Eighteen

I left the car in Clovers' lot, and we waded through waves of heat to the door. The world seemed to have shuddered to a stop. The stillness was absolute and unnerving. I didn't even hear birdsong or the revving of a motor on Crispian Road. When Leonora opened the door, even the tinkling of the clover wind chimes was muted.

The blast of cooled air shattered the spell. Surprisingly, the little restaurant was almost empty. Apparently people had taken the weather forecaster's warning to stay home seriously.

Afraid the ice cream would begin to melt if left in the car, Leonora carried the Blackbourne's plastic bag inside, looped over her wrist, along with her purse.

"I can't wait till I get home." She touched her arm lightly. "I think I'm getting a sunburn."

"You can't be," I said. "We haven't been in the sun that long."

Except for our twenty-minute lunch in the school courtyard, the rather long walk from the parking lot to Blackbourne's, the few steps to Clovers...The sun was relentless, and with her fair complexion, Leonora burned easily.

"Well, I'm getting something." She scratched her arm, leaving a long red streak from her wrist to her elbow.

At the counter, Annica presented a young man with two bulky bags and gave us a smile, also muted. Her red-gold hair had a freshly washed shine, and she wore a new pair of earrings, a fall of turquoise and pearls wrapped in gold. They didn't jingle but provided a perfect complement for her aqua midi-dress.

"We came for take-out," I said.

"And the coldest drink you have," Leonora added.

"Is the heat getting to you?" Annica asked.

"There's a heat advisory in effect," I pointed out. "People were advised to stay in. But our district wouldn't dream of dismissing school early."

"That's life in the real world," she said. "I had a class this morning, but before that..." She glanced at Marcy who gave her a barely perceptible nod. "Something interesting happened."

She led us to the booth with the best view of the woods. Our booth. "I'll have an iced tea with you."

"I'd like something different to drink," I said.

"How about a lime cooler? It's delicious and it looks pretty."

Leonora and I decided to try it and to take out orders of beef stew with garden fresh vegetables. It sounded somehow appropriate for a hot day.

Annica jotted down our orders and soon returned with the drinks. They were light green and topped with a small scoop of whipped cream and a sprig of mint.

"What's in it?" I asked.

"Mint and lots of good stuff. Just drink it and don't ask how it's made."

She eased herself into a chair a bit awkwardly. "I had a fall this morning," she said. "Two aspirin later, and I'm still aching."

"Should you be working?" Leonora asked.

"Oh, sure. It's best to keep moving. Okay. This is what happened. I saw the ghost in white again. She was standing this time, facing me and holding a big bouquet of fresh flowers. I called out to her, but she didn't answer. She looked right through me, so I decided to meet her in the wildflower field."

Leonora gasped. "How brave!"

"I didn't stop to think. I just started walking, trying to stay on one of the paths, but it was hard. They're almost covered by vines and trailing plants. I estimated I was about eight or ten yards from her, but it was funny. The farther I walked, the farther away she seemed. Pretty soon I could hardly move through the flowers, and I couldn't find the path. It was like a dream. And all the time she never moved."

"But you kept walking," I said.

"I'd gone that far. No way was I going back. But pretty soon I couldn't make my feet move forward. The flowers were too high and dense."

I recalled the day Crane and I had walked through the wildflower field without the prospect of meeting a ghost. The wildflowers were lush, so tall and close together that for one heart-stopping moment, I thought I had lost Crane.

"You and Brent planted a monster," Leonora said. "You created a whole garden of beanstalks."

Annica nodded. "We must have had magic seeds. We knew it would be beautiful but not unnatural."

I took advantage of the lull to take a sip of the lime cooler. I could taste lime, vanilla, and mint. It was more of a dessert than a drink and I suspected I'd want another one.

"What happened then?" I asked.

"Before long I couldn't move through the flowers, not if you paid me a million dollars. It simply wasn't possible. And I couldn't see the ghost anymore."

"Did she vanish in a white fog like before?"

"There was no fog. She simply vanished. So I had to turn around and make my way back, but this time the walking was easier and I caught an occasional glimpse of the path. All that effort and suspense," she added. "It was all for nothing."

"The wildflower field is bewitched," Leonora said, determined to hold onto her fairy tale interpretation.

"Or something. Before I reached Huron Court, I caught my foot in one of those infernal vines and fell, right into the prettiest pink flowers. They're squashed to a pulp. And ever since then my throat has been sore."

Her tale done, she drank her iced tea. When she set the glass down, at least a fourth of it was gone.

"You might be allergic to the flowers," Leonora said.

"Maybe. Some of the fragrances are potent, and they were constantly brushing against me."

I marveled at Annica's resilience. Hurting from a fall and nursing a sore throat, she still looked radiant.

"Did you see the violets?" I asked.

"I did. There are more of them now. Some are lighter purple with white streaks." She picked up her glass again but drank more sparingly. "What do you think the apparition means?" she asked.

I didn't have an easy answer. Ghost returns to earth to gather wildflowers? How un-ghostlike and not particularly frightening, except for the flowers. They appeared to have the power to protect the apparition in white from unwanted intervention.

"Well...Once I saw a young skater fall through a hole in the ice on a lake," I said. "It turned out that's the way she had died. She kept reliving the moment of her death."

Annica frowned. "I hardly think my ghost fell over dead in a field of flowers."

"Don't forget. That field didn't exist until the pink Victorian burned and Brent bought the property."

"Then this doesn't make sense," Annica said. "No sense at all."

"I agree. Not at the moment. But I don't see how it could possibly be a forewarning of your death."

"I don't think it is anymore, not since we talked to Lucy. Jennet..." She tapped the long spoon against the side of the iced tea glass. "You've gone to Huron Court with Crane. Would you come with me sometime?"

I didn't answer at once, not wanting to make a commitment I'd later regret. To be sure, nothing earthshaking had occurred on that occasion, but I'd had the security of Crane's company. Because of that trip, I had the watch, the wonderful watch I didn't want to give up. I had to admit I was as curious about the girl in white as Annica and remembered that I'd told Annica I'd try to find out who she had been in life.

So much to consider.

In the end, there was only one answer I could give her.

"Let me think about it," I said.

~ * ~

That night I dreamed of giant flowers. They encircled me, trapped me, and hid the sky from my view. They threatened to overwhelm me with their cloying fragrance.

Thick stalks touched my bare arms, creating a burning sensation. Some plants I knew were best avoided. Like poison ivy. Or another rare plant whose poison can kill a person.

Was that happening here in the wildflower field that Brent had planted in memory of the late Violet Randall?

I woke to find that my head had been lying on my arm. The air in our bedroom was cool and fresh. Crane slept by my side. The dogs in the doorway didn't stir. I was safe.

Although this wasn't a dream to remember, I lay still, trying to capture its elements before they dissolved. Unnatural flowers. Blended fragrances. A trap.

As a child I'd read a fairy tale in which flowers bled when they were picked. Who thought that image was appropriate for an impressionable young person? But so many fairy tales were similar to horror stories.

The last of the dream, the unpleasant medley of scents, floated away from my conscious mind.

Suddenly I knew I didn't want to go to the wildflower field with Annica.

Nineteen

Dreams tend to dissolve in the bright morning sunlight. By the time I began to mix pancake batter for breakfast, the last memory of flowers and fears had gone, along with my resolve to stay away from the wildflower field. In the coming days I'd be busy grading my final exams, and Annica had several poems to read for her Victorian Literature class. I could take plenty of time to think about her request.

Then, when school was over, I would accompany her to Huron Court. Chances were we wouldn't see a supernatural apparition and nothing untoward would happen.

That day after school Ronda called me. "My surveillance camera caught a person throwing a rotisserie chicken over my fence," she said. "It was still warm."

"Oh, no! Did Starla find it?"

"She smelled it, but I got it in time. It happened yesterday around ten in the morning. This person is pretty bold, operating in daylight," she added. "Anyone could have seen him, but apparently nobody did. But then he worked fast. He got out of a beige car, tossed the chicken into the yard, and took off. It must have taken him a few minutes, if that."

"What does he look like?" I asked.

"He wore black pants and a jacket with a hood pulled down low over his face. His height and build were average. I guess it could have been a woman. I couldn't tell."

I had just come in from inspecting the area around our house. We owned ten acres, but the collies rarely roamed far afield and didn't run in the woods, which made the job of policing it easier.

For now, for today at least, our property was free of lethal substances.

Still, I couldn't relax. The poisoner was moving from place to place and targeting one dog owner at a time, or so I assumed, but we couldn't count on his not returning to the houses on Jonquil Lane.

"I took the chicken to the police station to be tested," Ronda said. "I'm sure this is part of the poisoner's scheme."

"It must be. Who would throw a whole chicken away?"

"Yeah. That's seven or eight dollars."

Inviting me to view the tape whenever I had time, Ronda ended the call. A picture of the chicken formed in my mind, crisp and golden brown. Irresistible, just waiting for a dog or perhaps a human hungry enough to eat a dinner found on the ground. With that image, a troubling thought came to me.

Like every community, Foxglove Corners had a homeless population. At times vagrants had taken possession of one of the unfinished houses in the abandoned development on Jonquil Lane. The site had been steeped in dark and gloom—some said haunted— ever since the developer had gone bankrupt and left the state, giving the acres back to nature.

At least one structure was barely habitable, albeit with whole walls and windows missing. Bitterly cold in the winter, stifling during a heat wave, still it offered shelter and safety to one who had no other dwelling. The surrounding woods provided berries for food, and the dangers of venturing in the ruins assured the vagrant a measure of privacy.

The drawback? Occasionally the police raided the dying development and sent the squatters on their way.

What if one of that shadowy fringe had chanced on a warm, ready-to-eat rotisserie chicken? He wouldn't have heard of the attempted poisoning of dogs. He would eat it and die a painful and lonely death. Somehow before that happened, we had to find the miscreant responsible for scattering tainted food across the countryside.

But maybe—my mind gave me another fearsome thought—maybe it had already happened.

~ * ~

After talking to Ronda, I decided a second surveillance of our property was a good idea.

Most of the collies were resting in various parts of the house, but Halley and Misty joined me outside and followed me as I inspected every flower bed and shrub on the property. I peered into Raven's house and walked slowly to what I called the perimeter, the invisible line the dogs didn't cross when they were off-leash.

Recent winds had deposited bits of trash here and there. I picked up a page from the *Banner*, an empty candy bar wrapper, and a circular from a new pizza place. Halley sniffed at an empty package that had contained oatmeal cookies. I added it to my collection.

I thought I was finished when Halley and Misty began barking. They had found a white box and were play-struggling with each other to possess it.

Losing no time, I broke up the impromptu tug-of-war and lifted the prize high above their heads. It had been hiding under a plant so large and leafy that it might have seeded over from Brent's wildflower field.

Halley gave up with good grace, but Misty jumped up on me.

"Down," I said, and examined the box. It was empty except for crumbs and dabs of frosting on the sides.

Where was the cake?

In the end, Misty led me to it. She glanced at me over her shoulder and turned back to her new discovery. A dollop of strawberry frosting glittered on her nose.

Dear God! My heart skipped a beat, then speeded up. When did that happen? In the last heartbeat? She'd just been squabbling with Halley.

I hurried to her, grabbed her collar, and uttered a quick prayer. When whole, the cake had been one of those handy eight-by-ten sizes, ideal for tea or lunch. A chunk of it was gone, about a third.

"Misty," I cried. "You didn't..."

She wagged her tail, dark eyes a-sparkle with mischief.

"Did you?"

I didn't think so. She had thrust her long nose into the frosting, but no tell-tale crumbs clung to her face. She looked happy but not guilty.

A hawk soared high in the sky, and I had a sense of eyes watching me from the woods. My dogs weren't the only ones who would succumb to the lure of cake.

It's all right, I thought, and told myself to believe it. Nonetheless, I'd better call Doctor Foster and watch Misty for any sign of distress.

"In the house," I told the dogs and started walking to the door. As soon as everyone was safe inside, I would go back and scoop up the rest of the cake.

One more item to be tested for poison.

~ * ~

I finally found the rest of the cake. It was intact, only the frosting disturbed.

Later, after receiving assurances from Doctor Foster that Misty probably hadn't eaten any of the suspicious cake, I had one of those thoughts that sometimes appear in the wake of an incident.

Ronda had found a rotisserie chicken in her yard; I'd found pork chops and cake. This reign of terror had begun with roast beef left at Sue's ranch.

I saw a clear connection. We were members of the Lakeville Collie Rescue League. Our dogs were all collies.

The realization stopped me in my tracks. I sat at the kitchen table, trying to divine the significance of that connection. Then I remembered the other cases of attempted poisonings, the ones chronicled in the *Banner*. I didn't know the breeds of the dogs involved. One of them had ingested tainted meat and barely survived.

Perhaps that meant we weren't dealing with a would-be killer of dogs who had a special vendetta against collies and those who rescued them.

Crane stacked old papers in the basement until we recycled them. It took a little while, but finally I found Jill Lodge's article.

The known victims were a golden retriever, a six month old German shepherd puppy, and a rescued greyhound. All large dogs. No collies. And no way to anticipate the poisoner's next move.

What we needed was a clue. What *I* needed was a cup of tea.

Could the connection I thought I'd found have been a coincidence? There could well be other dogs whose stories hadn't yet been documented. Logic told me that not every home owner was as scrupulous about checking the grounds as I was, and not every canine death was investigated. And what about the strays?

Candy placed her paws on the table, searching for the doughnut or roll I usually ate when I drank tea. Aside from a vase of fresh wildflowers, the table was bare. As a pilfered snack wasn't possible at this time, she ran to the door and raked it with an imperious paw.

She wanted to go outside, and I was reasonably certain no one had left a poisoned treat on our property in the brief time I'd been in the house, but I couldn't be positive. No dog owner could be satisfied with "reasonably certain" these days.

Twenty

Sunshine poured in through the window of my classroom, sending the heat index soaring and spreading a message far and wide: *The last day is here. Summer vacation begins. Come walk in the sun.*

In fourth hour American Literature, it was quieter than it had ever been. Heads bent low over desks, hands moving, this was the kind of class I had longed for all semester and the one before.

No one talked or even whispered. Nobody claimed to be in dire need of a drink of water. Teachers without exams to give patrolled the halls, and, best of all, Grimsley had left the building for the day. Amazing how the atmosphere changed with this simple act. Everything, even the air, was lighter. It was a minor miracle.

I stole a glance at the clock. Another half hour. Then I turned my watch around. The hands were still moving in the wrong direction. One day I'd look and they would be moving forward. At least that was my fantasy.

I turned back to the class. Everyone was still working quietly on the exam.

I had deliberately added a few extra pages to it to make sure no one finished early and began to fidget and disturb the others. This meant it would take me longer to correct the tests, but no matter.

As I waited for my students to finish, I reveled in a sense of satisfaction, of achievement. I'd taken my class from the first recorded words of the earliest American settlers to twenty-first century classics while battling indifference, disruptive behavior and defiance. Now every one of them was going to pass the course.

That was achievement, indeed, and next fall when I faced a new group and the same archaic pieces of literature, I'd move forward with renewed enthusiasm. Such was the life of a high school teacher.

The bell rang.

Tests piled up on my desk. Bianca and Will told me to have a 'good summer' as they filed out into the hall amid erupting chaos. I wouldn't see them again except in passing unless I taught English literature for seniors next year.

All teachers are expected to remain in the halls between tests and especially at the end of the last day. Grimsley had repeated his mantra until it seemed to echo from the walls.

In that he was justified. Exuberance takes many forms. Happy looking-forward-to-fun screams. Confetti made from notebook paper torn to tiny bits, making the floor slippery. Entire notebooks discarded. Lockers emptied. A yellow jacket that appeared new left on the floor to be trampled.

I bent to retrieve it and felt a burst of cold water on my neck and hair.

Darn!

Not a water balloon.

Then a water pistol? The forbidden toy that could cause a student to be expelled. If you could catch him.

On the last day?

Mindful of Grimsley's edict, I looked down the hall but couldn't see anything except streams of young people heading for the doors as if a tornado bore down on them. The water bandit had chosen his moment well. I stood in the hall, enjoying the touch of cold on the hot day.

Finally the hall was quiet, the floor littered, the school year over. Oh, we teachers would be back tomorrow to grade papers and neaten our rooms for their long summer nap, but the school year was essentially over. I was more than ready to walk in the sun.

~ * ~

"How shall we celebrate?" Leonora asked as I entered the freeway.

"With a treat at Clovers," I said. "I'd like another lime cooler. Or two or three."

Leonora smiled. "And take-out."

She had come a long way from the days when she hesitated to serve her brand new husband a restaurant dinner.

Congratulations, Jennet, I told myself. *Another job well done.*

The drive to Foxglove Corners seemed shorter. The familiar roads swam in haze, lending the countryside a touch of magic. If only we could capture the lunatic who traveled around the Corners leaving raw meat in his wake for unsuspecting dogs. If only Annica and I could solve the mystery of the ghost in the wildflower field. And Minta...I'd have to see if she had received any more anonymous messages.

My summer was going to be busy, and Crane and I hadn't even planned a vacation.

When we entered Clovers, Annica swooped down on us in a jangle of silver—bell earrings, a charm bracelet, and a long necklace adorned with more charms. To set off this extravaganza of silver, she wore black with a ruffly pink polka dot apron that contradicted the sophisticated image she liked to project.

"I hoped I'd see you, Jennet," she said. "Now that school's over, can we plan our trip to the wildflower field?"

"It isn't quite over yet," I said. "We still have two work days."

"Can I tag along?" Leonora asked. "I'm feeling brave."

"The more the merrier," Annica said.

Leonora cast a covetous glance at my wrist. "I'd like to find a magic watch like Jennet's."

"I can't promise that. It'd be easier to find a needle in a haystack."

"Crane found your watch."

"Have you seen the ghost or heard the dog again?" I asked.

"No, it's been quiet, but Huron Court was all foggy early this morning. Especially in the field."

"It was the same till we entered the freeway," I said. "Then it burned off by the time we reached Marston."

"Remember, the apparition came and went in the fog," Annica reminded me.

I couldn't have forgotten. Mist and fog lay frequently on that strange road, sometimes accompanying the ghosts in their visitations.

"We're going to have lime coolers," I said.

"And take-out dinners," Leonora added.

Annica whipped out her order pad. "Mary Jeanne made forty-eight stuffed cabbages today, but they're not selling. I guess people think they're too heavy in this heat."

"Not for me," I said. "We'll take four of them off your hands."

"Make that eight."

I smiled. Leonora usually ordered what I chose.

"Now that I have so much time, I'm going to do more cooking," I said. "Camille gave me her recipe for stuffed cabbage."

"You have lofty plans," Leonora said.

I thought of other summers, other plans. Like New Year's resolutions they tended to fall by the wayside in the first weeks.

Not this time.

Annica served our drinks, and with my first sip, I felt as if she had added a special ingredient, a blend of energy, enthusiasm, and determination.

For once, I thought. *Let me accomplish everything I set out to do this summer.*

It was, after all, up to me whether I did or not.

~ * ~

A dead animal lay by the side of Jonquil Lane. A dog? I didn't think so, but similar. A coyote then? Yes, a coyote.

I left the idling car in the lane and walked over to the motionless body of the wild creature who had once prowled the woods. No more. It hadn't been run over. What had happened to it?

When I'd first become aware that coyotes were our close neighbors, I'd seen them everywhere. Their eerie cries in the night disturbed my sleep. I'd heard tales of cats and small dogs being stolen for food, and irrationally feared for my dogs, even though I walked them three at a time and any one was a match for a marauding coyote.

What killed it?

I took one last look at its lifeless face. It could have been poisoned. Ever scrounging for food, it could easily have come across a chunk of poisoned meat intended for somebody's dog.

Well, I didn't want to leave it lying on the lane. I, or more likely, Crane would come back with a shovel and bury it. Ever the southern gentleman, Crane would tell that this was no job for a woman. And today I wouldn't contradict him.

The sight of the dead coyote had cast a shadow on the otherwise golden last day of school without students.

Almost an omen.

I took one last look at it.

No, it was no such thing.

I only wished I knew what had killed it.

Twenty-one

The sky darkened, and thunder rumbled in the north. A storm was brewing over Foxglove Corners. Safe in my silent classroom in Oakpoint, I thought about home. Sky would take refuge in the most secure place she knew, under the dining room table. I didn't worry about the rest of my collie brood. They were troopers, used to riding out thunderstorms.

If this were only a run-of-the-mill thunderstorm and nothing worse. I was optimistic. It had been described as intermittent afternoon showers.

I could almost see what was happening in the house on Jonquil Lane. Misty would find her toy goat and carry it to safety, most likely to where Sky lay under the table. There both dogs would stay until they sensed that the worse was over. It wasn't that Misty feared storms; she wanted to protect Sky. My good dogs.

I turned back to my work.

With the exception of stacks of graded tests and a half pack of copy paper, my desk was bare. I'd already stored the books I used every day—like teachers' editions of texts, the Roget's *Thesaurus*, and *Bartlett's Quotations* in the closet.

I had one more set of tests to grade and bulletin boards to take down, for who wants to come back to school in the fall with sun-faded pictures of a summer gone by?

I also had an accumulation of abandoned items to drop off at the front office. One was a water pistol, left on my desk after fourth period. I hadn't seen its owner and was glad I hadn't had to demand its surrender. No teacher needed confrontation and commotion during a final exam.

I stared at the pistol, marveling how real it looked. A little water had dripped on the desk's finish. I blotted it with a tissue and considered.

Why leave a perfectly good summer toy behind? Grimsley's restrictions didn't apply to the rest of Oakpoint. One of the secretaries would probably just toss it in the wastebasket, along with others of its kind.

In that case...I opened my shoulder bag and dropped it inside. The dogs might enjoy being sprayed with water on the next ninety degree plus day.

Leonora came into my room with a thermos and her lunch in a paper bag and sat at a student desk. She reached for two sheets of white paper and made herself a placemat, shaking her head at the pencil sketches on the freshly polished wood.

"If it rains, the courtyard will be too wet," she said. "How are your tests?"

I was grading World Literature exams. "So far, they're good. My first hour has always been a bright group."

"Are you ready to take a lunch break? I brought brownies."

"Just a minute." I finished reading an essay and wrote a large 'A' on the first page.

We could have as long a lunch period as we wished today. Some teachers were going out to a restaurant as a department. But old habits are hard to break. I would rather stay in, especially with the threatening weather. Obviously so would Leonora.

"Grimsley is still out of the building, but he left us a message. As soon as our work is done, we can leave. It's a sort of strange end to the school year."

In past years, we had a brief meeting that amounted to a thank you for our hard work, cake provided by one of the secretaries, and punch. And a time to wish everyone a happy summer.

Well, we could provide our own cake and punch. Instead of punch, another lime cooler at Clovers, perhaps?

"That's an incentive to work hard," I said.

Then we were free for the next several weeks. But a celebration, even a low-key one, would have been a nice way to wrap up the school year.

~ * ~

"There's no way the ghost is going to show herself today," I said as I parked the Ford Focus on Huron Court. "Every time I've seen a supernatural apparition, I've been alone."

Every time?

I thought of the phantom Christmas tree again. Two of us had witnessed its last manifestation— my enemy and I.

"Do you think my presence is jinxing you?" Leonora asked.

"Not at all. It's like Annica wants a ghost on demand. That's not the way it works. We may see it today. Or not."

Annica said, "I object. I just don't want to miss anything, and I can't be here every minute."

Leonora aimed her cell phone at the lush expanse of vibrant wildflowers, some of which were taller than we were. "It's gorgeous. Whichever way you look, there's color. Could we walk in it a little way?"

"You can, but don't forget what happened to me. When I fell."

"The ghost was here then," I pointed out. "You were advancing on her."

Leonora said, "I want to take pictures from different angles. Then I'll take some of you and Annica so everyone can see how tall the flowers grew."

They were still growing. New splashes of color appeared in what had been green spaces during my last visit. Who would believe that a large Victorian house had once stood on this land?

It must be something in the earth, some secret ingredient that encourages unnatural, wild growth. A case in point? Violet's mysterious African violet plants.

"Those seeds we planted were magic," Annica said. "I should write to the company."

"Who's coming with me?" Leonora asked.

Neither Annica nor I rushed to answer. "Try to stay on the walkways," I said.

"What walkways? I don't see any."

"They're there."

I knelt and ran my hand over the ground. It was still damp from yesterday's rain. Pushing aside a trailing vine, I uncovered a square of concrete.

"Just follow the trail," I said.

"And don't fall," Annica added.

For a moment Leonora hesitated, then took a few tentative steps into the flowering jungle.

I thought I heard a sound, a dog barking far away. Not in the wildflower field.

Not on this earth?

In the next instant, the first tendrils of white fog rose out of the ground—or dropped down from the sky. It was difficult to tell. All I knew was that a certain area of the field was wreathed in fog. And I couldn't see Leonora.

~ * ~

The fog spread. It thickened, seemed to crawl out to meet us.

An illusion, I told myself. *It isn't a Stephen King fog.*

No? How could it have developed so rapidly then? Fog didn't do that.

I slipped into full panic mode. "Leonora!" My voice bounced back to me, an echo in the stillness.

Why was it suddenly so quiet?

"I don't see her." Annica grabbed my arm. "Maybe she fell."

It could be. Suddenly encased in a moving wall of white. Losing your sense of direction. The floor of the wildflower field was thick with heavy vines.

I called her name again. Annica joined her voice to mine.

No answer.

"We have to go after her," I said.

"Go through the fog?"

"Where else?"

A moment ago, it had appeared closer to the road. Not that it was breaking up, but...

I lost my thought. Glancing at my watch, I saw that only minutes, perhaps three, had passed since Leonora had entered the field. The hand moved in the wrong direction, but I'd learned to make adjustments.

I found the large patio stone I'd uncovered for Leonora. Already the vine had sprung back. Vine? There were more than one.

"Take my hand, Annica," I said. "Don't let go."

With her free hand, she pushed a thick stalk away. Judging by its tight green buds, it was going to be a lily. But whoever saw a lily that tall?

"It's like it was before," Annica said. "The flowers are so thick. It's hard to move."

I took a deep breath. Then another. Potent fragrances assailed me, conjured images of walking into a funeral parlor, which I always dreaded.

"Well, it isn't water," I said. "Follow me."

The fog held its arms open to receive us. Long white fronds dripped down to the ground.

Dear God, I thought. *This isn't natural.*

Not the least bit natural, but it was for Leonora.

Twenty-two

We hadn't walked far into the fog when I stumbled and would have fallen if Annica hadn't tightened her grip on my hand. A muffled moan told me I'd come into contact with a body part. With Leonora.

She lay sprawled at our feet on top of a batch of flowers resembling Queen Anne's Lace. They were pink and twice as large as the common white ones growing around Foxglove Corners. She was awake but seemed stunned. The fog was rapidly dissipating, allowing us to see her clearly.

"Are you hurt?" I asked.

"My ankle hurts. I hope I didn't sprain it." Her voice was hoarse. "I thought you left me."

Annica helped Leonora to rise. She stood but leaned heavily on Annica.

"We came as soon as we saw the fog move in," Annica said a little defensively. "Right away. We'd never leave you here."

"Even though we couldn't see you," I added.

Even though for one very brief moment I'd thought the fog had taken you away. I could think that, now that we'd found her.

"It seemed a lot longer," Leonora said. "I called and called."

I glanced at Annica who shook her head. We hadn't heard Leonora's calls. It was as if the fog had trapped her with its moist folds and tentacles. This was no time to debate the issue, though.

Leonora held her hand to her head and took a step. "I'm a little dizzy...Oh...Something's holding me down!"

I knelt. "It's just a vine." As I tugged at it, long red welts appeared on my palm. The vine didn't move.

"Get it off me!" she cried.

"Let me." Annica ripped the vine away from Leonora's sneaker. The movement almost made her fall backward. "This is a killer field."

"Let's get out of it," Leonora said. "Wait! My phone. I dropped it."

"It can't have gone far." I knelt again and felt along the ground, pushing plants out of the way. At last my hand closed on the phone, warm from its time in the sun and, I hoped, unharmed. "I found it!"

"Then let's get out of here," Annica said.

The fog was gone, seemingly in moments, leaving the multi-colored wildflower field baking under the sun. The view would be spectacular, if one were standing on Huron Court. Here, at the field's center, the mix of cloying fragrances and the harsh, unavoidable brush of leaves and stalks overrode the beauty.

"My ankle," Leonora murmured.

"Can you walk?" I asked.

"Yes, anything to get back on land," Leonora said.

Her word choice puzzled me. We *were* on land. She meant Huron Court, of course, and how unusual to think of that accursed road as a place of refuge.

"Let's get you in the car," I said. "You should have your ankle looked at. There's a new Urgent Care in Lakeville."

I expected her to object, but she simply said, "That may be a good idea, but if it were sprained or broken, I couldn't walk on it. Could I?"

"I wouldn't think so."

"I just feel all banged up," she said.

"How did you fall?" Annica asked.

"I heard a dog barking and turned. Just turned. Something grabbed my foot, and I lost my balance."

"It must have been the vine," I said. "The field is crawling with them."

"I thought it was a snake."

Annica frowned. "We never planted vining flowers. Where did they come from?"

"Lots of annuals have vines," I said. "If you'd planted them in a window box, they'd trail down. Here they just spread on the ground."

And grow as strong as rope and impede walking. What a chilling thought! Was that their purpose?

"When did you call us, Leonora?" Annica asked. "Before you heard the dog or after?"

"Before—I think. When that fog came out of nowhere. I couldn't see anything, and I panicked."

We had reached the road, reached the safety of the car, and concentrated on helping Leonora into the back seat. She seemed to have changed her mind about her ankle, as she began to rub it.

"It really does hurt. I don't suppose you have Aspercreme your rescue kit, do you?"

"Sorry, no. I don't even have any in my medicine cabinet."

"I do. I can wait. Can we just go home? Now my head hurts, too. I'm sorry to be so whiney," she added.

"You'll feel it more tomorrow," Annica said. "And the next day and the next."

"Thanks for that, Annica."

I walked around to the driver's side and started the engine, anxious to leave the wildflower field far behind.

"Are you *sure* you didn't hear me calling you?" Leonora asked. "Because I did. Five or six times at least."

"We didn't," I said.

What else was there to say? Leonora claimed she'd called to us. We hadn't heard her. But why be surprised or confused? In other circumstances, I would wonder if Leonora had fallen on her head, but this was one of the strangest places in Foxglove Corners, Home of the Strange. The unearthly fog had snatched her cries away from us.

Something occurred to me then. "But we all heard the dog barking."

~ * ~

After some discussion, we decided that the dog had no connection to the wildflower field. In all likelihood, it was a stray roaming the countryside. In other words, not part of the apparition.

"It's odd that he didn't come near us, though," I said.

"Not so odd if he didn't want to get caught," Annica countered. "I wish we'd seen the flower ghost."

"Or found something interesting like the watch," Leonora added. "I'm glad I came today, but I don't intend to set foot in that field ever again."

I'd said something similar about Huron Court, and this was the second time I'd ventured onto what was once forbidden territory.

"I can't say the same," Annica said. "I intend to go back again and again. I have a feeling this haunting has only begun. It has significance for me. I just haven't figured it out yet."

By the time we reached the outskirts of Lakeville, Leonora decided that she didn't want to stop at the Urgent Care.

"I'll just take a hot bath and a couple of pain pills," she said. "I took a few good pictures before the fog rolled in. We can look at them later."

"Tomorrow," I said.

Now that the adventure was over, I began to think of recording it in the book I was writing about my supernatural experiences in Foxglove Corners. To be sure, this wasn't *my* apparition, but I'd stood on its fringes, and who knew what the future would bring? It would be a good companion piece to my chapter on the pink Victorian.

Mentally I added working on the chapter to my summer's 'to do' list, but before I could do that, I had to understand what was going on in the wildflower field that Brent and Annica had so blithely planted.

~ * ~

At home, the day's adventure caught up to me. Anyone would think I was the one who had fallen. My arms and legs ached from plowing through the tall, close-growing plants.

They were super plants that had grown into something more than Brent had intended when he'd purchased the acreage on Huron Court. He had wanted to erase all traces of the fire that had leveled the pink Victorian, thereby eradicating the memory of what had happened there. As if that were possible. He wanted, moreover, to create a place of beauty for travelers as they drove by.

He had certainly attained his modest goal. The seeds grew, the rich soil nourished the perennials, and air, rain, and water had done their best. The flowers were stronger and brighter than others of their kind, their colors richer, their fragrances sweeter.

Too sweet.

I couldn't forget the violets. Their sister plants had left them behind. I didn't recall seeing them.

Suddenly I wanted to talk to Brent about his masterpiece, to see what he thought of it now that a ghost had smiled on the flowers and two healthy young women had fallen while walking through them.

I decided not to wait for one of his impromptu visits to invite him to dinner tonight.

Twenty-three

Brent scooped up the last forkful of his strawberry pie and set the dessert plate on the coffee table where Candy eyed it with unmistakable desire. Did he leave a crumb? Maybe more? And how soon could she make her move?

"Jennet has a never-ending supply of homemade pies in her kitchen, Sheriff," Brent said. "Each one tastes better than the one before. I hope you know how lucky you are."

Crane winked at me. "I think I do."

"Flatterers."

I had half a pie left. We might as well finish it. "It's only strawberries and meringue with graham cracker crust."

"All my favorites," Brent said.

"Who wants another piece?"

They both did, and Candy whimpered. Misty was in her pre-whimper stage. The other dogs were aware and alert, waiting for exciting developments. It was time to raid the Lassie tin.

"I wish we had strawberries in the wildflower field," Brent said. "Can you imagine how big and sweet they'd be?"

Only too well, I thought, as I divided the rest of the pie into three pieces. It was the first time he had mentioned the wildflowers, which was the reason I'd invited him for dinner.

By then, the dogs had congregated in the kitchen. I spilled the contents of the Lassie tin on a sheet of newspaper and moved out of the way as they advanced on it.

"Michigan berries aren't ready yet," I pointed out as I carried the last of the pie in on a tray. "These came from California."

"I wonder if it's too late to plant them for this year?" he said.

"I'd say so, but you don't want to add anything to the field. There's enough there already."

With this opening, I told him about Leonora's experience and my own, which paled beside hers.

"Don't forget Annica's ghost." I touched my watch but decided not to mention it. "And that fog. It comes and goes over the field at will."

"Are you saying I created a monster?" he asked.

"Not really."

"What then?"

"Mmm. Just a second." I swallowed. This particular strawberry was on the tart side. I'd use more sugar in the next pie.

"Something's going on there," I said. "I don't know what. Are you aware that Annica is driving out to Huron Court every day before her classes or her shift at Clovers?"

As soon as I spoke, I wished I could take the words back. Maybe he already knew. More likely, Annica didn't want him to know about her obsession. In any event, it wasn't my story to tell.

"If there's another manifestation, she doesn't want to miss it," I added.

Crane said, "Jennet, if you want to go back to the field someday, I'll go with you. It's too easy to fall in that wilderness. What if you were alone?"

I shuddered as I visualized that improbable scenario. Trapped by vines, unable to get up and away from the relentless sun, and no one to hear my cries for help.

Leonora's calls had gone unheard, while Annica and I had been within hearing distance.

That wouldn't happen, though. At the first sign of fog, the first telltale wisp, I would backtrack immediately. But could I move as fast as that accursed fog? All beside the point.

It won't happen.

"Don't worry, Crane," I said. "I won't put myself in harm's way again. Annica, though...I worry about her."

"I'll have a talk with Annica," Brent said. "And I'm going to check out the place myself. Jennet, I think you're exaggerating. My flowers are healthy, but they aren't..." He trailed off, searching for a word that eluded him.

I helped him out. "Excessively tall and vibrant? Unnatural? Deadly?"

"Deadly?" He stared at me. "You're serious, aren't you?"

"It can be a frightening place," I said.

"Well, I never intended for anyone to go tramping through it," he said.

"You used those large patio stones to make walkways, though."

"Walkways, sure. Rows. In case we wanted to cut flowers for a bouquet."

I couldn't resist. "Or sprinkle them with Miracle-Gro."

"We never did that. You're getting carried away, Jennet. It's just a prime location for the flowers we planted. There are no trees to block the sun, and we had plenty of rain this spring."

"What about Annica's ghost?" I asked.

"You of all people know that the supernatural fringe loves to hang out in Foxglove Corners," he said. "You and Lucy are in touch with ghosts, and Annica feels left out. Now she's seen one herself. That's what I think."

I swirled my fork through the meringue, feeling suddenly guilty. "Annica would hate to know we were talking about her."

"You're both concerned about your friend," Crane pointed out. "That's good. I don't like to think of Annica visiting that place every day either."

"Because sooner or later something will happen to her?" I asked. "She already fell."

"I was thinking it's unhealthy. Also, how does she have the time with her busy schedule?"

"I'm going to make Annica the same offer you made Jennet," Brent said. "If she wants to go ghost hunting, I'll go with her. Otherwise, from now on, she can keep her distance."

I turned a laugh into a cough. Did he really think Annica was going to stay away from their field at a word from him? Obsessions don't understand reason. Not even if the rational one is a man you wanted above all to please.

He glared at me. "Did I say something funny?"

"Annica makes her own decisions," I said. "She'll never listen to you."

"We'll see," he said.

Yes, we would. It had been clear for a long time. There was a definite mystery in the wildflower field, and it was my duty, as Annica's friend, to solve it. Or at least to try.

~ * ~

Another one of my friends was in trouble. Minta had received another anonymous message in the usual way. This one warned of specific danger to Sparkle.

"I haven't entered Sparkle in any shows," Minta said. "I haven't gone to any alone. We've been lying low, staying close to home."

"Doing what he told you to. What does he say this time?"

"That it was too late. I should say goodbye to Sparkle. Her days are numbered."

"I don't understand," I said. "We thought he was a competitor wanting a clear field for his own dog."

"I don't think that's his motivation anymore."

"Where are you now?" I asked.

"On the back porch with Sparkle. It's nice and private. I took her for a walk early this morning. We only passed a few runners."

"She should be safe then."

Except I knew too well that if a determined ne'er-do-well had targeted a dog, she would never be safe. There would come a time out in the yard, for example, when Minta would be distracted by adjusting the water in a sprinkler, by picking a flower, or by a quick 'hello' to a neighbor over the fence.

She wouldn't see a chunk of raw meat laced with a lethal substance.

"Why don't you and Sparkle take a ride out to Foxglove Corners today," I said. "Bring the message, and we'll brainstorm."

She accepted by invitation so quickly I thought that had been her reason for the call all along.

Twenty-four

We sat on the porch, Minta and I, with a pitcher of ice cold lemonade and eight collies in various stages of repose—except for Misty. Her attention was riveted on the woods across the lane. My collies often appeared to see something invisible to the human eye. At times, when we were in the house, they stared at the ceiling, which, in my opinion, was the most unnerving of all.

I had grown used to this bizarre behavior, figuring that something was there, or had been there, whether I could see it or not. With Misty, my psychic collie, the object of her surveillance could well be a supernatural apparition. If I were meant to see it, I would in due time, so it was pointless to stew about it.

I stirred the lemonade, setting the ice cubes to tinkle against the pitcher's glass sides, and refilled our glasses. Minta accepted hers and drank immediately. Seeing that it was refreshment time, Misty tore her eyes off the woods and lapped water from the dog's large pail, splashing it on the wood floor.

Minta laughed. "I love to see a collie drink."

She wore a short denim skirt and cornflower blue top trimmed in white with a silver necklace, always colors chosen to complement Sparkle's fur.

I should dress to match my collies, in black and tan for Halley and Candy. Or white for Misty or blue for Sky. All it took was planning.

Minta was saying, "I've decided I'm not going to stay away from the shows."

What had I missed while I'd been woolgathering?

"You don't mean you changed your mind about showing Sparkle, do you?" I asked.

"Oh, I won't take her with me, but whoever's sending me these messages might be a dog hater masquerading as a dog lover hanging out at the shows."

"You may be right," I said.

"Except for the heir aspirant, there's no one in my life who would want to hurt me by doing something bad to Sparkle."

"No one?" I asked, thinking of her boyfriend, Gavin, who didn't like dogs. "We can't always know what a person is really like, deep down."

"If I had an enemy, I think I'd know it."

"It depends on how clever and devious he is and also his motivation."

She pulled the latest message out of her pocket. "This is the worst one yet. Listen:

You chose to ignore my warnings. Now you're out of time. Enjoy Sparkle while you still have her. Her days are numbered.

"I can't take any more of this," she said. "He wanted me to keep Sparkle out of the shows. I've done that. It's like he changed his plan from one message to the next."

"Because he's unbalanced," I said. "And I wonder if it's Sparkle he has the grudge against—or you."

"I've never, ever harmed anyone. Not intentionally," she added.

"There it is. 'Not intentionally.' You have a lot of thinking to do, Minta. Go back over the past year and even further. Examine all your relationships. You said you've been in college?"

"Yes, and concentrating on my studies. I was never part of the college social scene. I started with a certain amount of savings and needed to complete my course work before my money ran out. I just made it."

"How about boyfriends?" I asked, hoping to turn her thoughts to Gavin.

"Well, you can tell if you're in an abusive relationship, can't you? Fortunately I've never had that experience."

"How about Gavin?"

"He isn't abusive. He just doesn't like dogs. Gavin is a lot of fun, but I'm not planning a future with him, so what he likes doesn't really matter."

Minta knew Gavin. I didn't. But I couldn't help be suspicious of a person who didn't like dogs.

"There must be someone, somewhere," I said. "You'll have to identify your own possible enemies. No one else can do it for you, and it doesn't have to be at a dog show."

"But you'll come to the next show with me, won't you?" she asked.

I had promised. Drat. But she might be right. Whoever was determined to kill Sparkle— and that was how I interpreted the threatening note— would probably go to all the shows, trusting that Minta would also attend, hoping she'd bring Sparkle.

"I will," I said, "and I think Annica will want to come, too."

"Good. It's next Saturday. We should be there around one."

Would the threatener leave another message between now and then? I wondered. This newest note conveyed a sense of time running out. Sparkle's time.

Her days are numbered.

I bent down and swirled my hand through Sparkle's thick coat, ignoring that old adage, 'Let sleeping dogs lie.' She flattened her ears and wagged her tail. Misty, instantly alert, pushed my hand away from Sparkle, dowsing me with water.

Most of the collies had dozed off, except for Halley who had brought her Nylabone out to the porch to chew. The scene was so tranquil, the view so soothing, it seemed impossible that evil could ever invade our piece of paradise, that we should sit with our dogs anticipating violence to one of them.

After a while, Minta asked, "Have you found any more poisoned meat in your yard?"

"No," I said, "and I haven't heard that anyone else has, but I did find a dead coyote on the lane, possibly poisoned. Crane buried it."

How much time had elapsed since I'd found the beef roast at Sue's ranch and the pork chops at mine? Weeks. I'd viewed the footage Ronda had captured and agreed with her. It wasn't much help. We couldn't even decide if the figure was male or female. I guessed a male with a slender build.

Could I dare hope that the terror was over? Except for the coyote, if he'd chanced on meat intended for a dog.

No, I told myself. *Let your guard down and it'll happen again.*

"It looks like your problem may be solved," Minta said. "I'm so happy for you. Now we can work on mine."

"We'll find your enemy or die trying. Uh-oh. Bad word choice."

"Let's hope it won't come to that." She set her empty glass on the wicker table and reached for her car keys. "I'd better get us home. See you Saturday."

I watched her drive out to the lane and decided to stay on the porch for a while and enjoy the scenery. Misty had returned to her surveillance of the woods. Halley turned her bone over with her paw, and Raven laid her head on her paws and closed her eyes. And I contemplated hamburger tossed into the shrubbery.

Our tormentor wasn't the kind to give us anonymous warnings. In a way that was unfortunate. Forewarned is forearmed, I always said. Was he just going to ride off into the sunset?

If so, that was all right as long as he never returned to Foxglove Corners.

~ * ~

The next day I checked Annica's schedule and drove to Clovers to remind her about our promise—my promise, rather—to accompany Minta to the collie show at Maple Creek.

She looked like the spirit of summer with her red-gold hair, seashell earrings, and an impractical white sundress.

"I'm one step ahead of you," she said. "I already arranged with Mary Jeanne to have the afternoon off. Is Minta bringing Sparkle?"

"Not this time."

I followed her to the booth I always thought of as mine.

"I'll have a lime cooler," I said. "That's my new favorite drink."

"It's our most popular item. How about a piece of key lime pie to go with it?"

I considered but decided to order only the drink.

When she returned with it, and one for herself, I told her about Minta's latest message. "It sounds ominous."

"So, our job is to watch for a suspicious character at a collie show." She sighed. "It sounds impossible, Jennet. We didn't see any likely suspects at the last one."

"So far as we know," I said. "Still, what else can we do?"

"I can't think of anything, but one way or another we have to find out who's threatening Sparkle. We can't let anything happen to her. My money is on that guy who thought he was going to inherit his aunt's money."

"I'll think it's the boyfriend, Gavin. Minta claims no one would try to hurt her through Sparkle."

"Obviously someone is."

"Our goal is to find him in time to save Sparkle's life," I said, "and the best place to look for him is at the Maple Creek show."

"Looking for the writer of those warnings will take my mind off the wildflower field," Annica said.

"I thought checking it out was your favorite pastime."

"Brent's developed a weird attitude toward it. He wants me to stay away from the field. He forgets it was our project together. As a team."

This, of course, was no surprise. Still, I asked, "Did he say why?"

"Something about danger. Just because Leonora fell, he thinks it's going to happen to me."

"What? Get trapped in the fog? Risk breaking an ankle? You already fell," I reminded her.

"He says he doesn't want me to go there alone anymore. I'm the one who bought those 'No Trespassing' signs for him at the hardware store. Now he's using them against me."

"Look at the upside," I said.

"Which is...?"

"Lots of time with Brent."

She smiled. "There's that, but no man tells me where I can and can't go."

"Okay, but it *is* his property."

She couldn't think of an answer to that.

Twenty-five

It was my day for unexpected company. The silver Honda turned into the drive, glided slowly up to the house, and parked in the space recently vacated by Minta. I recognized the newcomers as Diane Weatherall and Kristie Martin, the girls who had helped us track down the Silverhedge collies.

On the porch, the dogs came instantly alert to another of their kind inside the car and set up the requisite clamor.

Diane and Kristie, both in shorts and sequin-sprinkled tops, sprang out of the car. Diane led a bouncy tricolor collie out onto the lawn while her cousin Kristie closed the doors. The sunlight gave the tri's black coat a mesmerizing blue shine.

Rilla! How I loved tris!

"Hey, Jennet," Diane called. "Is it okay if I bring Rilla closer?" She adjusted Rilla's red-white-and-blue bandana and gave her a quick pat on the head.

"Sure," I said, as I became aware of a low growl. Most of the collies were wagging their tails, but Candy had bared her teeth. She'd never been the most welcoming of our brood, but she seemed especially testy lately.

"Candy! Behave!" I took hold of her collar and looked for Sky. She had taken refuge under the round wicker table. Sky had been calm during Sparkle's visit, but the arrival of another strange collie so soon proved too much for her to deal with.

Diane flopped down on the bottom step, keeping her hand on Rilla's chain, while Kristie waded through wagging tails to the wicker rocker.

"Doesn't Rilla look great?" Diane asked. "She put on a little weight, and her coat is fuller."

"I can see that." I caressed her soft, warm fur and hated to move my hand. I was sure Rilla remembered me. "You are *so* beautiful, Rilla."

Rilla was one of the lost Silverhedge collies rescued from their villainous caregiver whose nefarious plans we'd thwarted. Now reunited with Diane, she couldn't have looked happier or prettier.

"Did you bring Rilla out for a ride?" I asked.

"We're on our way to an orientation at Ms. Appleton's ranch," Kristie said. "We're going to be working there three days a week helping her with the dogs and horses."

Diane said, "Ms. Appleton has four new riding students. She says she can use the help. We're going to work mostly with the collies."

I knew Sue had been considering hiring the girls for the summer. As president of the Lakeville Collie Rescue League, she had managed to take care of her own collies, along with fostering an occasional rescue. But the arrival of the Silverhedge dogs, all but two of whom she'd kept, had significantly added to her workload. Then with additional riding students and Rescue League business, she would be unusually busy.

"I'll bet you girls would like some lemonade," I said. "There's another pitcher in the refrigerator." I started to get up, but Diane was already at the door.

"I'll get it," she said, and slipped inside with Sky close on her heels.

"Ms. Appleton said someone's been putting poison down for the dogs," Kristie said. "We can help her make sure the coast is clear before the collies go outside."

"Sue is lucky to have you. I found a package of pork chops and a cake but nothing lately. So far, none of our dogs have taken sick or died, but the threat is always with us."

"That," she said, "is pure evil. Whoever's doing this is worse than that horrible woman who kept Rilla away from Diane."

I agreed. "Much worse."

"I found it," Diane called, "and I'll bring more glasses."

Kristie held the door open, and Diane proceeded to fill the glasses, while I indulged in a pleasant fantasy about having a maid to wait on me instead of fulfilling the servant's role for one husband and seven collies.

Dream on, I told myself.

"I heard what you guys were saying just now," Diane said. "Why are our dogs always under attack? They don't hurt anybody. All they want is to love us and be loved back."

"You know why, Di," Kristie said. "Because some people are naturally evil."

"And because almost everybody is passionate about their dogs," I added. "If some disgruntled sub-human wants to cause another person pain, there's no surer way to do it than to go through her dog."

I was thinking of Minta, of course, whom the girls didn't know.

"That's not what's happening here," Diane pointed out. "This serial poisoner wants to cause a ton of pain at random to lots of people—and to dogs. He's killing two birds with one stone."

"We're going to help you stop him," Kristie announced. "Like we stopped that woman at Silverhedge."

She spoke with an enthusiasm born of youth and confidence. Listening to her made me feel as if we were going to be successful. After all, we now had two extra pairs of eyes.

~ * ~

Having arrived early in Maple Creek on the day of the show, Annica suggested that we stop for a pancake breakfast before going on to the show. Naturally I had no objections. We found a small restaurant, the Breakfast Bar, and ordered their specialty, blueberry pancakes with fresh blueberry syrup. According to the menu, the blueberries came from the Breakfast Bar's own bushes.

I settled back with a cup of coffee while Annica drank water, hoping to fortify herself for the hot, humid afternoon ahead.

"It's great being waited on for a change," Annica said. "I could get used to this."

"When you get your degree, you'll be able to get a better job."

"Yes, but I'm going on to grad school. I guess I'll be carrying trays for the foreseeable future."

She didn't seem disheartened at the prospect. Annica loved her English courses. She was happy in school and satisfied with the status quo, even when applied to Brent.

"Now..." I pulled my orange juice closer and tore the paper off the straw. "Let's strategize for a minute. We're under a deadline, and this may be our last chance to mingle with possible suspects."

Hurry! my wise inner voice urged. *Sparkle's days are numbered.*

"Here's what I propose we do," I said. "Mingle. The last time we were pretty stationary, just standing with Minta and talking."

"That was too passive," Annica added. "We have to work the room."

"Exactly. We'll separate and talk to as many people as we can, exhibitors and spectators both. We can ask leading questions."

I broke off as our waitress served the pancakes. I'd fixed breakfast for Crane this morning and had coffee and toast with him. How could I be so hungry so soon? Probably the effect of going somewhere different.

I lost no time in pouring syrup over my pancake stack. Annica was already eating.

"Here's what we'll say, or some variation of it," I said. "We have collies we plan to enter in the next show. Also we're in the market for a show prospect puppy. And whatever else you think of."

"And we look for...?"

"Anything suspect. Maybe a lack of understanding of the breed standard. Special interest in the blue merle entries. Or even some criticism of Minta."

"And names," Annica said. "We need names. Maybe Minta can supply backgrounds."

"We'll look at people with a new perspective. Afterward, we'll arrange to meet Minta for coffee or something so we can compare notes and brainstorm.

"It could work."

"It has to," I said.

Twenty-six

I knew as soon as I entered the crowded parking lot that we had come to the right place to search for our villain. For every collie at the show, there would be at least one person, be he collie fancier or ill-wisher. And if he was here, I was going to find him.

Vehicles and even trailers, most sporting collie-themed decals on their windows, had taken the best spaces. After cruising up and down aisles, we found a shady spot a short distance from the action next to an SUV that proclaimed 'Collie. Best Family Pet.'

Grabbing a bottle of water for each of us, Annica said, "Let's do it."

The sun beat down on our heads and arms, and the air was thick with humidity. Putting one foot down after another reminded me of wading through the wildflower field where each stem seemed to push us back to the road. But no flowers lived here, only rain-deprived trees on the fringe of the lot.

From the tented enclosure ahead, a cacophony of canine and human voices rode out on the air to greet us, and a promise of festivity waved overhead like a banner. We might have been walking toward a summer fair. Well, this was a fair of sorts, a celebration of the collie.

He's here, my trusty inner voice whispered. *For his own demented reasons, he couldn't stay away.*

"First we'll find Minta," I said. "And remember, we're going to mingle."

A short, wiry brunette in denim clipped past us, looking straight ahead. She led two sable collies who could have been twins. One, slightly smaller, looked back at us, tail wagging happily. Her lookalike companion padded stoically ahead.

"I wish I had entered Angel," Annica said.

"Did you ever take her to conformation classes?" I asked.

"It's on my to-do list."

"If you don't, she won't know how to gait or what to do. Showing well doesn't just come naturally to a dog and it's essential."

"Angel is awfully playful and skittish. Well, I can dream, can't I?"

"There's no law against dreaming."

Especially in this place of dreams.

We strolled past vendors selling souvenirs and collie novelties, past noisy lines in front of a hot dog stand and a portable ice cream 'palace,' and found Minta inside the tented enclosure. Here it was cool, courtesy of the many fans whirring in front of crates to keep the dogs comfortable. Wearing a grass-green sun dress, Minta stood out in the milling crowd, elegant and lovely.

She wasn't alone. A tall man with cropped light brown hair had stationed himself as near to her as possible with his arm draped around her shoulder. The man had all the attributes beloved of the romance novelist, from rugged, chiseled features to a dark tan, set off by a blue shirt. Oh, but it was too hot to be quite that close to another human body. At least in my opinion.

He could only be Gavin. What a pity he didn't like dogs.

"What a doll," Annica said.

"Hush."

"Chill, Jennet. I'm talking about that big collie over there," she said, but her mischievous wink said otherwise.

With a Coke in one hand and a hot dog in the other, Minta's cousin, Randi, stood a little apart from Gavin and Minta. As we approached, Minta's eyes lit up. "Jennet, I'm *so* glad you could make it."

She knew we planned to attend the show as I'd called her this morning. Her surprise must be for Gavin's benefit. I couldn't remember if she'd told Gavin about the warning messages. I didn't think she had.

"I couldn't stay away," I said.

Gavin let his arm fall to his side, and Minta moved imperceptibly away from him. "Girls, this is Gavin." She paused and gave him a hint of a mile. "Gavin, meet Jennet and Annica."

Gavin reached for my hand and all but squashed it. "Hi, Jennet. Anna...?"

"Annica," she corrected.

"Hey, what do you know? That's my mother's name."

Annica smiled. I didn't believe him. Surely Annica didn't.

Minta moved away from Gavin, closer to ringside, and pointed. "See that gorgeous tricolor with the narrow white ruff? She's going to be a big winner today. She's Woodwyn's Black Susiana. Call name Suzy."

"She *is* a beauty," I said.

But then so were all the collies in my view. All the collies I'd ever seen. God had never made an ugly one.

Annica said, "That hot dog looks good, Miranda. I think I'll get one."

After downing six blueberry pancakes? Was she serious? Then I realized she was going to mingle.

"Can I get one for you, Jennet?" she asked.

"No, I'm good," I said. "Only call them franks, okay? We don't use the word 'dog' in front of them."

She rolled her eyes. "Oh, right."

"So Jennet," Gavin said. "Are you another one of these collie fanatics?"

"You could say that."

"Are you showing a dog today?"

I had a fleeting vision of my own collies at home. Sky drowsing under the dining room table, the other dogs in their preferred spaces in the air conditioned house. They always gravitated to the vents.

"Not today," I said.

"Yeah, it's too hot to go prancing around in those heavy coats. As for myself I'd rather be on the golf course."

"Isn't it just as hot out there?" I asked.

He reached for Minta's hand again. "It's a different kind of heat. You have to be a golfer to understand. Anyway, I'll go anywhere to make my girlfriend happy," he added.

"Well it's nice enough in here. No one's going to let their dog get overheated. See that silver blanket over that crate? It's just another way to keep a dog cool."

"Oh, no," Minta said. "Not him again."

At first I thought she was referring to Gavin. Then Randi said, "It's Jeff. The heir. Talk about luck."

Good or bad luck, I wondered, recalling Randi's admiration for him.

Minta's serene expression turned into an indignant scowl. "That jerk is following me around. I'm going to get a personal protection order."

We'd lived through this scene at the first show. The heir aspirant waved to us and threaded his way through the crowd.

I didn't have to mingle. Yet.

"Hey, Minta," Jeff said as he forced his way into our group. "You're looking nice and cool."

She maneuvered her lips into a half smile. "Thanks. I don't feel cool."

Jeff looked cool himself, every blond hair in place, although he wore a crisp white shirt and tie, not exactly a dog show outfit. He fixed all of his attention on Minta, oblivious of Gavin and Randi.

"If you'd let me know you were coming up to Maple Creek today, we could have driven together."

Like that would ever *happen*, Minta's expression said, but she knew her manners.

"This is my boyfriend, Gavin," she said. "You met Randi and Jennet."

Jeff barely acknowledged the introduction. "How's the Sparkler today?"

"She's fine. I left her home where it's cool. My neighbor is babysitting her," she added quickly.

"It's not so bad in here," Randi said.

Were these people saying anything that popped into their heads? In spite of the efforts of numerous fans, it was stifling. I swiped at the moisture dripping from my neck to the collar of my top, hoping no one noticed.

Minta fixed Jeff with a sharp glance. "Why are you here, Jeff?"

He shrugged. "It's something different to do. I'm flying back to California next week."

"Where's your collie?" she asked. "Your girlfriend's collie, that is."

"She didn't want to come. Look, Minta, how about having a farewell dinner? We can get caught up on Sparkle and things."

"She's busy," Gavin snapped.

Jeff bristled. "The lady can speak for herself."

"When?" Minta asked.

"How's Saturday? I found a great new restaurant. Oakpoint sure has changed since I lived here."

"Saturday is good," Minta said.

I stared at her. A personal protection order one minute, a dinner date the next? Or was this part of her plan to drill Jeff for information? It must be, and it must have just occurred to her. Otherwise she wouldn't have been so snippy a few minutes ago.

"I'll give you a call," he said and strolled on, for all the world as if he were unaware of the burgeoning storm in his wake.

"Did you forget?" Gavin demanded. "We're going to a concert in the park this Saturday."

"Jeff is leaving next week. I won't have another chance to see him," she said.

"And that would be bad?"

"He *is* Sparkle's former owner's nephew."

"So?"

"Don't fuss, Gavin," she said. "It's too hot. I know what I'm doing."

During this testy exchange, Randi had wandered off. I couldn't see her but guessed she was hoping to connect with Jeff.

In many ways, wandering off was a good idea.

Twenty-seven

I hadn't gone far when I found myself walking into a virtual rainbow—Jacelyn Holloway spilling out of a swingy low-cut sundress. She had a collie with her, a frisky sable girl so small I wondered if she were a sheltie.

"Hey, Annica," she said. "Have you seen Minta?"

"It's *Jennet*," I said, "and I just left her. She's over there."

I pointed vaguely in what was probably the wrong direction. It was easy to lose track of where I'd been after weaving through the crush. In truth I couldn't see Minta and Gavin now. Maybe their disagreement had grown more volatile and one or the other had left the show.

I didn't care for Gavin's possessive streak. On the other hand, if he had plans to attend a concert with Minta and she had cast them aside to accept Jeff's offer...Well, I could sympathize with Gavin. To a point. He was still my primary suspect.

Jacelyn ran her hand along her low neckline as if checking to see that a bra strap was still in place. I had to admire her dress. Streaked with lime, orange, and raspberry, it reminded me of a large serving of rainbow sherbet. As accessories she wore two rings. One was a large ruby set in gold, the other an emerald. When she placed her hands together, they looked like a Christmas decoration.

"Is the puppy yours?" I asked.

Jacelyn smiled proudly. "All mine. Her name is Valentine. Say hello to the nice lady, baby girl."

Valentine wagged her tail. I let her sniff my hand. Yes, she was small, petite with snapping brown eyes, perhaps forty-eight pounds.

"Are you showing her today?"

"We just came to see all the pretty little collies. I really want to introduce Valentine to the Blueberry Muffin."

That would be Sparkle, of course. I cringed when people assigned their own nicknames to others to replace perfectly good names. Except for Leonora, that is, who often called me Jen. That was Leonora; that was all right.

"You're out of luck," I said. "Minta didn't bring Sparkle today."

"I wonder why she isn't showing her. Did she say?"

"I don't know. Maybe it's too expensive."

"That never mattered to her before. I know Minta was going to school, and showing dogs is expensive, but she always said she'd make any sacrifice for her dog. I guess most of us would."

"I feel the same way," I said.

"So why isn't Minta showing Sparkle?"

Had she forgotten she'd already asked that question? When I didn't answer, she said, "Sparkle isn't sick, is she?"

"I'm sure she's all right. I'd have second thoughts about bringing any dog out in this heat myself, let alone a rough collie."

"Nonsense," Jacelyn said. "It's summer. It's going to be hot. You know what they say: the show must go on. They do everything in their power to keep it cool for the dogs."

"Yes," I said. "It must. Well, if you'll excuse me..."

"Wait!" She grabbed my arm.

I wrenched it away from her, not the least concerned about hurting her feelings.

"I need to ask you something," she said. "It's important."

All right. I'd give her a minute. But what could this acquaintance of Minta's possibly want of me?

She stepped close, leaned closer, almost stepping on Valentine's paw, and lowered her voice. "Could it be that Minta's afraid something will happen to Sparkle?"

An alarm bell began to ring, faint and far off, but I heard it.

"Something like what?" I asked

"Oh, she might pick up some illness or other. The first time I took Valentine to a show, she was sick for days after. It's because all these people bring in their dogs from other states. Think of all those germs mingling together. It's asking for trouble."

"That didn't stop you from bringing Valentine today," I pointed out.

"No, I don't hide from germs myself. I don't think it's possible. Just saying."

I was growing tired of the conversation, weary of rainbow sherbet colors and sun-gold lips and sharp gold-flecked eyes.

I gave Valentine a pat on the head. "Excuse me, Jacelyn, I have to go. I see my friend over there."

Without another word, I moved away, walking a little faster than usual, hoping to melt into the milling crowd.

It wasn't a fabrication. I *did* see Annica.

~ * ~

We stationed ourselves alongside a crate from which a magnificent tricolor surveyed us solemnly and silently.

"Some people are just plain mean," Annica said. "There's a grumpy old man who doesn't have a nice word to say about anybody's dog. He has a long gray beard," she added. "He looks like a Civil War general."

"I didn't see anyone that unique, but Minta's friend, Jacelyn Holloway, is here. She's looking for Minta."

"This general— maybe he's a suspect," Annica said. "To hear him tell it, every collie has a flaw. And his voice is so loud. He doesn't care who hears him, even if it's the dog's owner. He'd even find something wrong with Black Beauty here."

The tricolor was still watching us. Watching and listening, or so it seemed.

"Everyone else I talked to seems normal," she said. "They're excited, anxious to take their dog into the ring. Did you learn anything?"

"Jeff's here. He asked Minta out in front of Gavin, and she accepted."

"No! She doesn't trust him."

"She must have a plan.

A scream brought the happy-busy buzz in the tent to an abrupt stop. More screams and angry shouting followed. Suddenly it seemed as if all the dogs at the show were barking. Everyone was stampeding toward the sound, generating more noise and confusion.

"What on earth...?" Annica stepped quickly out of the way of a youthful sprinter.

"Over close to the door," I said. "Where we were talking to Minta."

Who wasn't there now.

We moved with the crowd, holding on to each other lest we be knocked of our feet.

The handsome sable collie Annica had jokingly claimed she was looking at instead of Gavin pawed at the floor of his crate. A little red-headed girl of eight or nine stood by cradling what looked like a golden kitten or perhaps a stuffed toy. She was crying as if her heart were breaking, tears streaming down her face onto her *Colliecote* tee shirt.

The woman with her—her mother, I assumed as the two wore matching outfits—didn't even attempt to control her anger. She clutched her cell phone so tightly it might have crumpled if not made of sturdier material, and her face was as red as the proverbial beet.

I couldn't immediately see what the problem was, but bits and pieces of dialog swirled around me. I tried to catch each one.

How could it happen so quickly?

With scissors?

Did you see anyone near the crate?

Where's Security. Don't they have security in this place?

Someone meant to cut his throat?

Call nine one one...No, I'll do it.

Don't cry, Katie. It's only hair. It'll grow back.

"What are they talking about?" Annica asked. "What happened?"

By then I had a pretty good idea. The child was holding a gob of golden fur, no doubt cut from the shoulder of the big sable collie, leaving a large saucer-shaped area scalped and unsightly. The dog's magnificent coat, bathed, brushed, ready for the show ring, was ruined. He wouldn't win any ribbons this day.

"I'm sorry. Sorry." The child let the golden fur fall from her grasp, as the mother's shrill voice sliced through the chaos.

"You had to have seen something, Katie. I wasn't gone five minutes. I left you here to watch Raider. Who did this?"

The girl wiped her eyes with her long copper braid. "I don't—didn't see anybody."

"Don't tell me that. What happened?"

"I don't know."

"Poor kid," Annica murmured.

Poor collie.

"He's ugly now," the mother said. "Ruined. After all my work..."

I've wished I could intervene. Impossible, of course, and inadvisable, given the mother's explosion. I understood that she must be upset, but she was making matters worse—for her daughter and for the dog who had been attacked, who had no idea he was now worth less than he'd been only minutes ago.

In one person's eyes, anyway.

I wished I could comfort the dog, although that, too, was impossible. I'd learned long ago that collie fanciers take a dim view of anyone touching their masterpieces even when they hadn't been vandalized. If I so much as tried to touch Raider, I'd be immediately suspect.

"Don't anybody move," the mother ordered. "The police on their way."

Twenty-eight

By the time the officer arrived, most of the crowd around Raider's crate had dispersed. The shocking incident was now in the hands of the law. It was time to return to the business of the day. Showing dogs. Competing. Winning.

The show must go on!

It might be business as usual, but the festive air had vanished. Still, our curiosity held us in place. The crying child, the blustering mother, the tall officer whose concern seemed genuine, amounted to a story ended in mid-scene.

"I want to see what happens now," Annica said.

The answer proved to be not much. A teary Katie confessed that she'd stepped away from Raider's crate, but only for a few minutes, to talk to a friend. In that tiny timeframe, someone had sliced a huge chunk of fur from Raider's left shoulder.

The police couldn't do anything as no one admitted to seeing anyone suspicious approach Raider's crate or loiter near it. Nobody saw a flash of scissors or a figure moving surreptitiously away from the crate, blending into the crowd.

The assailant was long gone by then, and who were the losers? Raider and his owner. Raider wouldn't know his appearance had been damaged, but being a collie and sensitive, he would know Katie's distress and her tears and her mother's anger.

What did I do wrong? he might have asked. *How can I fix it?*

The question that lingered was chilling. Had the assailant intended to shove the scissors into Raider's throat? Whatever his intent, he or she had done the deed and disappeared. She, I suspected, as women outnumbered men at the show.

"It had to have been premeditated," Annica said as we finally tore ourselves away from the chaos and walked through the emptying parking lot to the car. We agreed we'd spent too long at the show.

"Not necessarily," I said. "There were plenty of scissors around and lots of totes and carry-alls. Not that anyone would hide them."

"It must have been awkward for the assailant to squeeze his hand through one of those small openings and make that cut."

I agreed. Easier to plunge the scissors' lethal points into the target. Perhaps mutilating Raider's fur wasn't the primary goal. I shuddered. It could have been so much worse.

"It was a horrible thing to do," Annica said. "I wonder if whoever did this targeted Raider specifically."

"They were saying Raider was a formidable opponent, already halfway to his championship. It might have been a case of eliminating the competition."

"Like what might have happened to Sparkle if Minta had continued to show her. Just imagine doing something like that with all those people around and hoping to get away with it."

"Well, apparently she did, but we don't know that she staked out Raider. Maybe any unwatched collie would have done as well. In which case, eliminating the competition wasn't the motive. We'll probably never know why it happened."

We reached the car, and I opened the doors so the oven-like interior wouldn't bake us. We stood outside for a few minutes, melting in the humidity, anxious to be on our way.

"I'd like a lime cooler about now," Annica said.

"No reason we can't stop at Clovers. Camille is looking in on the collies."

"Let's do it then. I need something to look forward to. This didn't turn out the way we planned it."

"Once we're back in Foxglove Corners, and I can't tell you how much I wish it were only a five-minute drive, we can sit down and think about what we learned."

"What *did* we learn?" she asked.

"So many things. Dog shows can be dangerous. Minta has her own plan to nail Jeff for sending her those threats. Your bearded general insults dogs at will, hardly an example of good sportsmanship. And Jacelyn Holloway talks about disease spreading at dog shows but brings her own collie to the show anyway."

"Hey, I wonder if the general did it," Annica said.

"Someone would have been sure to notice a bearded man with a pair of scissors in his hand," I pointed out. "And anyone planning to attack one of the dogs wouldn't go around loudly broadcasting their faults."

"Someone inconspicuous then."

I entered the northbound freeway and was happy to see it wasn't particularly busy. Now. Out of Maple Creek, on to Foxglove Corners and that lime cooler. I couldn't wait.

After a time, Annica said, "I don't want to show Angel after all."

I nodded. "You've never seen me enter one of my dogs in a show."

"Well, how could you? Only Halley would qualify. Your other dogs are rescues."

That was true but hardly the point.

"I love my collies whether they're champions or not," I said, "and I think they have a better life than the average kennel dog. But to each his own."

I was missing those collies and the country peace and quiet of Foxglove Corners, where, I could only hope, nothing bad had happened in my absence.

~ * ~

After enjoying lime coolers at Clovers, Annica and I parted. She went home to Angel where she planned to finish reading one of her long (and boring) Victorian novels. I took care of my dogs and fussed over them. They acted as if I'd truly abandoned them. Then, with a tall ice-filled glass of lemonade, I sat on the porch surrounded by collies and country peace.

Dinner was hours away, and the rest of the day gloriously unplanned. I sat quietly, stroking Gemmy's fur and reviewing our day at the show.

One happy memory took the edge off the traumatic end. I'd watched the photographer take pictures of a stunning tricolor collie with his handler in a surround of flowers and ribbons proudly won.

Who was to say that a dog didn't revel in such a golden moment? As I'd told Annica, "To each his own."

The collies came to sudden attention and congregated at the top of the stars, barking and jostling one another out of the way.

"Stay!" I told them, hoping they'd do it. I'd rarely seen them so excited.

A long white vintage Plymouth, its green fins shining, glided up the drive in a shower of flying pebbles.

Tails whipped the sullen air into a passable breeze. Sky, left behind by her more boisterous sisters, whimpered softly. The dogs knew what was imminent. Or I should say who. Brent with his roughhewn affection and treats from Pluto's Gourmet Pet Shop.

"Hey, Jennet! Hot enough for you?" Brent waded his way through his welcoming committee, dropping a light hand on each bobbing head. He sank into the wicker rocker, and, to the dogs' chagrin, tossed the Pluto's bag on the table. Anticipating a treat, Misty jumped on him. I took hold of her collar and eased her into a Sit.

"Like everything in the garden, I'm wilting," I said.

"Where were you this morning? I stopped by."

"In Maple Creek. Annica and I went to a dog show."

"So that's where she was. I was looking for her, too."

I waited for him to tell me why. When he didn't, I said, "This seems to be an unlucky time for collies."

As he listened to my tale of the scissors-wielding maniac at the show, his genial expression grew dark. "Give me two minutes with the fiend who did that."

"A dog can't be safe anywhere," I said.

I let my gaze roam lovingly over our lane. Ten acres and woods across the lane that I didn't let the collies explore, largely because of ticks. Still, an evil-minded invader had tossed poisoned pork chops in front of Raven's dog house.

"A dog should be safe in his own home," Brent said.

"And when they find the lowlife that hurts a dog, they give him a slap on the wrist. There's no justice for our animals."

"This country's laws are made of mush," Brent said. "I'm a firm believer in vigilante justice. Let me catch someone trying to hurt one of my dogs and he'll be missing a hand."

Although Brent already owned dogs, he'd adopted two of the Silverhedge rescues. He had a special love for dogs. Especially collies.

Collies...Suppose...

The thought wasn't new but it forced itself into the forefront of my mind. Were all of the dogs who'd been victimized collies? Not all, but most.

If so, did their tormentor have a specific grievance against the breed? A demented grudge? And if such a person prowled through yards and dog shows in search of a victim, what did that signify for those of us who loved and cherished our precious collies?

Twenty-nine

"I'd ask you to stay for dinner, but it's going to be leftovers," I said, thinking of the hot roast beef sandwiches I'd penciled in on my mental menu board.

"It's going to be pizza," Brent countered. "Don't you read your messages?"

I hadn't thought about my phone all day. It had been in my purse, silent and unconsulted.

"I ran into the sheriff at lunch," he said. "He's bringing two pizzas home, and I'm already invited."

Good grief. How had I fallen so far from my reality? At least I hadn't sliced the beef and warmed the gravy. Bless Crane for making my day easier.

"You'll just have to make a salad or something," he said.

"It'll be a salad." I had all the ingredients at hand, and it wouldn't take long to assemble. So I could forget about dinner preparations and sit in glorious idleness a little longer.

"Why were you looking for Annica?" I asked. "If I'm not prying."

"I was going to take her to the wildflower field. I don't want her to go out there alone."

I, of course, knew all about Brent's new restrictions and Annica's resolve to ignore them. This was the first morning she'd missed visiting her flowers in weeks.

"Again, why?"

"She might take it into her head to go walking through the field and get hurt. You know what happened to Leonora."

"She's fine."

"She's lucky. After Violet Randall's house burned, I only wanted to wipe the slate clean of evil," he added. "At the same time, I thought I'd do my part to beautify our planet."

"You did. And it's beautiful."

"Too beautiful. It's unnatural. Like that crazy Huron Court."

I sat forward, surprised to hear Brent expounding in so fanciful a manner about his property. He sounded like Lucy or me, not the earthbound, plainspoken man I knew him to be.

"What specifically are you afraid of?" I asked. "A revolt of giant tiger lilies and monster coneflowers?"

"I don't know exactly," he said. "There's the ghost."

"She hasn't been back in a while. Maybe she was a one-time phenomenon."

"Annica keeps looking for her."

"That's natural. Sort of."

I was curious about Annica's apparition, too, but not so much that I'd tried to find out who she had been in life. More important matters had claimed my attention.

"There's something else," Brent said. "I read about an invasive plant that's been spotted in Michigan. It's called giant hogweed. The leaves can burn your skin if you come in contact with them and even cause temporary blindness."

"Well, you didn't plant any hogweed seeds, did you?"

"No. We didn't plant the violets either."

He had a point. I recalled a moment when I had felt the brush of a stalk against my leg. It hadn't been pleasant. Brent and Annica had chosen seeds and plants at random, and some strange flowers had sprung out of the soil.

"Maybe I should bulldoze the whole area," he said.

"No!"

The dogs looked up at me in alarm, no doubt wondering if I were talking to them. I hadn't realized I'd spoken so sharply.

And why had I done that?

"They wouldn't like it," I said.

"What?"

The bizarre thought had simply insinuated itself into my mind—and my speech. White Queen Anne's Lace that resembled hogweed, the towering yellow carnations and red lilies...They'd grown used to the freedom of the wildflower field. Freedom to spread out and grow. All the way to the sky.

"Who wouldn't like it?" he demanded.

"What I mean is, you turned those desolate, burned-out acres into a paradise. You can't just destroy them. Anyway, they'll die in the winter."

"Okay. They can stay. I'll put in a few more 'No Trespassing' signs and keep Annica away."

"Good luck with that," I said.

~ * ~

Crane held the pizzas high above seven collie noses as I opened the door. We trooped inside. All except Candy.

"You got my message, honey," Crane said.

"Eventually." I took the boxes from him. "You two relax while I make a salad."

"I have wine in the car," Brent said.

"Oh, bring the dogs' treats inside, too," I said.

We might have forgotten the bag from Pluto's on the porch, but Candy hadn't, judging by the whining on the porch.

"Did you and Annica have fun at the dog show?" Crane asked as he locked his gun in the cabinet.

"Until something horrible happened."

Quickly I told him about the attack on Raider and the chaotic aftermath. I couldn't get Katie and her tears out of my mind and hoped her mother didn't keep telling her she was to blame.

"That can be a cut-throat game," Crane said.

"It might have been—literally. Fortunately all Raider lost was a hunk of his hair. But for a show dog that's major."

"There was another case of suspected dog poisoning today," he said. "A lady found a whole cooked chicken on her front porch. She pulled her dog away from it and got bitten for her trouble."

"Please tell me it wasn't a collie," I said.

"The biter was a Vizsla. That's a hunting dog. But there was a collie in the yard, too, an older dog."

I stared at the vegetables on the counter, at the red pepper and tomato waiting to be chopped, at the radishes. I attempted to hold the knife steadily, but my hand was shaking.

"They're all collies," I said.

"Except for the Vizsla, and I read in the paper about another breed."

"But most of the victims were collies. And the show today was just for collies."

"It looks like someone wants to get rid of the breed."

"In the most horrible way possible."

Candy nudged my leg. As always, she hoped a sliver of food would fall to the floor.

It had happened last week, a sliced of bell pepper that time. She had sniffed it and left it alone, waiting in vain for a sliver of cheese to follow.

"We're looking for a maniac with a vendetta against collies," I said. "We have to find him before he pays us a return visit."

Brent came into the kitchen and discarded the empty bag. Misty followed him, licking her chops.

"How do we do that?" he asked. "We already have a video image. It's useless."

"There've been stories in the *Banner* so people are aware of what's been happening. Nobody can be on guard twenty-four hours a day."

"We almost have to be," Crane said. "We can hope sooner or later he'll slip up. Then we'll nab him."

That was the way Crane often looked at similar situations. Sometimes it worked. But I hoped no more collies would succumb to the lure of a tasty bit of food before that happened.

The next time collies would be together in any number was the annual get-together and picnic in Everlasting Park outside Lakeville, set to take place in a week. As at the show, there would be crowds, people coming and going, catching up with old friends, showing off new collies, eating hot dogs and ears of corn, and taking pictures. In other words, a perfect opportunity for our enemy to work his evil.

"If we don't catch the poisoner before then, let's all plan to go to the Everlasting event," I said. "Sue, Camille, Annica, Ronda—all of us who have collies. That might be our last good chance this summer to catch the poisoner.

Thirty

The next day the *Banner* carried the story of the assault on Raider. The only new information was the intention of Raider's owner to sue the club that had sponsored the event. The reporter didn't link the incident to the poisonings, but why would she? Those atrocities had happened in Foxglove Corners and Lakeville. Perhaps she didn't know about them.

The incident with the Vizsla suggested that the poisoner was still in the area. Again I toyed with the idea that the same person was responsible for wreaking havoc in all three communities. Once again the task of apprehending him overwhelmed me.

At present, he was faceless and nameless. He might as well be invisible. As usual when I let the collies out after Crane left for his shift that morning, I all but fine combed every inch of the property which they frequented. For now, the coast was clear.

Danger aside, their lives and mine had to go on. We didn't live in a bubble. When I brought the dogs inside, I sat at the kitchen table planning the weekend's dinners, then shopped for groceries at Blackbourne's. On the way home I stopped at Clovers, knowing Annica would be working.

After a brief nighttime rain, the heat and humidity had returned. More than anything I wanted to sit in a cool place, drink a lime cooler, and set aside my concerns for a while.

I opened Clovers' door to the soft jingling of the green chimes and spotted Annica at her favorite station, the dessert carousel. She was filling it with generous slices of a new dessert, strawberry shortcake pie.

As she often did, she dressed to advertise an item on the menu. Today she wore a short bright red sheath with a white collar as soft as whipped cream. Miniature strawberry shortcake earrings peeked out through errant strands of her red-gold hair.

"You have to try these, Jennet," she said, setting the last plate in the carousel. "Mary Jeanne let me and Marcy create our own desserts. This is mine."

"Well..." I spared a thought for the waist of my denim skirt. It seemed a bit tight. "I'll take two for tonight. Make that three, and a lime cooler for here."

"I'll have one with you," she said. "Grab the booth. I'll ask Marcy to cover for me. I have some exciting news."

My favorite booth was empty as were most of the tables, it being too early for the lunch crowd. I seated myself and contemplated the woods across Crispian Road. If only it would rain again. So far it had been a dry summer. The leaves looked parched and—horrors!—were some of them already yellow? It couldn't be. It was still June.

"Here you go." Annica set down my take-out dessert and two lime coolers in tall tumblers.

"What's this exciting news?" I asked.

"You'll never guess. I saw the ghost this morning, and I heard the dog. Professor Brown at Oakland says perseverance is its own reward. I'm ready to believe him."

"About the ghost?" I prompted.

"I'm coming to it. It was raining, so I almost didn't drive out to the wildflower field, but then I did. As soon as I turned on Huron Court, it cleared up.

I nodded, understanding. Huron Court had its own weather patterns. Let it rain on the rest of Foxglove Corners. If Huron Court wanted snow, the temperature dropped thirty degrees and snowflakes fell from instantly appearing clouds.

"It was still misty but just over the wildflower field," Annica said. "First I heard a dog barking, but I didn't see it. Then she appeared. Just like that." Annica snapped her fingers. "She was all in white, standing, facing me, and holding a bunch of flowers. She looked like a bride."

"Are you sure you didn't see the mist and imagine the rest?" I asked.

"I'm positive. The mist was all around her, kind of like a light. I saw her as clearly as I see you."

"What happened then?"

"She started to walk toward me. I thought I'd meet her halfway, but before I could take a step, she disappeared into the mist. And the dog howled."

Annica came to a stop and played with her straw, leaving her drink untouched. During the telling of her tale, her rosy glow had turned ashen.

I took a long sip of the lime cooler and felt a wondrous cool sensation envelop me. Uh, no, it was a chill generated by Annica's eerie story. Even I would be unnerved to see a ghost walking toward me.

"What does she want with me?" Annica asked.

"To tell her story? Forgiveness for something she did in life? To warn you about some danger? Maybe to warn you away from the field."

"I wish I knew. I'd love to tell Brent, but I don't dare," she said. "He's gotten as bad as Lucy, always spouting gloom and doom."

"He cares about you."

"But I won't let him dictate to me."

"No, you shouldn't, but he's afraid of something connected with the field. He wants you to be safe."

"I won't rest until I know why this is happening," she said. "Will you help me find out who the ghost used to be when she was alive? If we knew that, maybe we could figure out why she's haunting me."

Annica had asked me to help her before. Although I had no idea how to begin, I had promised her I'd try.

"You're so good at research," she added.

"Well, so are you."

"I'm behind in reading for my novel class."

"And I've been sidetracked by what's happening to our collies, but..."

Her eyes lit up, and a hint of the rosy glow returned to her face.

"Oh, thank you, Jennet, and I'll keep looking for the ghost, but don't tell Brent."

I finished my drink, planning the first steps. You could find practically anything on the Internet, but the library was almost as good, and more pleasant. Miss Eidt would be intrigued and willing to help. In truth, I had time to delve into any source I could unearth.

To begin, I'd need a name.

~ * ~

The old white Victorian on Park Street was a popular cooling station in summer for the denizens of Foxglove Corners, as popular as The Ice Cream Parlor. It had been the family home of librarian Miss Eidt before she donated it to the town, along with the first books from her own collection. In a sense, the library was the heart of Foxglove Corners.

Miss Eidt's cat, Blackberry, lay on a plump cushion in her wicker chair, bestowing a cold, jewel-eyed glare to all who entered her domain. She didn't move as I passed her with a casual, 'Hi, feline.'

Delicious cool air washed over me as I went through the doors. Miss Eidt, looking serene in an aqua suit with a three-strand pearl necklace, sat at her desk rifling through catalogs. Her welcoming smile always made me feel as if I had come to my second home.

"I was thinking of you this morning, Jennet," she said. "I just shelved two dozen old paperbacks in the Gothic Nook. Debby and I found them at an estate sale."

Miss Eidt knew my love for Gothics and always made sure I was the first to check out a special find. She had one today, a vintage paperback as pristine as if it had just arrived from a bookstore—for an incredible sixty cents. *The Secret in the Hidden Cemetery* featured the requisite maiden in a long misty gown poised as if frozen amidst the gravestones.

"This is for you, not the library," she said.

I thanked her and slipped it into my shoulder bag. "I'd like to have a look at your vertical file."

No request could have made Miss Eidt happier. While she had computers and knew how to use them, she would never give up her longtime habit of reading with a pair of scissors in her hand and clipping articles or pictures that caught her interest. These she kept in manila folders. In the past I'd found many a gem in her collection.

"Do you have a new mystery?" she asked.

"It's been around for a while. What I'm looking for..." I paused, wondering how best to explain it. "It won't be easy to find. I don't have a name, only a location. It's Huron Court where the pink Victorian once stood."

"Where the most exotic plants this side of heaven bloom. I know it. In fact, when I first saw it, I took pictures and started a new file. So you're looking for a flower?"

"Not exactly. I'm looking for a ghost who wears white and likes flowers."

"How romantic!" she said. "Let's see what we can find."

Thirty-one

I had come to the right place. Miss Eidt's vertical file practically overflowed with material on Brent's wildflower garden. That surprised me as it had only been in existence for two seasons.

I emptied the folder on the table in Miss Eidt's private office and divided the material into two sections: pictures and newspaper clipping. The earliest pictures depicted a charming springtime palette in greens and pastels when the tender plants were at the beginning of their lives.

I arranged them in approximate chronological order, using height and color to guide me. In the end, I almost had a video, could almost hear the wind sloughing through the blossoms and hear faint stirrings.

It was creepy.

Apparently Miss Eidt or her young assistant, Debby, had visited the field every day, recording changes large and small. What was the nature of the hold this wild garden held over certain impressionable people?

A disturbing thought tugged at me. We were still in June, nearing July. Would the wildflowers continue to grow thicker and taller throughout the rest of the summer and fall until ultimately they reached up to the sky?

Come back to earth, Jennet.

I gathered the pictures into a neat stack and turned to the printed material.

Miss Eidt had clipped several news stories detailing the fire that had burned the elegant pink Victorian to the ground. Skimming the longest article swept me back in time—figuratively, that is—to my first sight of the house in all its rosy-tinged glory and my meeting of Violet Randall. To the deterioration wrought by passing decades. And to the deadly battle I'd waged within its walls.

I didn't want to think about that time. It still had the power to alter my heartbeat and turn the blood in my veins to ice water.

Miss Eidt pushed open the office door. She set a large white box on the table.

"How about a break, Jennet? I sent Debby to the Hometown Bakery for cupcakes."

She knew me well enough not to wait for an answer but cut the string with her scissors. Taking a plate from the cupboard, she began to lift the cupcakes out of the box.

"They're all ours," she said. "Debby is on a diet. The silly girl thinks she needs to lose weight."

"Well, it's summer," I said. "Bikini weather."

I refiled the material and peered into the box at the little cakes topped with mounds of swirling frosting.

"We have lemon, coconut, strawberry, peach and chocolate, of course," Miss Eidt said. "Help yourself. I'll put the water on for tea. Is Darjeeling okay?"

"Perfect."

"Did you find what you're looking for?" she asked.

"Not yet. I've been browsing through your pictures of Brent's wildflower field. It's a truly magical place."

Miss Eidt picked up a close-up of a red lily-like plant and smiled softly. "I feel connected to it. Before Brent and Annica sowed the first seed, they were here poring through gardening and wildflower books. They wanted a natural, wild look, and see what they have now. An exotic garden amidst acres of wilderness."

"In the end, they just threw a mixture of seeds and plants down and let them grow."

"Sometimes that's best."

"My present ghost, the one I'm researching, haunts the garden," I said.

"It has good taste."

"I should clarify. I haven't seen her, but Annica has. She asked me to try to find out who she was in life. Annica is a little obsessed," I added.

"Then you should be looking at my supernatural files. I save everything I come across, even if it only mentions a ghost. And we have a good collection of books on the subject, but you're familiar with them."

"I'm searching for a ghost that appears on Huron Court. She's been seen...Rather, Annica has seen her picking flowers in the field. She wears white and is usually accompanied by mist.

"That doesn't ring a bell. Didn't you see the ghost of the girl who lived in the house that burned down?"

"Violet Randall, yes, I saw her from a distance walking away from me on Huron Court. Her dog was with her. Neither one noticed me, so we didn't interact. I don't think Violet is the spirit Annica saw, though."

"I have a separate file on Huron Court," Miss Eidt said. "Let's have our tea and cupcakes, and I'll find it for you."

As she poured the tea, I chose a strawberry cupcake. I had a passion for all things strawberry this summer. From Annica's unique strawberry shortcake pie to a simple concoction of graham cracker crust, strawberries and whipped cream—when I looked back on these happy summer days, I knew I'd think of strawberries.

~ * ~

For a road that for many years had only been home to a single domicile, the pink Victorian, Huron Court had seen a modest share of psychic activity.

In the nineteen forties, a man had crashed his car after being forced off the road by an old Model T Ford. No trace of the Ford had ever been found, and so far as I could tell, no one else had ever encountered it.

But it made sense that a car from yesteryear had found itself trapped in one of Huron Court's famous time shifts.

A woman I'd met in the library, a self-proclaimed ghost chaser named Edwina Endicott, had seen the spirit of a young girl and her dog walking down Huron Court. That could only be Violet Randall and Ginger, the ghostly pair I had seen myself from a distance.

Then, in a Halloween feature story about local ghosts, I found an unverified tale of a boy and a girl, luminous in appearance, who dashed in and out of the woods on Huron Court. A one-time visitor to the pink Victorian had seen them. She could never be persuaded to pass through its door again.

Neither the luminous pair nor Violet had worn white and stopped in the midst of their haunted trek to pick flowers.

I realized that Annica's apparition could have lived in the house before Violet and her family. The long white dress suggested an earlier period, the first decade of the twentieth century, perhaps. But if anyone else had seen a ghost in white in the vicinity of Huron Court, they hadn't bothered to record it.

And if the ghost belonged to an earlier period, she wouldn't be picking flowers in Brent's wildflower garden because a grand Victorian house had occupied that space.

I amused myself with the thought of a spirit wandering blithely down Huron Court and coming across an extravaganza of brilliant blooms.

I must have some of these beautiful red lilies, she'd think, and detoured into the field to gather her ghostly bouquet.

Good grief. What a thought! I'd been reading and thinking about the mystery too long. My watch told me I had been reading and taking notes for two hours. I had dogs to take care of at home and dinner to make.

I rinsed my teacup and replaced the left-over cupcakes in their box, marveling that we'd only eaten half of them. Stacking the file folders neatly, I left the library, saying goodbye to Miss Eidt and telling her I'd save a visit to the Gothic Nook for another day.

In spite of the air-cooled library, I felt as if I'd been trudging through a murky landscape. I longed for a breath of fresh air.

Thirty-two

The air outside the library was thick with humidity, but it was as fresh as it was going to be today; and the sun was unbearably hot. In the brief walk to the parking lot, I felt damp and crumpled. I lost no time getting inside the Ford and turning on the air conditioning.

There! Delicious cool again.

I passed The Ice Cream Parlor with a wistful glance, but made myself drive out of the Corners. I had ice cream at home and sherbet and lemonade— and seven collies waiting for me.

So far the day had been a disappointment. Two hours of research had revealed nothing useful. Annica's ghost in white remained elusive. And why not? She had no interest in me. I didn't even know her name, and Annica had never described her features adequately.

Surely a ghost had a describable face, the same as it'd had in life.

I hated to tell Annica that I'd failed, but at the moment, I didn't know where else to turn. Meanwhile, other mysteries had a claim on my time. The danger that stalked our collies, for example. The poisoner and the vandal who had cut out a chunk of Raider's fur. I had to find out if they were the same person.

I couldn't imagine a villain so twisted that he would harm our gentle, sweet collies. All they wanted was to love their owners and please them and perhaps herd their sheep.

No punishment was too extreme for such a person.

I turned on a quiet lane bordered by trees and wildflowers and steeped in silence. Having the road to myself with nothing to do but drive was conducive to thinking.

I hadn't heard from Minta lately. I'd better call and see if she had received any additional messages. That last one had been truly frightening, indicating that Sparkle had run out of time. Maybe Minta had indeed received the last message. No. I had to stay positive.

The next gathering of collies at Everlasting Park was drawing closer. Most of my friends planned to bring their dogs to the event. All except Camille, who was busy writing a new cookbook, and Lucy.

Lucy had said, "I dislike crowds with a passion, Jennet, and I was never a fan of the outdoors, not even when I was a child."

And in truth, I couldn't see Lucy dressed in black with her gold chains and bracelets, sipping a coke in a paper cup with the ethereal Sky at her heel. I always pictured her in the sunroom at Dark Gables, drinking tea from a white bone china cup and waiting to read my tea leaves.

Minta's adversary had no way of knowing that Minta wouldn't bring Sparkle to the Everlasting gathering. I couldn't afford to stay away. The annual event might draw over a hundred collies. People milling around, exchanging news and gossip, and collies being collies would provide a rare opportunity for a person who nurtured a demented vendetta against the breed to strike again.

If he did, I would be on hand to apprehend him or at least describe him to the police.

However, I didn't have to do anything heroic today, nothing at all except care for my collies and make dinner for myself and Crane. Feeling optimistic about the immediate future, I left Jonquil Lane, parked in my driveway, and stepped out of the cool into the heat again.

Inside the house, the dogs set up their usual clamor. One day, one of them, Candy perhaps, would break through the door in her desire to be the first to greet me.

"Okay," I called. "I'm here. Settle down."

With my next step, my shoe sank into a squishy mess. I slid and looked down in horror at the obstacles thrown down in my path. At least three dozen jumbo-sized meatballs lay cooking in the relentless sun. No doubt laced with poison and they would definitely appeal to a perpetually hungry canine or to any animal that chanced to wander onto our property.

The poisoner had targeted my dogs again!

I didn't want to open the door for fear they would fly out and pounce on the meatballs. I couldn't assume that more hadn't been tossed into flower beds and rolled under leaves. For a moment I stood there frozen in horror.

I wished Crane were home. He wouldn't be, not for several hours. *Think!*

I had to scoop up these lethal chunks of meat and set them aside to be tested. But I needed a trowel or a rake, both in the house.

Suddenly I knew what to do. I kept a roll of paper towels and a paper bag from Blackbourne's in the trunk. The bag held books I intended to donate to Lila and Letty Woodville at the animal shelter for their summer fundraiser.

The dogs kept barking. Misty and Candy added their eerie howls to the cacophony. As I walked back to the car, a headache appeared out of nowhere and began to pound behind my eyes.

How quickly my world had changed! I'd gone from serene to traumatic in the blink of an eye.

I spilled the books out into the trunk, then picked up the meatballs one by one with a paper towel. I was correct in my estimate. I gathered thirty-six meatballs. As soon as I had collected the ones in my sight, I set out on a meticulous search of the property all the way to the invisible line that marked the beginning of the woods.

Our collies didn't venture into the woods. The poisoner wouldn't know that, but likely thought it more effective to toss the bait on the walkway where the dogs would see them as soon as they left the house.

My collie girls kept barking. Why wouldn't they be quiet? I was doing this for them.

Finally. All clear. Safety restored.

I used paper toweling to clean my shoe and locked the meatballs in the trunk, then opened the door to the kitchen and plowed through cold nudging noses, waving paws, and wagging tails.

Even my timid Sky seemed to be asking, *what took you so long?*

"Sorry, girls," I said. "How about some biscuits?"

The sight of the Lassie tin in my hand drove thoughts of abandonment out of their minds. As for myself, a sudden nausea derailed me. Sooner or later I had to move the meatballs out of my trunk. I couldn't do it yet, though. I sat at the kitchen table and slipped water slowly, trying to regain my equilibrium, but didn't feel any better.

You should, I told myself. *Once again you averted disaster.*

The next step was to eliminate it.

~ * ~

Crane swore when I told him about the meatballs, which was unlike him. "This has gone far enough. Our dogs are under attack in their own home."

"And still I don't know what to do about it."

"We have to catch him. Somehow."

"I called Sue," I said. "She found meatballs outside her front porch, too. The poisoner appears to be getting desperate. It's like he has a deadline and time is running out."

"He must have made a study of the houses on the lanes. I talked to Doctor Linton up the lane the other day. He hasn't had any trouble."

"He doesn't have any dogs. The vile wretch knows where the collies are...Oh, no! Camille! Her dogs are also at risk."

But neither Camille nor Gilbert were home.

"I'll leave her a voicemail," I said.

"Do that," Crane said. "I'll check out their place and get a sample of the meatballs Sue found."

"It'll be poisoned," I said. "The same as the ones I picked up. Then hurry home. The stew's ready."

He left, still wearing his gun, without taking a dog with him, which resulted in a bit of grumbling from Candy. I stirred the stew vigorously, thinking how much dogs loved beef and how their enemy must know that. I still felt a little ill and my headache hadn't gone away, but I had to eat something. I needed to be well and strong to meet the next challenge that came my way.

Thirty-three

In Camille's cozy country kitchen, treachery seemed far away. Here sunlight turned the cobalt glass bottles on the windowsill to glittering sapphire shapes, and the smell of cinnamon hung lightly in the air. We sat at the table drinking tea and sampling Camille's peach muffins, and all was well in our homes. For this sliver of time.

As I told her about the meatballs, she called Holly to her and buried her hand in the thick fur of the black collie's ruff. When she reached for a second muffin, I saw that her hands were shaking.

"Thank God, he's bypassed me again," she said. "But for how long? He must know I have Holly."

Hearing her name, Holly placed her front paws on the table, her eyes fixed on the plate of muffins. The Belgian shepherd, Twister, watched her, occasionally licking his chops, but being older and more laid back, he made no move to join her. In her consternation, Camille had forgotten to give the dogs a hand-out.

"Yesterday I was weeding most of the day," she said. "Twister usually lies on the porch in the shade, but Holly had her nose everywhere. What if a hawk or creature carried a meatball from your yard to mine?"

What she described was a possibility, but a quick glance at Holly was all I needed to know that Camille's fear was just that. A fear. Full of energy and bouncy, with a touch of mischief in her dark eyes, Holly couldn't have looked healthier.

I hastened to assure Camille that an even number of meatballs had landed on our walkway and that Holly was all right.

"But until we find out who's doing this and put a stop to it, be extra vigilant," I said.

"Gilbert always checks the property. Every day. So do I."

"But he's away at the university, and some days you stay in your kitchen. The poisoner comes and goes at odd times."

Like a ghost. And living as we did on our ten-acre plots, chances are no one would see him toss his poisoned meat into passing yards.

"I know," she said. "It seems that he's making you and Sue his special targets. I wonder why."

"That's easy. Sue and I are involved in collie rescue. You have one collie, a pet, and you're pretty much a homebody."

"While you pose a threat to him," she said.

"I hope so. I hope he knows it." I drained my teacup. My plate was empty, even of crumbs. "I'm going to get him, Camille."

I stood. Seeing her chance for a bite of muffin passing by, Holly yipped.

"I don't know how, but I am," I added. "For Holly and all our collies."

~ * ~

At Clovers, I discovered it was still Strawberry Week extended by Mary Jeanne because Annica's strawberry shortcake pie had been such a hit.

"I'm running out of strawberry outfits," Annica said.

She looked demure in a pink and white striped shirtwaist dress with a new pair of crystal earrings that resembled strawberries.

"How about a piece of my pie and iced tea?" she asked.

"It's tempting, but..."

I'd come for take-out, having told Crane it was too hot to cook. The day's feature was short ribs and potatoes, a meal we would both enjoy.

"I'll take a whole pie for dessert," I said. "But now I'd just like a lime cooler."

"One cooler coming up."

When she came back with our drinks, she looked so happy that I hated to tell her the result of my library research. I had to, of course. And she had to know about the meatballs.

"As far as I can tell, nobody else has seen your flower-gathering ghost," I said.

"How disappointing." Then she brightened. "That means I'm the first to see her."

"Which would explain why I couldn't find a record of her."

"I'll have to write one then."

"You can't until you discover why she haunts the wildflower field."

"Sure I can," she said. "I'll just describe how she comes and goes with the mist. We don't have to know why she appears. We don't know why Violet walks on Huron Court."

"She was killed there."

"Okay, but what about those kids who go running through the woods? Are they Foxglove Corners' version of Hansel and Gretel?"

"Maybe they died in the woods."

But I didn't think that was likely. If two children had perished in the Foxglove Corners wilderness, Miss Eidt or somebody would know about it. That was a ghost story for another time.

Annica said, "And what about the Model T?"

"That's easily explained. A person from the past drove into another time, caused an accident, and drove back to his own time again. Remember, we're talking about Huron Court. Most of the accounts I read just detailed the circumstances surrounding the ghost's appearance. They weren't short stories with neatly tied up endings."

Annica had brought a lime cooler for herself but didn't appear to be in a hurry to drink it. Instead she played with her straw. "I'm just talking. I'm too busy with my classes to write about the ghost. But I *do* want to see her again."

"Did you drive out to the field lately?" I asked.

She nodded. "Every day. It was misty this morning, but she didn't show up."

I sipped my drink slowly, thinking I'd like to try again to identify Annica's ghost. But I needed more details.

"You mentioned she had long dark hair," I said. "Can you describe her features?"

"The first time I saw her, she wasn't facing me. Later, her face was sort of blurred. You know the way they obscure the faces of innocent victims in a picture?"

"Did you notice any details at all? Think."

She shoved the straw into her glass, took a first sip, and gazed out at the woods across Crispian Road. "I'd say she had a heart shaped face. Her hair was brushed back off her forehead. I couldn't tell about her figure because she wore a loose fitting dress. She wasn't wearing make-up, but she had nicely shaped eyebrows."

"That could be Violet, but Violet wouldn't halt her trek up and down Huron Court to pick flowers, and she wouldn't appear without Ginger."

"Don't forget the dog, though. We heard it barking." Annica smiled. "You know a lot about ghosts, Jennet."

"It's mostly guesswork. I can't see a ghost applying make-up. I suppose they'd look like they did when they passed on."

"Would they wear the same clothes?"

"Who knows? Probably."

"She must have died a long time ago because her dress was so old looking."

"You can't be sure about fashion," I said. "I see dresses with a vintage look in the stores all the time."

Annica drained her drink. "That was good. We should start making double lime coolers."

"Suggest it to Mary Jeanne," I said.

She sighed. "It's fun to talk about ghosts, but it isn't getting us anywhere."

"I don't agree. One of us might say something that triggers an idea."

Suddenly Annica said, "You're wearing your backwards watch."

"I haven't worn it much since school let out, but I felt like dressing up today."

"Are the hands still going the wrong way?"

I glanced at it. "Yes. One day I'll look at it, and it'll be moving forward. It'll have the same time as every other watch in Michigan."

And that particular mystery would be over, if unsolved.

"Will you go out to the wildflower garden with me again sometime?" Annica asked.

"Why?"

"The ghost may be more inclined to appear if you're there. I asked Lucy, but she wasn't interested. You're the ghost magnet."

"I guess we could." I attempted to inject a modicum of enthusiasm into my voice. "But if your ghost appears, it'll be when you least expect it."

I frowned, realizing that applied to the poisoner, too. Before I left I'd have to tell Annica about the meatballs and remind her that we were going to the gathering at Everlasting Park.

"The ghost doesn't want me," I added.

As if all she'd heard was 'I guess we could,' Annica said, "When can we go?"

Thirty-four

Is it misfortune that comes in threes? Or death?

I sat on the porch with the collies ranged around me, soaking up the peace of my home while I contemplated the latest ripple in the summer.

Yesterday Crane learned that the meatballs had been poisoned. Now, today, Minta called with an appalling tale. Sparkle was gone, stolen yesterday from her backyard. In the end, all the shows she had skipped, all the precautions she'd taken, hadn't ensured the pretty blue merle's safety.

"It was a trap, and I fell right into it," Minta said.

I could hardly make out what she was saying, which happens when one tries to talk through tears.

"How did they get to her?" I asked.

"We were in the backyard playing ball. I heard the landline ring and went inside to answer it. When I came back, the gate was open, and my dog was gone."

"Don't you keep it locked?" I asked.

"Well no. Sparkle is never outside alone."

Except for the one day when it mattered.

"Randi and I have been driving around, looking for her. I called the police, the animal shelter, put up flyers, did everything I could think of. It's no use. He has her."

"Who?"

"Jeff Whitman. Who else? This morning I found a ransom note in my mailbox. It said I could have Sparkle back for ninety thousand dollars, and it was signed 'Retribution.'"

Retribution? If a clue was embedded in the signature, I couldn't see it.

"How odd," I said, "but that's better than no message at all. Or worse, one that told you Sparkle was dead."

"I don't even have a thousand dollars in my savings account."

"I wonder why he wants that specific amount."

"Don't you remember? It's Sparkle's inheritance from Nessa Whitman. It comes in monthly payments."

"That's weird," I said.

"That's Jeff. It's the money he thought should be his."

"Did you confront him?" I asked.

"I can't. He checked out of the motel. For all I know, he's back in California."

I leaned back in the wicker rocker and contemplated the myriad clouds in the sky. Did one of them look like a running collie? It was moving rapidly toward the west, already changing shape.

"I think Sparkle is with him," she said. "She must be."

"In California?"

"Wherever he is."

That didn't make sense to me. At first the person who sent Minta the messages appeared to be threatening Sparkle with death. Now it turned into a dognapping for ransom. There was more to the story than Minta was telling me, or perhaps more than she knew.

"Back up," I said. "If Jeff is counting on you paying the ransom, he can't have gone far."

"I didn't think of that. I can hardly think at all. The police won't help me. I can't give them evidence that Jeff stole my dog."

"They probably think someone opened the gate, some kid, and Sparkle ran away."

"I know better." She paused as if to grasp the last bit of her courage before it flew away. "Do you think you can help me?"

"I'll try."

But I sighed. Once again I was being asked to do the near impossible. But then this was for Sparkle. For a collie.

I said, "What can we do?"

"I don't know. We can get together and brainstorm maybe. Things work out for you." Her voice broke. After regaining control of it, she said, "I want my dog back."

I imagined a large piece of Minta's heart breaking off and floating away. Suppose one of my collies were held for ransom. I'd do anything in my power to get her back.

"Should we meet in Oakpoint?" I asked.

"That's a long way for you to drive. I could go to Foxglove Corners. I need the diversion."

"Come anytime." Something occurred to me. "By the way, who was the caller?"

"It was one of those telemarketers," she said. "Now I think it was a setup. Maybe it was Jeff himself. I wouldn't recognize his voice."

"Wait. If it was Jeff on the phone, he had to have an accomplice waiting outside your house for a chance to take Sparkle."

"You're right," she said slowly. "Maybe the girlfriend he talks about, the one whose collie he brought to that first show. It might have been a legitimate call, but it was too well timed.

"That seems like a cumbersome way to arrange an abduction. I take it you told the police about the previous threats."

"Again, it isn't evidence. If I can't find Jeff, how could they?"

"They have ways."

"But they're not going to help me."

"Probably not. I supposed finding a dog that might have run away is low on their priority list. However, it's at the top of ours. We'll move heaven and earth to find her."

"If she's still alive."

"Don't even say that," I said. "If we're to believe the note, Sparkle is worth a lot of money to her abductor. To Jeff, if you think he's the dognapper."

"Then there's hope," she said. "For a while I didn't know where to turn."

"There's always hope," I assured her.

But sometimes it was hidden from our view, like Annica's ghost covering herself with the mists that hung over the wildflower field.

I stood, and my collie contingent came to life. Any change was good.

"Try not to worry. I'll see you soon, Minta."

As I ended the call, I glanced again at the sky but couldn't see the cloud that looked like a runaway collie. I hoped its absence wasn't a bad omen.

~ * ~

I took three loaves of banana-nut bread out of the oven and set them as far back on the counter as possible. A large jar of sun tea was brewing on the porch, but the circumstances called for soothing hot tea. Thinking about the meatball incident and now Sparkle's disappearance made me feel as if Evil were once again coming close to my home.

Well, it was. Closer and closer.

Tuning quickly around, I almost stepped on Candy's paw.

"Not for dogs," I said.

Misty gave a pathetic whimper. *Give us our biscuits then.*

That was a good idea. The dogs were due for a snack, and I had to check to see that the property was clear of poisoned meat before I could let them out. I wanted to do it before Minta arrived.

I passed out treats from the Lassie tin and stepped outside to check the yard. What if the poisoner were to drop by with another lethal delivery at this very moment? I couldn't apprehend him, but I could see what kind of car he drove and possibly manage to memorize his license plate number.

That would be a happy coincidence, but, of course, it didn't happen. There was no traffic on the lane, nothing at all except a deer that promptly melted into the woods. Once again all was clear. I let the dogs out and watched them dash around the yard, barking and chasing one another, nudging me to join in the fun.

My gaze fell on my own blue girl, Sky. Collies with blue merle coats were rarely seen outside the show ring. The color and markings were so distinctive that surely someone would notice a Lassie dog with a frosty blue coat and call Minta if they happened to see one of her flyers.

Unless the dognapper kept Sparkle hidden away. He'd take no chances with a dog worth ninety thousand dollars.

I remembered the last time I'd seen Sparkle. Her coat had shone as if it were made of crushed sapphires and gold and snow. A beauty among beauties, with her shining personality radiating from her dark eyes.

Where was she now?

The optimism I had tried so hard to maintain started to fall away. First more poisoned meat, then a stolen dog. Was there going to be a third misfortune?

Thirty-five

By afternoon the temperature had soared to eighty-seven degrees, and the humidity was unbearable. Minta and I sat at the kitchen table slowly demolishing a loaf of banana bread. I was surprised to see that worry hadn't diminished her appetite until she said, "This is so good. I didn't eat today."

"Would you like a sandwich?" I asked. "I have chicken and cold cuts."

"Mmm, no, thanks. Just another piece of this heavenly bread."

Fortunately I'd baked three loaves. Candy, ever hopeful, lay under the table, certain I'd slip her a hand-out, which I'd probably do if I didn't have to give one to all the dogs at the same time.

No matter how hot the day, Minta always managed to look cool in her favorite color, light green. But her face showed signs of strain that even carefully applied makeup couldn't mask.

"When I had dinner with Jeff, he was so nice he had me believing I was wrong about him," she said. "He told me I deserved the inheritance for being kind to his Aunt Nessa and giving Sparkle a home. Now this. They were all lies."

I wasn't convinced, still suspecting that the abductor was Minta's boyfriend, Gavin. "Maybe. We don't know."

I reached for my mystery notebook, opened to a new page, and wrote "The Sparkle Mystery" at the top.

"Let's review the people you see regularly at the shows and your other friends. Just for now, we'll set Jeff aside."

"But he's the one. I know it."

"Even so," I said. "Even though you know they're innocent, let's consider everyone you come in contact with. Your cousin, Randi, for instance."

She couldn't have been more shocked if I'd thrown a cup of tea in her face.

"No, no, no!" she cried. "Randi is family. She was heartbroken when I told her about Sparkle. She came right over and helped me look for her."

"It could be an act," I said, seeing a chance to play the devil's advocate. "Could she use ninety thousand dollars?"

"My Aunt Miranda has money. Randi doesn't want for anything. I've known her since she was a baby. No, it can't be Randi."

"How about your friend, Gavin?" I asked.

"Well..."

I noted that she wasn't so quick to rush to Gavin's defense.

Finally she said, "I admit Gavin is possessive. He doesn't like other men talking to me and makes no secret that he thinks dogs are superfluous. Sparkle never warmed up to him."

"Always trust a dog's instinct."

I wrote his name and put a checkmark next to it. Minta looked at it and frowned.

"But he wouldn't do anything illegal. He's a lawyer, for heavens' sake."

Still the frown remained. Apparently she was reconsidering her opinion of Gavin, perhaps wondering how well she could know him in so short a time.

"No," she concluded. "Gavin wouldn't do this to me."

"Okay, now think about the shows," I said. "Who did you know well enough to talk to?"

"Lots of people, but no one to socialize with. I never saw them outside the shows."

"Did anyone show a particular interest in Sparkle?"

"Everyone who saw Sparkle admired her. Lena Hunt wanted to buy her."

Ah! A new name. Someone Minta had never mentioned, a person I'd never seen.

"How would you describe her?" I asked.

"Lena is all about winning. She has a pretty sable, Cinnamon. She hopes to finish her this year."

"She's a competitor then?"

"Yeah, a serious one, but I can't see Lena dropping threatening messages in mailboxes or stealing a dog, and she didn't know about Sparkle's inheritance. Don't add her name."

I did anyway. A serious competitor could be a sore loser, a woman desperate to give her kennel a boost. Anything for the points, the glory, the money. But stealing a dog?

"What about the lady who wears color that clash?" I asked.

Minta smiled. "You must mean Jacelyn Holloway. She's just annoying, always calling Sparkle silly names like Blueberry Muffin and Crumble. I've corrected her a million times, but she keeps doing it."

"She wanted to know why you weren't showing Sparkle," I said. "I'd say she was nosy."

"She is, but she's a talented artist. One time she brought some of her collie sketches to a show. She's harmless."

So were they all, according to Minta. I began to think she was naïve. She talked about several people but didn't appear to know any of them well and always came back to Jeff.

"I know he's is the one who stole Sparkle," she said. "I'd stake my life on it. We have to find him, Jennet. Maybe I should hire a private investigator."

I had a feeling that Sparkle's abduction would be resolved before Minta could find a P.I. Besides, by her own admission, she couldn't afford to hire one.

"If you're right, and if he wants the ninety thousand dollars, he'll find you," I said. "That's how a ransom works. Now let's proceed on the assumption that the abductor isn't Jeff. Who else should be considered?"

Although she'd left the show by the time Raider was assaulted, Minta knew the bearded man, the one Annica called the general. His name was Edward McAllister, and he was always critical of collies, especially the winners. He didn't have anything nice to say about people, either. It was his way, and nobody took him seriously.

Still, I added his name to the list. How could I find more information about him and about Lena Hunt and Jacelyn Holloway?

On the other hand, it was obvious that only Jeff knew the amount of the money Nessa Whitman had left to Sparkle.

"What puzzles me is the way the anonymous messages kept changing," I said. "First, you were told not to take Sparkle to the shows because of diseases like dog flu. Then he flat out warned you that something unfortunate was going to happen to Sparkle, but it turns out that he's interested in money. What does that tell us?"

"That he's nuts," Minta said. "We're dealing with a certifiable lunatic. Or maybe two people with different agendas."

"I agree that our enemy is a lunatic, but I don't think two people sent you the messages."

"Oh, Sparkle," she said. "I promised Nessa I'd take care of you."

I had no answer for her. It was true that sometimes the matter of care was out of our hands.

An hour passed. I made a fresh pot of tea, took another banana loaf from the counter, and sliced it. Candy and Misty were beside themselves with excitement, while the others napped in pleasant air-cooled comfort. When I opened the Lassie tin, the sound of biscuits falling lightly on newspaper brought them all into the kitchen.

"How I envy you to have all your collies safe," Minta said.

"To a point. I have to be on perpetual lookout for poisoned meat."

Speaking of meat, before long I'd have to begin dinner. Minta couldn't think of anyone else to add to her list. For a pretty, vivacious young woman, she seemed to be unusually solitary. Her friends from high school didn't share her interest in collies, and she didn't know anyone from her college days well. Gavin was her first serious boyfriend.

"I'd better be getting home," she said. "I'm expecting another message. After all, how am I supposed to pay the ransom?"

"He needs to give you instructions. If this isn't settled by Saturday, let's plan to go to the gathering of collies at Everlasting Park."

"That's only two days away," she said. "I won't have Sparkle."

"You don't have to bring a collie. Some people just go to look at the dogs and mix with the breeders. There'll be refreshments and souvenirs and even a fun match for puppies. I'm going to take Misty, and Annica is coming with her collie, Angel. It'll be a chance to look for suspicious people, and we'll be on hand if anything terrible happens."

"Randi will go with me," she said. "Maybe if I'm lucky, Jeff will be there and I can confront him again."

No matter how many names we collected, how many people we discussed, Minta always came back to Jeff Whitman.

"But this was helpful, Jennet," she said. "It forced me to take a good look at the people in my life."

Perhaps Minta was right and Jeff was the culprit we'd been seeking. Her enemy knew too much about her and Sparkle to be a stranger.

Thirty-six

Brent aimed his fork at his piece of orange chiffon cake, mangling the dainty frosting-flower I'd worked so hard to create.

"I'm taking Annica out to the wildflower field tomorrow," he said. "She's been good about staying away from it, but it's time we saw what's growing there."

I didn't say a word. Crane, who knew about my latest adventure with Annica, sent me a surreptitious wink.

"Are you hoping to see the ghost?" I asked.

"That'd be a blast, but she only shows herself to Annica. I wonder if she's there when we're not around to see her."

"It's like the tree falling in the forest when no one's around to hear it," Crane said.

"Good comparison, Sheriff. I'd like to know her name, if nothing else. We should hire a ghost hunter to bring her out into the open."

"That's sort of extreme," I said, "and, like you say, she's a one-woman ghost. You can also just let it go. In time, Annica will forget about her."

What had I just said? I didn't believe for a minute that Annica would ever abandon her hope of seeing the spirit in the wildflower field again.

"The ghost is just picking flowers," Crane said. "That doesn't hurt anyone."

Brent stared at his empty plate, which was my cue to refill it. "Annica thinks the ghost has a message for her."

"I wonder what she does with the flowers," I said, as I cut him another piece of cake. "Put them in a heavenly vase?"

He laughed. "She takes them up to her living room in the sky. Hey, Jennet, how about if I bring you a bouquet from our home-grown garden?"

"No! You'll make them mad."

They stared at me. I'd spoken without thinking. "That is, no thanks. I'd rather have a bouquet from a flower shop or the farmers' market."

"You'll have them." Crane covered my hand with his. "Only the best for a lady who can make a cake like this."

His plate was empty, too. I stood. "We might as well finish the cake. I can bake another one tomorrow. And if anyone is inspired to bring me flowers, I'd like yellow roses."

~ * ~

When morning came, it was too hot to bake. I was considering going to Clovers for a strawberry pie when Diane and Kristie turned into the driveway. I hadn't been expecting them; then I recalled it was their day to work at Sue's horse farm. Diane had Rilla with her.

The girls looked hale and sun-kissed, and Rilla's black coat had a blue sheen in the sunlight. She had regained the spark she'd lost under the dubious care of Ella Davidson, otherwise known as Cruella.

My dogs rushed out to greet the visitors, forming a happy circle around them. They saw Rilla rarely but had readily welcomed her into their pack. And dogs don't forget. We watched them play-fight over Gemmy's blue Frisbee, and all was well with our world as long as collies were a part of it.

Kristie said, "Did you hear that Sue found poisoned meat at her place yesterday?"

My heart sank. It lay especially low because only moments ago it had been soaring, enthralled by the joyful sight of eight collies playing.

"What was it this time?" I asked.

"A couple of pounds of ground meat. Turkey, Sue says."

"Our poisoner is going for variety."

"He's spending a lot of money," Diane pointed out.

"So far, yes, and thank God, he hasn't been successful. Only one dog got sick, and she recovered. He must be getting frustrated."

"We have news," Diane said. "Kristie and I found a clue. At least we think it's a clue. Someone left a silver ring with a stretchy band behind. It's the kind that can slip right off your finger if you're not careful. It has seven oval panels with different floral designs. Each flower has a small clear stone."

"Where is the ring now?" I asked.

"Sue has it. She's calling her riding students and their mothers to see if one of them lost it. If not, that means it belongs to the poisoner. She must have lost it when she was planting her poisoned turkey."

"That *is* a clue," I said. "It tells us that the poisoner is a woman. All along I've been thinking it was a man."

"Most men wouldn't wear a fancy ring like that," Kristie said.

Diane nodded. "I can't believe a woman would be so cold-blooded."

"Some women are worse than men," I said. "Remember Ella Davidson."

"Ugh, let's not."

She would have euthanized healthy collies because they stood between her and her master plan. Even now the memory of Cruella's plan, happily thwarted, raised my blood to the boiling point.

"Then there were those women who spilled poison out of their rings like Lucretia Borgia." Kristie looked down at her watch. "We have to go, Jennet. Our first job is to check every acre of the farm and even inside the corral. Sue's afraid for her horses."

"That's how we found the stretchy ring," Diane added. "It was close to the turkey."

Would the police be able to find a fingerprint on a small object like a ring? I supposed so. But who knew if our poisoner's prints were on file?

I was anxious to see the ring and also to view Ronda's video again. Could I be wrong about Gavin, and was Jeff innocent? Was Sparkle's dognapping a separate issue? Following that train of thought, was Raider's assault the work of a disgruntled exhibitor?

"See if you can find anything else our poisoner left behind," I said.

Diane called Rilla, who dashed up to her and sat at her side, offering Diane her paw to shake. Why couldn't my collies do that?

I praised Rilla lavishly, then had to placate Misty and Candy, who thought themselves shortchanged.

"Tell Sue I'll be over later today when it cools down a bit," I said.

~ * ~

The ring was as the girls had described it. Silver with seven clear stones set in small oval panels, each with a different floral design. Seen from a distance, it could pass for a wedding band. I held it up to the sun and watched it burst into brilliance.

"I lost a birthstone ring once," I said. "It was too large for my finger. I was going to have it resized but put it off." Automatically I touched my engagement and wedding rings. They were secure.

Sue slipped the silver ring on her own finger. "It doesn't belong to anyone who came here legitimately."

"It's beautiful," I said. "I wonder if those are diamonds."

"More like rhinestones or cubic-zirconia," Sue said. "I can see how it happened. The poisoner drives up and tosses a mess of ground turkey through the window and her ring goes with it. She's in a hurry and doesn't realize until later that she isn't wearing it. And I didn't see or hear anything."

"She must have come at night." Sue moved the ring to a finger on her other hand. "Now that I think of it, the dogs were barking around two."

"Did you look outside?" I asked.

"Yes, but by then there was nothing there. I check the property every morning," she added. "When the girls are working, they do it."

"The only one who has seen her is Ronda, and that's on a video," I said. "We weren't sure if it was a man or woman."

"Well, now we know."

"A ring doesn't have to be expensive to be meaningful," I said. "Suppose the woman retraces her steps and comes back to the ranch. It'd have to be during the day. We could put the ring back where it was and pretend the girls never found it. Maybe you'll get lucky and see her."

"I'd kind of like to keep it," Sue admitted. "My finger swells sometimes. A ring that stretches would be ideal. But every time I looked at it, I'd think about poison."

"I'm sure you can find another one like it. It has an old-time look. Take it to the Green House of Antiques in Lakeville."

"If only it were engraved."

"I'll take what we can get," I said. "Let's not lose sight of the fact that it's a clue."

"Our first good one," Sue agreed. "Okay. The ring goes back on the ground. Let's hope no bird discovers it."

For the first time since the nightmare began, I felt as if we were one step ahead of our antagonist. We would set a trap for her. Now if she'd just fall into it.

Thirty-seven

Brent handed me a dozen yellow roses. Their fragrance drifted out of the green floral wrapping paper and scented the air. It was as if I held the essence of a never-ending summer in my hand.

"Guess what happened yesterday," he said.

Crane had brought me a similar bouquet, also yellow, now residing in my favorite crystal vase on the dining room table.

Which reminded me. I hadn't baked the promised orange chiffon cake yet. I'd better do it tomorrow. Well, we had that Clovers pie for dessert. Belatedly I realized that Brent was waiting for a reaction from me beyond "thank you."

"Something happened?" Crane asked.

Brent disengaged himself from the leaping collie paws. All canine company manners flew out the window when Brent held a shopping bag from Pluto's Gourmet Pet Shop.

"It happened in the wildflower field," he said. "I took Annica there."

He handed me the Pluto bag and sank into the rocker. Even before he'd settled himself, Misty jumped into his lap where she knew she was welcome.

I opened the credenza in hope of finding the perfect vase. "Tell me about it."

"When you're ready to listen."

"We're ready," Crane said.

I found a vase acquired by my grandmother at a place called Green Stamps.

"I'm listening," I said. "It's called multi-tasking."

"Okay then. When I turned on Huron Court, I drove right smack into a wall of fog. No surprise there. I wanted to turn around, but Annica said it was good ghost-seeing weather. So we drove on. The fog began to dissipate, but some of it still hung over the field."

I waited patiently while he smoothed Misty's white ruff with one hand and stroked Sky's head with the other. When Brent had a good story to tell, he liked to take his time and pause for dramatic effect.

"To make a long story short, Annica saw the ghost," he said. "I didn't. Annica said she was tossing flowers into a basket."

"What else happened?" Crane asked.

"Annica said, 'I'm going in.' I said, 'No, you're not,' but she was too quick for me. She went about five feet into the garden. Suddenly she stopped. I asked her what was wrong. Annica said, 'She's gone. I lost her again.' But get this. The ghost left her basket behind on the ground."

Brent followed me into the kitchen as I filled the vase from Green Stamps with water and set about trimming an inch off each rose stem. How fortuitous that our mysterious visitors left their possessions behind. First the silver stretch ring, now a basket of flowers.

"That's a breakthrough," I said. "The ghost may be a real girl. If she were a spirit, wouldn't the basket be part of the apparition? It would have disappeared along with her."

On the other hand, living girls don't vanish in thin air. Usually.

He shrugged. "You're the expert, Jennet. I'm just reporting what I observed."

"Did you or Annica take the basket out of the field?" I asked.

"Annica did. Afterward, she decided it would have been better to leave it where it was in case the ghost came back for it. I guess we'll drive out to the field again tomorrow."

I set the last yellow rose in the vase and decided to leave the arrangement on the kitchen table. Yellow roses in two rooms. I was indeed lucky.

Back in the living room, Brent dropped into the hard oak chair. "At first I thought Annica was hallucinating. How could she see something—er—someone that I couldn't? But there's the basket. That's a hard one to get around. Here's something else. All the flowers the ghost picked were dead."

That was the most chilling aspect of this latest apparition.

"How soon did they die?" Crane asked.

"Right away, as soon as they touched the bottom of the basket—unless the ghost picked flowers that were dead to begin with. Why would she do that?"

"The last time I saw your garden, all of the plants were healthy," I said. "No natural flower would start to wilt right after it was picked."

"Annica said the ghost girl chose the prettiest, most colorful ones, then something killed them. She says it was the ghost's touch."

"What did you do with the flowers?" I asked.

"Ditched them. Who keeps dead flowers around?"

Crane said, "I don't want you going there, Jennet. Fowler, bulldoze the entire field before someone gets hurt. It was a good idea, but it backfired."

"Don't overreact, Crane," I said. "There has to be a logical explanation. Like...I don't know. Maybe some kind of weed killer spilled in the basket."

"Or maybe we planted a diabolical garden," Brent said.

"The flowers will start to fade in autumn, and in the winter they'll be gone, naturally," I pointed out.

"Yeah, maybe," he said. "But summer's just started."

~ * ~

The next day I drove out to Spruce Road to visit Lucy Hazen. I couldn't stop thinking about healthy vibrant flowers that died as soon as they were picked. Fragments of a dream I'd had last night came back to bedevil me. I was climbing a giant tiger lily when it gave a strangled cough and collapsed. I came tumbling down to the ground into the embrace of a plant that looked like Queen Anne's Lace.

Only it was the dreaded hogweed. Immediately I felt intense burning on the arm that had come in contact with the toxic plant. It felt as if I had dragged it through fire.

It was a good time to wake up. Fortunately I did. The dream faded as I reached my destination, and there stood Lucy on her porch, all in black, waving a welcome.

Always ready to entertain company Lucy filled the teakettle while I told her about Annica's latest experience in the wildflower field, about the flowers that died so quickly.

"You could be right, Jennet," she said. "If some kind of powerful, fast-acting weed killer remained in the basket, it could destroy the hardiest wildflowers."

"Or," she added, "flowers picked by the hand of the dead soon die themselves. Don't forget. You're hearing this second-hand."

Lucy was particularly knowledgeable about supernatural matters. She would have to be as the books she wrote for teenagers often dealt with the denizens of the other world, and no critic is more discerning than a young reader. But a ghostly touch destroying flowers in an instant? I didn't agree with her. Deciding to be diplomatic, I changed the subject.

"Yesterday Sue Appleton found more meat at her ranch. She didn't have it tested yet, but we assume it was poisoned."

"Are her dogs all right?"

"She got to it before they did. Have you had any trouble?"

She laid a hand on Sky's head. "We're okay so far. Dark Gables is isolated and, as you know, all the evergreens hide the house from the road. Your poisoner may not know we're here."

"I hope it stays like that."

The teakettle whistled, and she made tea. Sky's ears pricked. She knew it usually meant treats, and the next sound was the ping of cookies hitting a plate.

"Let's see if this miserable woman shows up in your teacup," Lucy said. "She sounds dangerous. And not just to dogs."

I drank my tea and prepared my teacup for reading. Lucy could find joy or sorrow, good things or bad, in the patterns formed by the leaves inside the cup. Incidents that affected me closely appeared in my 'home,' which was near the cup's handle.

Sometimes events foretold came true or partially true. Sometimes they didn't. But this was my chance to be warned about approaching trouble, or forewarned, as I liked to say.

"There's something," Lucy said and fell silent.

"A person?"

"More like a storm. It's over your home."

"And that means?"

"Events blown out of control," she said.

I swallowed the piece of cookie I'd just bitten off. Pineapple-nut from Kendall's gourmet line, and safe for dogs. Why did I feel as if I'd just eaten sand?

"Do you mean I have no control over whatever happens?" I asked.

"I wouldn't go that far. Let's say you have a battle ahead of you."

"Lovely," I said.

Lucy turned the cup around. "I have faith in you, Jennet. And cheer up. I see your wish."

"Can you show me the storm?" I asked.

She pointed a glittery blue fingernail to a blob of dark leaves all clustered together. "As you can see, they couldn't be closer to your home."

"What if I take a napkin and wipe them right out of the cup?"

Lucy laughed. "You can try, but it wouldn't make a bit of difference."

"I wonder if this storm is associated with the ghost in the wildflower field or the threat to our dogs," I said.

"I couldn't say. Just remember, forewarned is..."

I finished for her. "Forearmed."

Sky laid her head in my lap. She wanted petting, but I chose to think she was offering me canine-style comfort.

"On a brighter note, we have the *Devilwish* premier to look forward to in July," Lucy said. "Brent reserved a room at the Hunt Club Inn and invited everyone we know."

Devilwish was the movie based on Lucy's best-selling novel. We'd been looking forward to seeing it for months. How wonderful it would be if we had caught the poisoner by then and identified Annica's ghost.

It could happen.

Thirty-eight

Which collies should I take to the Gathering at the Everlasting Park? Misty, of course, but who else? That morning I sat on the porch and watched the collies play in front of the house, feeling like a mother being forced to favor one child over the others.

I knew my dogs. Candy would never behave, and my older rescue, Star, would soon tire of the novelty of going to a new place and want to take a nap. Sky was too timid to enjoy an outing that included over a hundred people and their collies. That left Halley, Gemmy and Raven.

I had taken Halley to the Gathering three times. Gemmy and Raven, never. So—Gemmy or Raven?

Gemmy, I decided. Raven had recovered nicely from the broken leg she'd sustained when a careless vagrant had run her down, but maybe she needed more time to regain her energy. All right. That was decided. Gemmy and Misty.

Speaking of energy, Camille had announced she wouldn't attend the Gathering this year.

"It's too tiring," she'd said. "I'm not a spring chicken. I'll keep an eye on your house and the dogs, so you can stay as long as you like."

I looked beyond my collies at their play to the yellow Victorian across the lane. Twister was lying on the porch while Camille weeded her flower beds and occasionally stopped to throw Holly's ball. The homey sight infused me with peace. Still, I imagined the poisoner planning her next move as she shopped for steaks and chops.

With collie lovers from far and wide gathered in one place, she would be able to leave her poisoned meat in selected yards free from observation.

Or—and this was the more likely scenario—she would lose herself in the Everlasting crowd, a spectator without a collie in tow. She could admire this pretty puppy and that frisky sable lad, slip her next victim a tainted treat, then melt out of sight. The opportunity to work her evil would be too good to pass up.

I felt as if the tale of the poisoner were about to take a giant step forward. We'd apprehend her and be able to enjoy the rest of the summer without fearing for our collies' lives. While the storm in the teacup might be rapidly approaching, the forecast for tomorrow promised a perfect day.

~ * ~

Later that afternoon, Minta called. "Can Randi and I go to the Gathering with you? I'll help you with one of the collies."

I gave a quick thought to seating. Three people, two large collies. The Ford Focus could manage.

"Sure," I said. "I'm going to leave around ten."

"We'll be there."

"Have you heard from the dognapper?" I asked.

"Not a word." But her voice sounded upbeat, and therefore, hopeful.

"I have high hopes for the Gathering," she said. "Even though Jeff checked out of his motel, I'm hoping to see him there."

"I hardly think he'll approach you in a crowd and demand that you pay him the ransom money," I said.

"No, but I can talk to him. Reason with him. Maybe he'll bring Sparkle."

That then was the reason for her sudden optimism. I didn't share it. First, I wasn't convinced that Jeff was the dognapper. Then, whoever had taken Sparkle would keep her out of sight until he had the ransom money in his hands.

My hope centered on the poisoner. I'd be surprised if she didn't show up. Somehow she would give herself away, and I'd be on hand to apprehend her.

"I wish I had Sparkle," Minta said. "I could take her to the Gathering and not have to worry about someone harming her."

"You'll have her back," I said, expressing confidence I didn't entirely feel. "And there's always next summer."

"Yeah," she said. "It'll be over long before then."

~ * ~

Annica was excited about taking Angel to the Gathering. Mary Jeanne had given her the day off, and she had finished her last reading assignment to be ready for her next class.

"I've never had a chance to show Angel off," she said.

A strawberry pie in the dessert carousel might have had 'For Jennet' written on it in dough. Apparently it was still Strawberry Week at Clovers. Annica wore her pink and white striped dress again and her strawberry earrings.

"This is *Michigan* Strawberry Week," she said.

"We have the best. Set a pie aside for me and I'll have a lime cooler."

"You're a creature of habit."

"I won't deny it." When we were settled at a booth, I said, "Brent told me what happened at the wildflower field. I wonder if I could see the basket."

"You could, but it's gone."

"Gone where? How?"

"That's a good question. I left it on a shelf in the closet. The next morning, it wasn't there."

"Did Angel chew it?"

"She couldn't reach it. After the flowers died, I didn't want her to touch it. I should have left it in the field," she added.

"Are you sure you brought it inside?"

"I remember doing it."

"Did you put anything else on the shelf and push it to the back where you couldn't see it?"

"No."

"What you do think happened then?" I asked.

She shrugged. "It was supposed to go with the ghost. She came back for it."

"I can't see that. Ghosts don't leave the place they haunt. But I guess they could."

"This one did."

A lady drinking coffee at a small table next to our booth stared at us. Ignoring her shocked look, I leaned closer to Annica and lowered my voice.

"You interfered with her plan."

"This whole affair is crazy," she said. "From where I stood, I could see the colors of the flowers. She had a lot of red, some pink and yellow. They looked fresh and beautiful. Then after she vanished, I saw she'd left the basket behind. I picked it up. The flowers were starting to die. By the time I put them in Brent's car, they were dead."

"It happened that fast?"

"Amazing, isn't it?"

"That whole field is cursed," I said. "It's on Huron Court, after all."

"But remember the beautiful pink Victorian? The land couldn't have been cursed then."

I took a sip of my lime cooler. It was wonderful as always. "It's too hot out to untangle this..." I searched for the right, the perfect word, but settled for "...mess."

"Let's talk about dogs then," Annica said. "Angel is going to wear her new bandana to the park."

~ * ~

I've never made a study of dreams. I just have them and usually forget the details as soon as I wake up. But not always. Sometimes they stay with me, and sometimes, rarely, I have the same dream twice.

That night, when I expected to dream of the collies at the Gathering, I found myself in the wildflower field. Again I was climbing a tiger lily. It had grown since the last time I'd seen it— in my dream.

Like Jack's beanstalk, it reached up to the sky and disappeared in a low-hanging cloud.

I wanted to see the planet that lay above the clouds. It was said that humans could walk and breathe on the surface and be invisible to the inhabitants. The idea fascinated me. It could have been a plot for one of Ray Bradbury's Martian chronicles.

But when I was halfway to the top, the lily shuddered and coughed, a surprisingly human sound. Then it fell to the ground like a young tree blown down in a windstorm. I fell with it, hitting my head on the hard packed dirt.

But not before I'd passed through the noxious hogweed.

The dream was horrid, a bona fide nightmare, and I remembered it for longer than I should have.

Whatever its meaning, I thought it boded ill for me—if I went to the wildflower field again, that is.

Thirty-nine

We had agreed to meet at the park entrance and sit together. Yes, sit. Ronda was bringing four lawn chairs, for which I was grateful. I'd be inclined to stay longer at the Gathering if I didn't have to stand or walk for hours.

There would be eight humans in our party and several collies. Litter sisters, Starla and Rilla, would be reunited, and Sue was bringing Icy, Bluebell, and Scarlet. Annica's Angel was making her first appearance at a collie event, and I had Misty and Gemmy.

I was happy to see Silverhedge represented.

Before I could reach for my wallet, Minta pulled out three ten dollar bills. "This is my treat," she said. "I have a good feeling about today."

That must mean she thought she'd find Jeff Whitman at the Gathering. I also had a feeling, a bad one, but I kept it to myself. We wouldn't find Jeff, we wouldn't find Sparkle, but something would find us. Something was going to happen to mar this picture perfect day.

I'd never been able to banish the memory of little Katie turning away from Raider's crate to talk to a friend, never setting eyes on the assassin who cut a chunk of the show collie's beautiful coat.

We had to be aware of everything in our environment, even though it appeared to be innocuous.

I was fortunate to park in a shady section of the lot, and we exited the car in a happy mood. Misty and Gemmy were wagging their tails non-stop, eager for the fun to begin. Minta carried a basket containing collapsible bowls, bottled water, and treats for the dogs. I took Misty's leash, and Randi held onto to Gemmy.

"All these people," Minta said. "He has to be here."

We walked into the heart of the gathering, past the ring where the fun match was going to be held. The park was already crowded. Some people had brought multiple collies and Ex-pens with covers to drape over them. Most of the dogs were adults but some were puppies, and all were overjoyed to find themselves in the midst of so many of their kind. I wished I could translate their various barks and high pitched yelps into human language.

As for people, who would miss an opportunity to stroll in collie heaven?

I saw Annica immediately. As if she were advertising Lime Week at Clovers, she wore an emerald green sundress, no doubt chosen to match Angel's bandana, and her earrings were thin china collie puppies hand painted to resemble blue merles. They bounced between gleaming strands of red-gold hair whenever she moved her head.

She told Angel to sit, and the collie sat, raising her paw in Lassie fashion.

"You sweetheart," Minta murmured and obligingly shook hands with her.

"There must be over two hundred people here," Annica said. "We'll have our work cut out for us."

We were going to be on the lookout for foul play, as Annica termed it. "If we see anyone who looks like they're up to no good, don't let him out of your sight." She patted the slight bulge in her pocket. "Take a picture."

"Do you remember Jeff Whitcomb, Annica?" Minta asked. "You met him at the show."

Annica nodded. "He's drop dead gorgeous."

"On the surface, maybe. If you see him, come and find me right away. Take a picture. Start a conversation."

"I can't do all that at once," Annica pointed out.

"Do your best."

"I found a great place for us to set up camp," Annica said. "It's nice and cool, under a weeping willow. I left my chair and tote there."

"Ronda's bringing four lawn chairs," I said. "We'll make it our headquarters."

An enticing smell of franks and sausages cooking rode on the clear air, mixed with the fragrance of flowers—and dog. I was hungry, even after having a pancake breakfast with Crane.

"Did you see any blue merles, Annica?" Minta asked.

"A lot of them, and tris and whites. All colors."

"Halley's breeder, Ellen Grove, has a handsome blue at stud. She had four blues and four tris in her last litter. I'll bet she brought them today."

As if on cue, I heard a familiar voice.

"Hey, Jennet—Greenway, isn't it?"

I turned. Georgia Grove, Ellen's daughter, struggled to hold onto two wild youngsters, a tri and a blue merle.

"I thought I recognized you," Georgia said. "How've you been?"

"Fine." I stooped to pet two excited puppies. They were perhaps three months old, both with striking markings. Definite show quality.

"Who are the babies?"

"Blue Lace and Licorice. Didn't you bring Halley?"

"I left her home this year," I said. "I brought two of my seven instead. The white girl is Misty."

"She's a beauty. Who's her breeder?"

I smiled. "The Snow Queen."

Georgia looked puzzled.

"I found her on my porch one Christmas Eve," I said. "All of my collies except Halley are rescues."

Both Misty and Gemmy were wagging their tails madly, anxious to make friends with the frantic puppies. "The sable is Gemini," I added. "We call her Gemmy."

"Oh, I remember. Gemmy was accused of plotting her owner's death. Like that could ever happen. Some people are plain crazy."

"Gemmy is a gentle soul," I added.

"Can I hold the little blue?" Minta asked.

"Be my guest. Lace loves being held."

Minta lifted the squirmy puppy up to her face, to hide the tears, I suspected. The baby's head markings were striking, half blue merle and half tricolor, and one of her eyes was blue.

"Would you like a merle to go with your tri, Jennet?" Georgia asked. "We still have Lace and two males at home."

I could imagine Crane's reaction if I came home with another collie. In truth, I didn't want to imagine it.

"It's tempting," I said, "but then I'd have eight. That's a lot of fur and kibble."

"How about you, Minta?" Georgia asked.

Minta set Lace gently on the ground, and Licorice pawed her leg, hoping for her turn in the human's arms. "I already have one," she said. "Her name is Sparkle."

I thought Georgia would ask Minta if she'd brought Sparkle to the Gathering, but she said, "I'd better get these pups back to their Ex-pen. I'll see you around, Jennet. If you change your mind…"

"Thanks, but I won't," I said, suddenly remembering my underlying reason for coming to the Gathering. It wasn't to add a collie puppy to my brood.

~ * ~

In the next half hour our party grew. I held Starla's leash while Ronda set the lawn chairs in a semi- circle under a majestic weeping willow, perhaps my favorite tree of all, although we didn't have any on our property. It must be Misty's favorite tree, too, judging from her fascination with a strand that almost touched the ground. In a moment, she would seize it for a solitary tug-of-war game.

Sue arrived with Kristie and Diane. She led Icy and Bluebell on a brace, while Diane held tight to her beloved Starla and Kristie took charge of Scarlet.

Annica had wandered off with Angel, who wanted desperately to explore this wondrous world of dogs and people and follow the smell of something delicious cooking. Sue, falling prey to the same temptation, left with Kristie and Diane to buy hot dogs.

Minta and Randi were also roaming, no doubt searching for Jeff Whitman.

Alone for a moment, I sat in one of the lawn chairs, which was a signal for Misty and Gemmy to lie at my feet. I was thinking how perfect everything was in the shady, sprawling park. The warm sun, the gentle breezes, old friends and collies, collies, collies.

There was no reason for alarm, none whatsoever, but suddenly one of the gentle summer breezes turned chilly and wrapped around me. At the same moment a cloud blotted out the sun. It seemed as if a little of the light had gone out of the world.

The sensation passed quickly but not without delivering its message.

Beware! Even now something has invaded this perfect place.

Something or someone, malicious and unavoidable.

As I sat under the weeping willow, safe and content with my collies, it moved silently among the milling collie owners and their dogs. Every minute it grew closer.

Forty

Brent stepped out from behind a stand of pine trees. He led two familiar tricolor collies, Tempest and Lucky. The sun struck lights in his dark red hair, and his forest green shirt blended into the many shades of green all around us.

A lady with a platinum blonde braid wrapped around her head like a coronet led her collie past him, pausing to give him an admiring glance which he didn't see.

His eyes lit up when he saw me, and the collies almost leaped out of his grasp. Both of them were Silverhedge rescues, and Tempest remembered me.

"I didn't know you were coming to the Gathering," I said.

"Wouldn't miss it. Why are you just sitting here?"

"I'm waiting for Sue to bring the hot dogs," I said "and I'm recovering from a premonition."

"Uh-oh."

I told him about my certainty that trouble was even now making its way toward Everlasting Park.

"It's a good thing I'm here then."

"Minta and her cousin are looking for Jeff Whitman. She's sure he's holding Sparkle for ransom. I'm not."

"What do you think will happen today?" he asked.

"The poisoner may be here. Somebody's dog is in danger."

"Just let her try something. It won't be so easy for her to get away with anything. Too many people around."

"Just the opposite," I said. "She'll be able to lose herself in the crowd."

I could picture it. The vile woman would be casually dressed with nothing to set her apart from a genuine collie lover. She'd strike and be gone by the time her victim showed signs of distress.

"She can't get away on foot," Brent said. "Two of my boys came with me. I have one of them watching the parking lot. They can sound the alarm if they see somebody running to a car."

"Good."

"Have you seen Annica?" he asked. "She was supposed to bring Angel."

"She's around—somewhere. So are Ronda and the girls. Kristie and Diane are pretty sharp. We have a lot of people watching over the dogs."

"Yeah, we do. The whole Silverhedge gang."

"And Minta and her cousin."

I ran my hand along Tempest's side. Her massive coat hid her once prominent ribs, and her eyes had that endearing gleam of mischief common to the collie. I remembered a time shortly after her rescue when she didn't want to eat.

Not to be overlooked, Lucky pushed her out of the way.

"Your dogs are looking so good," I said.

"They all had baths yesterday," Brent said. "Guess we'll go find Annica. She's still shook up about the ghost's basket."

"That's a mystery for another day."

"Right. I'm off to patrol the grounds. If Annica comes back, tell her to wait for me here."

I said I would, but I didn't intend to remain in one place. As soon as our food arrived, I'd eat and give the collies their own hot dogs, then set out on a patrol of my own.

~ * ~

The lady who had admired Brent hurried her collie southward toward the exit. Her dog was on the small side, white with caramel markings on her back and sides. Like Angel, she sported a bandana. She made a sudden sound deep in her throat, not a growl.

Her owner stopped abruptly and knelt on the ground. "Are you all right, Spice?"

The dog seemed fine to me, interested in Misty, who quivered at the end of her leash, wanting to get closer.

I stopped too.

"Is the little one okay?" I asked.

Platinum Braid gave me a quick smile. "I think so, but I'm taking her home. This is her first time at the Gathering, and it looks like the excitement is too much for her. I guess."

Spice and Misty touches noses. I noticed the name tag pinned to her owner's white shirt: Monica LaBlanc, Huron Station Collie Club.

Huron Station was up north on Lake Huron. Monica had come a long way to attend the Gathering, but people did that.

"She threw up," Monica said.

"Are you going to take her to the vet?"

Megan rose and scrutinized Spice's face. Judging from the dog's demeanor, she was fine, over her upset.

It's like that with dogs sometimes. They throw up, it's over, and five minutes later they're looking for food.

"No," Monica said. "She'll be all right. She does that sometimes. You have a beautiful dog," she added.

Our collies did look good together, Misty with her tri head markings and Spice like a living sundae all fluffy white and caramel.

"It's just that I worry about bringing my girls to a place with so many collies walking around," I said.

"Because of that dog flu? I do, too, but you can't keep them locked up."

"I worry about people who look on an event like this as a chance to harm a dog," I said.

Monica's smile evaporated. "What a terrible thought. Who'd want to harm a collie?"

Who indeed?

"I'd better get Spice home." Monica tugged on the leash. With a little cough, Spice rose. "See you next year."

I said goodbye and walked slowly toward Everlasting Lake. Misty trotted along gamely at my side. Our picture-perfect day was rapidly growing warmer. After a refreshing stroll by the lakeside, I'd take her back to our station.

I couldn't help thinking that trouble would be out of place in the park. Everyone looked happy, fussing over other people's collies as well as their own, eating franks and sausages, and drinking various beverages. I didn't see my friends but did spy Licorice and Lace sleeping in their Ex-pens while Georgia leafed through a program.

Sue was back at the station watching collies, but where was the rest of our group? How was it possible that I hadn't come across at least one of them?

I walked on, conscious of admiring glances directed at Misty. We had missed the fun match, but the silent auction was scheduled to start in...I glanced at my wrist, frustrated to find that I was wearing the watch from the wildflower field.

Well, if that was my only false step today, it was good.

At the souvenir stand, I stopped to gaze at the offerings: collie-themed T-shirts and notecards, figurines, some of which looked expensive, and a watercolor head study of a blue merle collie priced at twenty-five dollars. The artist was gifted, capturing that mischievous gleam I'd seen in Tempest's eyes.

Should I buy it for Minta because I couldn't give her Sparkle? Or would the print only add to her sorrow over losing her own blue merle?

While I stood, considering, an unfamiliar voice said, "Hello, Jennet. That's mine, by the way."

I turned to find myself looking into a burst of color. Jocelyn— or was it Jacelyn?—wore another rainbow sherbet sundress with a long necklace consisting of chunky purple beads. She pushed her sunglasses up into her strawberry blonde hair.

"Hi, Jacelyn," I said. "What's yours?"

"The print you're looking at. I donated six of them for the rescue. This is the only one left."

"You do good work," I said. "The collie is so lifelike."

"I like to capture beauty when I see it. It's so transient."

That wasn't the word I'd used to describe a collie with its connotation of loss. But then dogs change every day, like the leaves, as one season merged into another.

"I guess it depends on the kind of beauty," I said.

"I've been looking for Minta. She must have brought the Blueberry Muffin."

I didn't want to discuss Sparkle with her. "She's here."

"Oh, good. I'll keep an eye out for her. My advice? Get the sketch while you can."

"I'm going to," I said, "but who do I pay?"

"Rosemary Webber. She's around somewhere."

I hoped she hadn't gone far. How easily those tiny figurines and notecards would be to slip into a pocket.

"Anyone could walk off with anything," I said.

Jacelyn held her hand up for Misty to sniff. "Nice collie you have."

Misty sniffed and pressed against my leg. She must be getting tired. I'd better forget the lake and take her back to the shade of the willow tree. But first I asked, "Did you bring a collie?"

"Not this year," she said. "I just brought myself."

I almost asked her why, then decided I really didn't want to know. Not as much as I wanted a drink of water or lemonade. That hot dog was making me thirsty.

"Hey, Jennet," she said suddenly. "You have collies, don't you? How'd you like a sketch of them, maybe in front of your home?"

At the moment, I couldn't think of anything I'd rather have. I could almost see all seven of my collies depicted in oils, framed and hanging on our wall.

"I'd like that," I said and jotted down my address. "We're on Jonquil Lane in Foxglove Corners."

She tucked the slip of paper in her pocket. "I'll be in touch. I don't think you'll be disappointed."

A woman who must be Rosemary Webber rushed up to the stand, carrying a drink in a paper cup. I paid for the sketch and bid Jacelyn goodbye. Taking my print and my dog, I retraced my steps and still didn't see anyone I knew. It was as if they'd all been swept away into another time.

Really, Jennet, I told myself. *You're in Everlasting Park, not on Huron Court.*

I especially didn't want to lose track of Brent. I felt safer with him in the vicinity. He could deal capably with any problem he encountered.

And maybe nothing untoward would happen. Could my premonition be false?

Forty-one

A scream shattered the conversational hum that permeated the park, and suddenly it seemed as if all the dogs at the Gathering were barking. It wasn't a 'Snake!' or 'Fire!' scream but one that held great anguish.

Sue swallowed the last bite of her hot dog. "What on earth?"

I pointed to the area behind the pines from which Brent and his dogs had emerged. "Over there."

"Let's go," Sue said. "Hurry!"

"Sue!" I stared at her, incredulous. "One of us has to stay with the dogs."

We couldn't leave them unattended, although every one of them seemed eager to investigate the scream, especially Misty, who had grabbed my hand lightly with her mouth.

Sue blushed as well she might. "Oh, right. I'll stay. You see what's going on."

Two husky boys, adolescents in gaudy T-shirts, dashed past me, followed by a man, then a small crowd. All headed toward the site of the commotion, while others stood immobile, their faces puzzled and anxious. The atmosphere in the park had changed, the air charged with electricity and filled with angry voices and shouting and frantic barking.

I joined the stampede. Hurrying, I stumbled on a rock and almost lost my balance but recovered. My heart raced and moisture dampened my skin. It was too hot for such exertion, but the cry was impossible to ignore.

Where was Brent? He should be here.

Coming to a stop, I peered over shoulders at a distraught woman. She knelt in front of her collie, forcing the dog's mouth open. The collie, a handsome young sable, appeared thoroughly cowed as if he had been caught stealing his owner's sausage.

And was that a sausage lying on the ground, torn from its bun? Or rather, a part of a sausage?

"I don't see anything in his mouth," the woman wailed. "Nothing. He already swallowed it."

"Look on the ground," a voice said. "Everybody, look."

Feet shuffled and the voices grew louder, but no one cried, 'I found it!'

"It came from over there." She pointed to a trio of pink flowering bushes about five yards away. They formed a natural barrier. "Somebody threw it."

"Let's roll," one of the husky boys said, and he and his companion took off running toward the bushes, even as the screamer said, "He's gone. He got away."

She rose and the collie wrenched himself away from her, no doubt upset by the unaccustomed rough handling. As I watched, filled with fear for him, he threw up on the ground.

"Oh, no! Dasher got to it before I could get to him. What am I going to do?"

A silver-haired man stepped forward, stabbing the ground with a black cane. "Do you have a napkin or something, ma'am?"

She looked puzzled, but pulled a paper napkin from her picnic basket.

"You're going to want to have this tested." The man bent down and picked up what was left of the sausage and the bun which had fared better, being whole. Gingerly he wrapped it in the napkin and handed it to her. "We can't be too careful."

"What do you mean?" she asked.

"That sausage may have been tampered with."

"Dear Lord."

Phone in hand, a tall dark man in the tan uniform of a park ranger jogged up to the group that had gathered around the woman and her dog.

"Hold on," he said and snapped a picture of the offending meat. "Okay. Did you see who threw the—uh—hot dog, ma'am?" he asked.

"No, it just flew through the air like one of those drones. I couldn't see anyone because of the bushes." Her voice broke. "My dog. What am I going to do?"

"Don't panic," the man with the cane said.

"But you're saying my dog was poisoned."

"It's a possibility," the ranger said. "A good one. Then again, maybe somebody didn't like the taste and threw it away."

Possible, but unlikely. Receptacles for waste were plentiful in the park, together with signs forbidding littering.

I was so tempted to intervene. What was Dasher's owner waiting for? She should be rushing to her car, taking Dasher to the vet. I was about to speak up when the woman said, "I have to find my husband."

I listened to the voices that floated around me, snatches of dialogue running into one another.

"Poisoned?"

"Yeah, it's been happening. Read the paper."

"Poor dog. I hope those kids catch the jerk that did this."

"No place in hell hot enough..."

"I lived here all my life. Never thought I'd see the day..."

I swallowed the lump in my throat and watched as Dasher's owner dropped the sausage in her picnic basket. On its way down, it tumbled out of the napkin. I could only hope the meat didn't touch other food, or, if it did, that she would have the sense to throw it away. She took hold of the basket handle and Dasher's leash, weeping openly. Dasher stumbled, and the ranger picked him up. "I'll carry him, ma'am," he said.

The onlookers began to drift away, as people do in the aftermath of an incident that doesn't touch their own lives. The suspected poisoning must have made more than one of them realize they'd better check on their own dogs.

A heavy hand landed on my shoulder.

"What happened here?" Brent asked.

"Our poisoner showed up with a sausage in a bun."

"The kind they're selling here."

"I think so."

"Damn it! I hope my guys caught her."

"She's sneaky and fast. The dog's owner didn't see anything but a flying object coming out of those Rose of Sharon bushes. She called it a drone."

"A drone is way bigger than a sausage," he pointed out.

"She was just upset. Anyone would be. Too bad she didn't get to the sausage before her dog did."

"She thinks he ate some of it?"

I nodded. He swore again.

We began to walk back to the weeping willow where I'd left Sue and the collies. "If I were her, I'd find a hiding place here in the park. It should be easy to do. Then after everyone cleared out, I'd drive away."

"And in her place, I'd hightail it out to my car and be out of here before anyone realized what happened," he said. "It'd help if we knew what she looked like."

"Sometimes I'm afraid we'll never catch her.

I envisioned having to look for poisoned meat in a drift of autumn leaves and in the snow. It would be next to impossible to see a steak or a chop that had sunk down into the leaves. In the snow, anything with color would be readily visible.

However, with luck on our side, this murderous woman would be apprehended long before the season changed.

~ * ~

We were finally together, sitting in lawn chairs. Our dogs rested around us, all accounted for, all safe. People had begun to leave the Gathering, taking their Ex- pens and their collies to the safety of their own kennels and homes. We should leave, too. We would, as soon as we shared our experiences.

I told them what I knew of the apparent poisoning, repeated what I'd heard. "The park ranger knows about it, but what can he do? If Dasher should die..."

"Don't say that," Sue said. "His owner must have rushed him to the vet. If he shows signs of ingesting poison, they can give him something to counteract it."

"Can they?" Kristie asked. "Won't they have to know what kind of poison it was?"

"We can hope he'll be all right," I said.

I tugged Misty's leash, pulling her closer to me. She had been watched every second, but what if the poisoner had tossed the sausage in her direction? She was quick. All food-motivated dogs were. Could I have moved faster than a ravenous collie?

What if I were the one sitting anxiously in an animal hospital, praying that the vet would be able to save Misty or Gemmy? Or any of the dogs I knew and loved?

Even if the poisoner were caught, I didn't think I'd come to the Gathering next year.

"Let's look on the bright side," Diane said. "Unless there's a story in the *Banner,* we won't know how it turns out, so we can hope the dog survived."

"Do you know her name, Jennet?" Brent asked.

"No," I admitted. "I didn't talk to her. I was a bystander."

"I'll see if I can find out something."

"I'd suspect Jeff Whitman, but I didn't see him here today," Minta said.

She held the watercolor head sketch of the blue merle. She'd taken one look at it and promptly burst into tears, but once she recovered, she thanked me repeatedly.

Randi touched her cousin's hand. "Well, it was a long shot. I can't see Jeff running around the park with a poisoned sausage. He's more the holding-a-collie-for ransom type."

Minta said, "We should be getting home, Randi. We have a long ride, and maybe there's another note in my mailbox."

We all rose and gathered our possessions, taking our own dogs and helping others who'd come to the Gathering without their animals. Sue cleared the area of any trash, and Brent took the lawn chairs from Ronda.

"I still have to meet up with my men," he said. "Could be they saw something. I'll call Jennet if they did, and Jennet can let the rest of you know."

I think we were all relieved to leave the park, but as we joined the stragglers, I thought about what Brent had said—that if he were in the poisoner's place, he'd wait in the park until everyone had gone home. Everlasting was a spacious, woodsy park with plenty of trees and bushes. In other words, plenty of places to hide.

Suddenly every shadow seemed suspicious, and even though the sun was still shining, the ambience reminded me of the abandoned construction on Jonquil Lane. Another place best avoided.

Forty-two

The *Banner* carried a short article about the incident at Everlasting Park. The collie had ingested tainted meat but was expected to recover. Dasher's owner lived in northeastern Michigan, in Huron Station. She had traveled a long way only to place her collie in danger. Well, she couldn't have known what would happen.

The reporter ended the account with a plea for anyone with information about the poisoning to contact the police.

Brent had called last evening with a progress report. His men had followed a running woman in gray slacks and a black top out of the park, but by the time they reached their car, she was out of sight.

Once again, the poisoner had eluded us.

Annica folded the paper and picked up a fork. We were having strawberry pie and iced tea at Clovers. Annica was a customer today but still wore a red dress with her strawberry earrings.

"I was wondering..." She scooped up a spoonful of meringue-topped strawberries and murmured, "Mmm, perfection. I baked it myself."

"Wondering what?" I asked.

"Whether the poisoner brought the sausage from home or carried a bottle of arsenic with her."

"Who knows? Probably she added the poison at home where no one could observe her. She wouldn't be likely to risk being recognized at the food booth. I think she must make daily trips to a meat department," I added.

Annica's musings set off some of my own. No one buys one of any kind of meat except a roast. Should we look for sausages in our garden now?

"What's important is that Dasher is going to be all right and no other dogs were targeted, that we know of," Annica said.

"We'd have heard if they were. These poisonings are so random. I used to think Sue and I were being singled out because we were in Rescue."

"This happened to a regular collie owner from out of town. As you say, random."

I nodded. "It's the breed this sick person is targeting."

"I don't understand," Annica said. "Everybody loves a Lassie dog. Who in their right mind would want to kill a collie?"

"A psycho. That's what we're dealing with."

"I'd die if anything happened to Angel," she said. "I just want this to be over."

"We all do."

"And that other matter, too."

"Which is?"

She set her fork down on the plate. "The ghost in the wildflower field. Specifically, the missing basket. How do you explain that?"

"Black magic?"

"And why did the flowers die as soon as they were picked?"

"I don't know."

I'd almost finished my pie, except for one tiny bit of crust topped with meringue. I'd have to order another piece.

Annica scooped an ice chip out of her tea and chewed on it. "I have an idea I want to run by you."

Uh-oh. This couldn't be good.

"I'm going back to the field and pick a bouquet of my own. If the flowers die, then there's something wrong with the soil or..." She let her observation trail off but added, "Brent said Crane told him to bulldoze the entire field. He can't do that."

The very idea appeared to upset her. I didn't know how she would stop him. It was his property, after all.

"No one tells Brent what to do," I said. "But if he were to bulldoze the field, you could always replant it in the spring."

"Then we'd end up the same way, with a garden filled with strange flowers. And what about the ghost?"

"She could still haunt the land."

I glanced around. The tables near the booth were empty. We'd already been overheard discussing spirits and haunting by a curious fellow diner.

"There wouldn't be any flowers to attract her," Annica said. "Just dirt." Abruptly she switched subjects. "What do you think about the basket?"

"That a ghost wouldn't need one."

"Seriously?"

"All right." I had given the missing basket some thought and come up with a possible explanation.

"A smart, determined dog can do anything. Angel managed to pull it down from the shelf and chewed it. Obviously my weed killer theory is wrong because Angel is fine. Someday you may find basket parts around your house."

"That's possible. Angel is smart, and she loves to hide things. Can you think of anything else?"

"If I have another piece of pie, maybe I can," I said.

"Sure thing. I'll have one too."

She started to rise, then remembering that she wasn't working today, tried to catch Marcy's attention.

"There's one more thing, Jennet," she said. "Will you come with me?"

I hesitated. Her plan sounded innocuous. I could wait on Huron Court while Annica gathered her flowers. She'd have the good sense not to wander deep into the field.

On the other hand...

"I've dreamed about that field twice," I said. "The same dream. I'm climbing up a tiger lily when it dies and I fall to the ground."

She laughed. "You can't climb a tiger lily."

"It was a dream," I reminded her. "It was able to hold my weight. I couldn't see the top of it."

"Jack-in-the-beanstalk," she said.

"Yes."

"I tend to dream about dogs and..." Her face turned a few shades lighter than her strawberry earrings. "Well, dogs. So, will you go?"

"All right." I wouldn't be climbing any flowers. "When?"

"Now?"

I glanced at my watch, the real one whose hands ran forward. It was still early, just after noon. I had hours to take care of the dogs and plan dinner.

"Let's go then," I said. "As soon as we have another piece of pie."

~ * ~

The summer days followed a similar pattern. Mornings were pleasantly warm, but by late afternoon, it grew hot and humid. By the time Annica parked on Huron Court, the sun was high in the heavens and the air was heavy with moisture.

I rolled the sleeves of my sheer white blouse up to the elbows and smoothed the wrinkles in my denim skirt. I knew I was risking sunburn, but this venture shouldn't take long. At least no mist hung over the field today, which meant the ghost girl probably wouldn't show herself.

"It's all so beautiful," Annica murmured.

I agreed. The color in the wildflower field had never been more vibrant. Blossoming was truly at its peak. I didn't think the flowers would begin to fade any time soon.

Hastily I revised the thought. As long as they were allowed to stay in the ground.

Somewhere a dog was barking. The sound came from a faraway place, perhaps the woods that backed up to the Randall property when the pink Victorian had still been standing.

"Do you hear that?" I asked.

"I've decided it's a stray, a real one," Annica said. "He won't bother us."

She stepped into the field, keeping to the edge, as I'd hoped she would. She held the sides of her dress away from the encroaching plants, which told me she hadn't planned this outing or she would have worn jeans.

"Do you want to pick some flowers, too?" she asked.

"No, thanks. This is your project."

She pulled a small pair of scissors out of her pocket and began snipping pink coneflowers. Their petals were a deep shade of pink and perfect, their leaves not yet nibbled by hungry insects. When she had about a half dozen, she took a step forward and added red lilies. Then golden yarrow and a dark blue flower, probably bachelor's buttons.

A steady hum intruded on the silence. It was a motor, a car coming closer. Speeding? Quickly I stepped away from the edge of the road and waited for it to pass. Huron Court seldom saw traffic, and drivers in Foxglove Corners were notorious for ignoring speed limits. But this road had one dangerous curve after another. Even if one were the only person on the road, it didn't make sense to race down it.

The car, yellow with long white fins, whizzed by and rounded a curve, its hum dying out. Except for the color it had looked like Brent's vintage Plymouth. I hadn't noticed the driver. But of course there had to be one. But did he live in the present? In my time? Or had he fallen prey to Huron Court's penchant for hurling a wayfarer into another age?

"Yikes," Annica called. "Way to take out the wildlife."

She'd moved farther back into the field, and her bouquet had grown. Surely she couldn't hold anymore. She began to walk toward me, her red-gold hair glistening in the light, the flowers in her hand so brilliant the sight of them hurt my eyes.

"What's the speed limit on this road anyway?" she asked.

I didn't answer, my mind elsewhere. Out of nowhere a memory had surfaced. Not long ago, two cars had collided on Huron Court. One of the drivers fled the scene, the other lay bleeding and broken, thrown from her vehicle. She would later die in the hospital.

Suddenly I knew the identity of the ghost in the wildflower. The answer was so simple I wondered why I hadn't realized it earlier.

Forty-three

Gail Redmond.

A young college student, Gail had died, the victim of a hit-and-run driver on Huron Court last fall. According to a witness, this had happened after she'd passed the wildflower field, driving toward the cemetery at the end of the road. She couldn't fail but be enchanted by the sight of the exotic, rainbow-colored display. Perhaps she planned to return on another occasion and help herself to a bouquet.

The "No Trespassing" signs hadn't been posted yet.

Gail couldn't know that she had so little time left, that her life would essentially be over before she turned off the road.

The wildflower field, then, was Gail's unfinished business, her last conscious intention. The last bright imprint on her mind.

Without a shred of evidence, I knew I was right, and I shuddered at the cruelties of fate. Of being in the wrong place at the wrong time. If Gail had pulled off the road and gathered her flowers as soon as she saw them, she wouldn't have crossed paths with the hit-and-run driver.

"Gail," I said. "I'm so sorry."

Annica stepped out of the field, clutching the most colorful, healthiest bouquet I'd ever seen. "What?" she asked.

"I think I've solved one mystery," I said. "I know who your ghost is."

As I told her my theory, color drained from her face.

"But I'm going to have to convince Lucy to come back with me," I said. "I'd like her opinion."

"Didn't that accident happen last year?" Annica asked. "My ghost is from olden times."

"What made you decide that?"

"Her dress, for one. It was long and white."

"A typical ghost uniform," I said, hoping to spread a modicum of light on what was a dark situation. "Let's go with the assumption that a ghost appears in whatever clothing she was last wearing." I thought of those ugly hospital gowns. "Or in her favorite outfit."

"Then if I died this minute and came back in spirit form, I'd be the ghost in red."

"With strawberry earrings," I said.

"And you'd be the ghost in denim. I wonder, would your sleeves still be rolled up?"

We were sliding into silliness, which was all right. It was better than being afraid.

"I'd like to be known as the ghost in red," Annica said. "Or the strawberry ghost."

"Maybe we can find a picture of Gail on the Internet or in Miss Eidt's vertical file. I remember reading she was from out of state, so she doesn't have family in the area. Not that we'd want them to know their daughter is still wandering around the earth as a spirit."

"That won't help," Annica said. "I never saw her face. Not clearly."

"Well, we can still look."

"Let's say you're right. It *does* make sense in a way. But why did she show herself to me? What does she want of me?

It was a good question, one I'd already considered but couldn't answer. "I have no idea. That's why we need Lucy."

"Could Gail have come to tell me that I'm going to die on Huron Court like she did?"

That grim thought accounted for her pale face.

"I doubt it, but it wouldn't hurt to stay from the field for a while."

"I want to go home," she said and walked quickly around her car.

She wrapped the flowers in a damp towel Mary Jeanne had given her to keep them fresh in transit.

"They're not dying," she said as she laid them carefully in the back seat.

"No, they're fresh and lovely."

"Do you want them?" she asked.

"No."

"I'll take them to Clovers then."

We made a U-turn on Huron Court and drove toward Jonquil Lane. I wasn't used to being a passenger, but it was a pleasure to lean back and gaze at Sagramore Lake, lying still and shining in the bright afternoon, its beach jammed with sun lovers.

"Your theory doesn't explain the basket," she said.

"I still think Angel chewed it."

"I mean, we still don't know where it came from."

"Or my watch," I said. "And we don't know what Gail wants besides flowers. We don't know how to help her."

I really needed to talk to Lucy.

~ * ~

To my surprise, Lucy readily agreed to accompany me to the wildflower field. Annica didn't want to go, claiming she had too much reading to do along with her shift at Clovers.

Apparently she was taking my advice to avoid the place seriously.

"If I can help Annica in any way, of course I'll go," Lucy said.

The next morning, Lucy and I stood quietly at the edge of the field. Fog lay lightly on the land, muting the brightness of the flowers. As soon as it burned away, the weather was going to be hot. Again.

Finally Lucy said, "You're right, Jennet. It's the spirit of Gail Redmond that haunts this garden. The wildflower field is her last memory. As to why she isn't at peace, I can't say."

"Then we can't help her?"

"She might not want our help. When the time is right for her, she'll cross over. Until then, let her linger in her happy place."

"Then it doesn't have any particular significance for Annica?"

"That we can't know. Time will tell, but I rather doubt it."

A clump of blue bachelor's buttons grew within my reach. I had a sudden desire to pick them, along with an aversion to touching flowers that might be cursed. In the end, I left them in the ground.

"Do you have any idea why the flowers in the basket were dead by the time they made it to Brent's car?" I asked.

"That's easy, Jennet. The girl who gathered them was dead."

We waited a few minutes. The fog continued to veil the view, and offhand, I couldn't think of another question to answer Lucy.

"This is a sad place," Lucy said. "It isn't evil, and I don't believe the ground is cursed. Brent created beauty here after the pink Victorian burned. He shouldn't try to eradicate the garden."

"I hope he doesn't."

"Don't forget that Violet Randall's amazing violet plants are part of the garden. They're certainly not evil."

And there was no way I was going to fall from a giant tiger lily. That only happened in a nightmare.

I would talk to Brent about the field the next time I saw him. However, that would mean telling him that Annica had ignored his 'No Trespassing' edict. Oh, well, he couldn't stay mad at her, and I didn't think she'd want to return anytime soon. Seeing the ghost of Gail Redmond had quite likely cured her of the desire to have a supernatural experience.

All's well that ends well. Again.

Except there was still the matter of the ghost basket.

~ * ~

"Nobody does what I tell them to," Brent said that evening as we sat in the living room drinking coffee and eating dessert. A strawberry pie, naturally. "I didn't think Annica was going to the field all this time."

"I'm glad she did yesterday. Otherwise I'd never have known about Gail Redmond."

"Just how did you happen to know about her?" Crane asked.

How did I know?

"It came to me out of the blue, and Lucy agrees with me."

"It could have happened that way," Brent said. "What do we do now?"

"Nothing. Let Gail roam through the field. She'll find another place to haunt when the flowers die in the fall. Either that or she'll finally be at rest."

"If I don't go straight to heaven, I want to hang around the barn with my horses and dogs," Brent said. "That's my ideal afterlife."

"I'd like to stay right here in our house on Jonquil Lane," I said.

Crane winked at me. "With me, I hope."

"With you and all our collies."

But I didn't want to think about the afterlife, no matter how glorious it proved to be. I was living in heaven on earth, and I wanted it to go on forever.

It wouldn't, of course.

I banished the thought and concentrated on pie. How could Clovers' strawberry pie be so good? All it contained was strawberries, meringue and graham cracker crust. And sugar.

Savor the moment, I told myself. *Who knows what the future will bring?*

Forty-four

"Waiting is hell," Minta said. "I don't even know if Sparkle is still alive."

Although she looked cool and serene in aqua denim and turquoise jewelry, her eyes had a haunted look. I wished I'd been able to help her.

She had driven up to Foxglove Corners this morning, frustrated and anxious to go someplace. Any place. Staying in her house and waiting for a new development had taken its toll on her.

I had been examining my flower beds for sausages or other lethal tidbits, and she had helped me search. When we didn't find anything suspicious, I let the collies out. We sat on the porch with a pitcher of iced tea on the wicker table between us, exhausted from the double dose of heat and humidity.

"It's comforting to be around your collies," she said.

Since the Everlasting Gathering, Minta had become especially attached to Gemmy, who sat by her side, happily soaking up pats and endearments.

"Are you sure there weren't any further messages?" I asked. "Some that fell out of your mailbox maybe?"

"I'm sure," she said. "I'm beginning to think Sparkle isn't being held for ransom after all."

"What do you think is happening then?"

"That she's stolen. I have an enemy who wants me to suffer. I'll never see Sparkle again, so it doesn't matter that I can't pay the ransom."

"Don't worry about raising the money," I said. "It doesn't appear to be a priority for whoever snatched Sparkle. Something else is going on."

"I can't imagine what."

At the moment, neither could I. At first the motive had been straightforward: envy and getting rid of the competition. Not anymore. Minta might be correct. An unknown enemy was determined to hurt her through her dog.

"I'm beginning to wonder about Gavin," she said after a while. "I'm thinking of breaking up with him."

"Because of Sparkle?" I asked.

"Partly. We went out to dinner last night. He said he likes it better without a dog coming between us."

I was flabbergasted. "How insensitive! A dog doesn't have to come between people who love each other. Crane and I have seven collies. We couldn't be happier."

"Then Crane is the right man for you," she said. "About that other man in my life, here's an update. I ran into Jeff Whitman the other day. It turns out he didn't leave town. He moved into a in a condo and is thinking about buying it."

"I thought his home was in California."

"So he said. Something changed. He's talking about earthquakes and wildfires. We don't have them in Michigan, not on that scale anyway."

"Could he keep Sparkle in a condo?" I asked.

"Maybe. It wouldn't be ideal."

"I was thinking about homeowners' restrictions."

"I'll look into it," she said. "Jeff was very nice, very solicitous. He asked about Sparkle, but it could be an act. How can you know?"

"With some men you can't."

I glanced at her glass. It was almost empty, and the pitcher was half full. Misty crossed in front of us and lapped water noisily from the dogs' pail, sending droplets flying in every direction. I kept a rag on the porch to mop up spills lest I or one of the dogs or company slip. As I reached for it, I tried to find another subject.

"Whoever took Sparkle has had her too long," Minta said. "I'm getting discouraged. Every time I look at the beautiful watercolor you gave me, I feel like crying. That dog *does* look like Sparkle."

"Well, it's a blue merle."

"She and Sparkle have the same markings."

"I hope it makes you happy until you have your girl back again," I said. "I forgot to mention, your friend, Jacelyn, is the artist. I was talking to her at the Gathering."

"She's not a friend, just a woman I run into at the shows. Every time she called Sparkle blueberry muffin or pancake I wanted to scream at her."

"You're too much of a lady to make a scene, Minta," I said. "Every person has their quirks."

"Jacelyn called me Minnie once. I wasn't very ladylike then."

"I shouldn't think so. Minta is a pretty name."

"It's Araminta really, but that's a mouthful and way old-fashioned sounding. People always called me Minta."

I refilled our glasses. Candy followed the motion of my hand, licking her chops. This was her way of telling me that treats from the Lassie tin were past due.

"What are you going to do about Sparkle?" I asked.

"I don't know what else I can do. Wait to hear from the dognapper, I guess. He must want something."

"If it's Gavin, he won't like it if you break up with him."

"Tough. We didn't have much in common anyway. I can't be with a man who doesn't like dogs. Is there a chance he did this?"

"There's always a chance." I reached back into past memories. "A woman I knew lost her dog when her former boyfriend surrendered him to a shelter without her knowledge."

She gasped. "What happened?"

"In the end she was able to get her dog back. Sometime later the man died. He was shot. Not by her," I added.

"Serves him right. If I find out that Gavin took Sparkle, I'm going to kill him."

I understood the feeling but felt obliged to discourage her.

"Don't," I said. "You might end up behind bars. Let Karma take care of him."

And while Karma was at it, let her punish the poisoner. People had to know they couldn't harm our precious collies with impunity.

~ * ~

After that visit, I didn't hear from Minta for a while, and other matters claimed my time. I searched through Miss Eidt's vertical file and found a picture of Gail Redmond clipped from the *Banner*. Annica looked at it and declared that Gail resembled the ghost. She said no more about returning to the wildflower field.

The next time I went to Clovers, Annica's flowers were still lush and lovely. Mary Jeanne had arranged them in a tall cream-colored pitcher and placed them on the counter close to the dessert carousel.

"Mary Jeanne put a special powder in the water to make them last longer," Annica said. "Lucy never did explain why my flowers lived and the others died."

She had said Gail's touch had killed them, Gail being a ghost. Annica, thank heavens, was still alive. But Annica was right. It wasn't a satisfactory explanation.

"Lucy can't have all the answers," I pointed out. "But I can't think of any other reason."

Neither one of us mentioned the ghost's basket.

I took two pork chop dinners home and another strawberry pie. Neither Crane nor I had grown tired of them.

The next day storms swept through Foxglove Corners. Our world exploded in a wild display of lightning, thunder, and hail. I stayed inside with the dogs while Crane's patrol took him out in the worst of the weather. On the day of the storm I didn't search the flowerbeds for poisoned meat, assuming that the she-devil was staying in her house while the ground turned to a gigantic quagmire.

The storms continued throughout the night, but in the morning the sun rose and the earth dried out. And Sue called to tell me that Kristie and Diane had found chunks of meat strewn along one side of the corral.

The poisoner was back in business.

Forty-five

Misty lifted her head and sniffed the air. Before I could blink, she flew past me in a mad dash to the front door. Seeing a rare opportunity, Gemmy pounced on Misty's beloved toy goat. Holding it in her mouth, she followed the pack.

Drat! I wasn't expecting company. I'd just finished baking a lemon cake, had just dried the last of the bowls and was looking forward to an hour with my new (old) Gothic novel. Not to entertaining.

Still, I couldn't be anything but gracious. With my Tennessee-born husband's influence, our house was a bastion of southern hospitality.

I passed Star, who always trailed after her sister collies, demanded quiet from the pack, and glanced out the front window. I didn't recognize the car, only registered that it was white. The woman stepping out of the vehicle was another matter. She was a vision in a bright orange sundress that clung to her curves and a Kelly green necklace. She carried an oversized tote with wide rainbow stripes.

Jacelyn Holloway.

I recalled giving Jacelyn my address and inquiring about a watercolor sketch of my collies. In the ensuing drama of wildflowers and attempted poisonings, my request had slipped out of my mind, along with Jacelyn herself.

Well, you invited her.

I ordered the dogs to stay and opened the door, summing up a smile as friendly as hers.

"Hi, Jennet," she said. "I hope I'm not imposing, but I thought I'd come over and get some ideas for the picture."

Misty and Candy seemed about to forget their training and jump on Jacelyn. I grabbed both dogs by their collars and said, "Come in. They won't bite."

"What beautiful collies," she said, undaunted by their high spirits. "They'll make a gorgeous picture."

"If they can stay still long enough to pose for one," I said.

"Oh, that's no problem. I take pictures and work from them."

Miraculously, my brood fell back. Jacelyn glided through the hall, and I ushered her into the living room. "Have a seat."

She chose the rocker, the one Brent always sat in. Misty eyed her warily and sidled up to her.

My chair!

As Jacelyn's hand moved to stroke Misty's head, I noticed her rings. One, a clunky turquoise set in a gold claw, the other a ruby in a circlet of diamonds. Or a red stone surrounded by rhinestones.

"Something smells delicious," she said.

"I have a lemon cake in the oven. It won't be ready to serve for a couple of hours."

I reviewed the possibilities for refreshment. I didn't have anything to offer her except something to drink.

"Would you like a glass of lemonade?" I asked. "I make a fresh batch every morning."

"Thanks, but I had a late breakfast," she said. "Why haven't I seen your dogs in the ring?"

"I only showed Halley once."

I looked for Halley, but, her greeting concluded, she had wandered off.

"The show ring life isn't for me," I said. "Besides, my other dogs are rescues."

"I see. So you don't have papers for them."

She made it sound as if my collies were somehow lacking.

"It never mattered," I said quickly. "They're wonderful dogs."

"I'm sure they are. Have you thought what background you'd like for a picture?"

I hadn't, but suddenly I knew what I wanted.

"The porch," I said. "Some of the dogs on the stairs, some on the ground. I'd like a ladder effect."

She nodded. "That's what I would suggest. You can place them in the order you acquired them, first to last or any order you like. It's up to you."

"I doubt if I can get them all together," I said.

Doubt? It would be impossible to arrange my collies in the order I could see so clearly in my mind.

"No problem," Jacelyn said. "I'll follow them around and take random snaps with my camera. Then I'll put them all together. Now, would you introduce us? Start with little Marshmallow over there."

"Her name is Misty," I said with an emphasis on *Misty*. "She came on Christmas Eve with the snow. I saved my blue merle, Sky, from a man whose hobby was abusing dogs. She's still timid. Candy..."

I smiled as I described my prime mischief maker, who was eying Jacelyn with a tell-tale gleam in her eyes. "An enterprising young man tried to pass Candy off as Halley when Halley was lost. He wanted the reward money."

I continued my recital until I'd told a mini-story about each collie. Jacelyn appeared to be suitably impressed. We went outside, and she took several pictures of them as they frolicked around the fountain and chased one another. Gemmy set her sights on a brilliant butterfly while Raven tried in vain to catch a bee.

"Who lives in that charming green doghouse?" she asked.

"Raven used to. Now she stays in the house."

"Then it's empty?"

I nodded. And it was going to stay that way.

"I could sketch your collies individually or grouped the way we talked about," Jacelyn said. "It's your choice."

"Let me think about it. May I have a copy of the pictures?"

"You sure can, and I'd better say goodbye now. I have a few errands to run this afternoon. I'll be in touch."

"Would you like a deposit?" I asked.

"That won't be necessary. I'm going to love painting your beautiful collies."

As I walked her to the car, she said, "I can't wait to get started."

And I couldn't wait to see the finished product. Products, I decided. I'd choose the porch scene with all of my fur family together and have the pictures she'd taken individually framed.

I knew I'd be happy with Jacelyn's work. In spite of my initial reluctance to entertain company, the time I'd spent with Jacelyn had been one of the more enjoyable interludes of a trying summer.

~ * ~

When Minta called that evening, I was hoping she had good news about Sparkle, but she sounded upset.

"I broke up with Gavin last night," she said.

"How did he take it?"

"Not well. He said now that Sparkle was out of the picture, we'd be better together. How does that sound?"

"Suspicious."

"I thought so, too. In fact he refused to accept that we're over."

"That's not his choice."

"I told him that. He said it was *our* choice, and he wouldn't go along with my decision."

How complicated relationships could become, even those that were relatively short. It wasn't as if Minta and Gavin had been together for years. And even then...

I wanted to assure Minta that this was just talk, essentially meaningless, intended to intimidate her. But how could I? A memory I'd recently recalled tugged at me. The man who had surrendered his girlfriend's dog to a shelter when she thought he was taking care of her.

Controlling men were capable of any atrocity.

In the end, all I said was, "What are you going to do?"

"I'll get a restraining order if he threatens me. I hope it won't come to that."

Everyone knew that retraining orders don't always ensure the victim's safety. I saw no need to point that out.

"The problem is, how can I find out if Gavin took Sparkle if I don't see him?" she asked

"I know you're angry and frightened now," I said, "but remember the ransom demand. That implies that you'll have Sparkle back if you come up with ninety thousand dollars. How does that fit in with Gavin's taking Sparkle?"

She was quiet for a minute, finally saying, "But I never got a message telling me how to pay it."

"True, but that demand didn't sound to me like it came from a thwarted lover."

"We weren't lovers," Minta said.

"All right. That was the wrong word."

"It's okay. I see your point."

"Did you ever mention Sparkle's inheritance to Gavin?" I asked.

"No, he hated when I talked about her. He just tuned me out."

"The way I see it, you have two separate problems. A former boyfriend who won't go away and Sparkle who's missing, presumed dognapped."

"I don't know what to do about either of them," she said with a sigh. "I feel so lost."

Thoughts of Lucy and her tea leaf reading crossed my mind. But Lucy dealt with the supernatural. Minta's problems were one hundred percent down to earth.

"I never saw that side of Gavin," Minta added. "Now I think he may have done something to my dog to get her out of the way."

The spotlight had moved from Jeff to Gavin. As for myself, I didn't know what to think. Either man could be the guilty party. Or neither.

"Come over anytime if you need to talk," I said, "and keep the police on speed dial. Just in case."

As I ended the call, Crane came into the kitchen trailed by Candy, who sensed a walk in the near future. Candy would have to wait.

I threw my arms around Crane and kissed him. "I'm so glad you're a kind, loving, thoughtful man," I said.

He returned my kiss. With interest. "I try."

"And I'm so fortunate you were on Jonquil Lane looking for acreage to buy the day I met you," I added.

"I have a confession to make," he said. "I'd seen you earlier that day."

"I didn't see you."

"You were looking at Halley when I drove by. I had never seen a black collie before— or a girl like you."

The gods of romance had smiled on us that day. Crane hadn't made up a story of wanting to buy acreage. Eventually he'd found the perfect site and built his log cabin.

I didn't want to let him go. How lucky we were to have each other. And how unfortunate that Minta, with her cool, classic beauty and bright future prospects, had become entangled with a man like Gavin.

"Do you think Candy can wait for her walk?" I asked.

His frosty gray eyes grew warm, the flecks of ice melting. "She'll have to," he said.

Forty-six

That night I woke with a certainty that all was not well.

I had been trapped in a nightmare. My unease, a vague dread, had its roots in that appalling dream, but I couldn't remember any of it.

Don't try to remember that which isn't real. All is well.

Crane slept beside me, and Halley and Misty lay close together in the doorway, guarding us from intruders. Moonlight streamed through the windows. Out in the night the coyotes were howling.

That must have been what had awakened me. Strange that their barks and howls no longer disturbed the dogs. Coyotes were a part of country life, and we'd all learned to co-exist with them.

I turned, still troubled by something I couldn't identify. If I kept trying to identify it, I'd never fall asleep again.

Unbidden, a line from *A Midsummer Night's Dream* slipped into my mind: *Wake when some vile thing is near.*

A large black spider crawling down the wall, a moving shadow, a shapeless menace...

In a moment I would be out of bed, wandering through the silent house, disturbing the dogs as I searched for something that wasn't there. I didn't want to do that. Closing my eyes, I kept thinking, *All is well*, over and over and over again. And finally slept.

~ * ~

When next I woke, I felt as if I hadn't slept at all. A dull pain throbbed at the back of my head. But the new day beckoned. Crane was downstairs, and the dogs were most likely with him.

Knowing I was out of bed, Misty bounded up the stairs to escort me to the kitchen where Crane was brewing coffee. The aroma was tempting, but I wanted tea and a pain killer, although...I pressed the back of my head. The throbbing was already receding.

Thank heavens. I didn't want to waste a moment of a precious summer day.

In his crisp uniform and shining badge, Crane looked bright and ready for the day. "Morning, honey," he said. "Did you sleep well?"

I filled the teakettle. "After a while. I woke up once and couldn't go back to sleep. I had a nightmare."

No sense saying any more about it. I couldn't remember what had frightened me. A spider climbing up the wall? I'd better check the house for cobwebs.

"Would you like scrambled eggs this morning?" I asked.

"That sounds good."

I opened the refrigerator and took out a fresh carton of eggs.

Crane set mugs and juice glasses on the table. "What kept you awake?"

"Subconsciously worrying about Minta, I think. She's afraid of her boyfriend. She tried to break up with him. That isn't what he wants."

"Break-ups happen all the time," Crane said.

"There's more. She thinks Gavin stole Sparkle to make their lives less complicated. His life, that is."

"What do *you* think?" Crane asked.

"It's possible. I suspected him from the first. Only she swears he doesn't know about Sparkle's inheritance, and the ransom message mentioned the exact amount. I can't get past that. Jeff Whitcomb knew about the money."

"Are they the only two suspects?"

"The chief ones," I said.

He patted my arm. "You'll figure it out. Only don't get caught in the crossfire."

"What crossfire?"

"You know what I mean."

I pulled seven eggs out of the carton. Three for Crane, one for me and three for the dogs to share. As if she could read my mind, Candy watched me crack the shells.

I thought about telling Crane we'd soon have a beautiful new picture of our collies to hang on the wall but stopped myself. Let it be a surprise.

~ * ~

After Crane left for his patrol, before the day grew too warm, I took Gemmy, Raven and Sky walking to Squill Lane. Since they still had energy to spare, we continued on to Sue's horse farm. This was the girls' day to work. I was eager to hear any updated news they might have about the poisoning at Everlasting Park.

I found everyone outside with all the animals. Sue's dogs were running around the ranch house like wild creatures, while the horses grazed quietly and watched them. The sun bathed dogs and horses in light, bringing out all their colors.

Seven collies, so like mine, gathered around us, tails wagging, eyes inviting me and my leashed trio to join in their fun.

So much elegance and beauty! It should be preserved. I'd have to tell Sue about Jacelyn's artwork.

An air of unrestrained excitement radiated from the three humans. Dispensing with a formal greeting, Kristie said, "There's good news, Jennet. The ring is gone."

"Good and bad news," Sue corrected. "We had a visit from Lucretia Borgia yesterday. She took the ring and left about two pounds of chocolate candy in its place. Ugh. It was a mess, all melted. I raked it and poured vinegar over the whole area."

Anyone with knowledge of dogs knew that eating chocolate could be fatal for them.

"The Arsenic Hag changed her M.O.," Diane said. "She must have run out of meat money."

Arsenic Hag! What a perfect name for our poisoner.

"Chocolates are expensive, too," Kristie pointed out. "She's spending a bundle on the off chance a dog will get sick or die."

"What part of this news is good?" I asked.

Sue frowned. "It proves the ring was hers. She dumped the chocolates in the same place she lost it."

Unless a bird or other wild creature had carried it away.

"True," I said, "but how does that help us capture her?"

"She fell into our trap."

"We're going to set another one for her," Diane said. "It'll be bigger and better. Any ideas, anyone?"

For a moment, no one spoke. Then Sue said, "This isn't a trap, but if we happen to see a woman wearing that ring…"

I sighed. What were the chances of that happening? And how many similar rings were in existence? "I wish I knew why she's been targeting collies," I said.

How many times had I said that? More than I could remember.

"Don't we all?" Kristie said. "I wonder if she was ever bitten by a collie."

"My mom told me a collie knocked me down when I was two," Diane informed us. "You can see how it affected me. I don't remember it," she added.

"If this goes on all summer, I'm going to lose my mind," Sue said. "It's hurting the rescue. This isn't a safe place to foster collies. If it weren't for you girls, I don't know how I'd manage."

"We won't let you down," Diane promised. "We love your collies, too."

"Did she hit your place, Jennet?" Sue asked.

"I haven't found anything that shouldn't be there lately, and she never left anything on Camille's property."

"So," Sue said, "do we have a Plan B?"

~ * ~

Later that day, Brent came over bringing a box of chocolates for me and something in a Pluto's bag that had a strong gamey aroma. I accepted the candy graciously while thinking of chocolate melting in the sun on Sue's horse farm.

"What smells so good?" he asked.

"Dinner," I said. "You'll stay."

It was a statement, not an invitation. Two chickens were roasting, and I'd prepared a huge salad filled with all the greens and vegetables I had on hand.

While we waited for Crane, I told him about the poisoner's latest attempt to take out Sue's collies.

"Drastic times call for drastic measures," he said. "We've let this reign of terror go on too long. She's one depraved person, but we outnumber her."

Perhaps Brent could provide a Plan B.

"Do you have any ideas?" I asked.

"Let's review what we have. We've seen her on video, but the picture isn't clear enough to ID her."

"She may be wearing her stretchy ring," I said.

"I'll start noticing what women wear on their hands."

"I hardly think she's anyone we come in contact with," I pointed out.

"I see women all the time," he said.

"I'll bet you do."

"Seriously. It helps to know we're looking for a woman."

"What about starting a rumor that one of Sue's dogs ate a chocolate?" I said. "But that would be tempting fate. It might come true."

"That's something Lucy would say. Besides, how do we know the rumor will reach her?"

I crossed with ease over the stumbling block. "With a fake story in the *Banner*? Jill Lodge might write it."

Or not. Jill was a stickler for the truth, for reporting unadulterated news. However, she could write another story about the poisonings and end it in such a way that the reader would suspect one of Sue's collies was in bad shape.

"How would that help?" Brent asked.

"It might make her bolder. She might come back to Sue's place, and we'd be waiting for her. One way or the other, I want this woman caught. The Arsenic Hag. That's what the girls call her."

"She *is* a hag." He looked through the window, his expression lost in thought. "I've got a lot of land around my barn. There's always someone coming and going."

"Including women?"

"Some of the owners of horses I board are women, yes."

We continued in this vein until the collies alerted us to Crane's arrival.

"We should all get together at Sue's and hash this out," Brent said. "The Silverhedge Saviors did the near impossible. We can ride again."

In the kitchen, I heard Crane's hearty greetings rise above the pack's frantic barking

"I'll call Sue and arrange it," I said and went to the kitchen to give Crane a greeting of my own.

Forty-seven

I couldn't stay away from Clovers and their lime coolers and strawberry pies— and a chance to chat with Annica, who should be working today. Feeling as if I'd melt if I had to take another step, I opened the door and was greeted by the sweet notes of the clover chimes and waves of cool air.

God bless the air conditioning.

The little restaurant was quiet. About a fourth of its tables were occupied, and the conversational hum was low. Everything looked good, especially the cherry pies cooling on the counter on a three-tier stand.

I didn't see the flowers from the wildflower field. They would have died by now.

Annica stood at the menu board adding items in white chalk: Stuffed cabbages, baked Virginia ham, roast turkey. She was plainly dressed in a blue and white gingham blouse with a long denim skirt, quite a departure for her, but her earrings, as usual, were unique: tiny mermaids holding tinier pearls.

"I hope you have strawberry pies," I said as she turned to greet me.

"Still in the kitchen. They'll be ready to be boxed up in about fifteen minutes."

"I'll have one and a lime cooler while I'm waiting."

"I'll join you," she said. "It's been a slow day. I have too much time to think."

She stirred her lime cooler listlessly while I drank mine in gulps. She seemed unusually quiet.

"What's wrong?" I asked.

"I feel like we left Gail Redmond hanging."

I hadn't expected this and tried not find humor in the visual she suggested.

"How do you mean?" I asked.

"If she's still wandering through the field, she isn't at rest. We haven't done anything to help her."

"Well..."

What could we do? What could I say? I decided on, "How do you know she's still there? Have you been back to the field?

"No," she said, "but I keep thinking of her picking flowers, and I wonder, what happens then."

"She disappears. Goes back into the mist."

"Then what's the purpose of it?"

I reminded her of my theory, of Gail stepping into the beauteous scene that had imprinted itself on her mind in her last moments of life.

"That's not supposed to be how the afterlife works," Annica said. "What about resting in peace?"

She had a point. Poor ghost girl. Alive or dead, gathering wildflowers would be a pleasure for about fifteen minutes. After that it would be tedious. Whenever I pictured rest eternal, I always thought there must be more to heaven than lying still in the everlasting light.

"I'd like to think we could help Gail cross over to the other side," Annica said.

"How could we do that?"

"Lucy might know. Don't you see, Jennet? We've left the wildflower field mystery unfinished. That's not what we do."

"Not every mystery can be solved," I pointed out. "Or should be."

She started drinking her lime cooler. "I remember the time she was walking toward me and the mist swallowed her up. I want to feel like we did something to help her. She needs help. That was the reason she appeared to me."

"All right," I said. "We'll visit Lucy. Have a cup of tea. See what's next?"

"Then there's her dog," Annica said.

I hadn't heard a dog barking since our earlier visits. I said, "We never saw him. Maybe he's just a living dog with no connection to the spirit."

"He's a loose end."

"Did you ever find basket pieces?" I asked.

She shook her head. "That's part of why I feel this way. The basket is another loose end. I believe I'll know when we're finished."

"All right. We'll visit Lucy and go back to the field one more time. That's all we can do."

I thought she looked marginally happier. "Don't tell Brent," she said.

~ * ~

Lucy arranged cups, saucers, and dessert plates on the coffee table in the sunroom. The Zodiac charms on her bracelet jangled. Sky watched her, eyes bright with anticipation.

Annica, who appeared uncharacteristically nervous, played with her seashell earrings and twisted a red-gold strand of hair with a mind of its own.

"Are you asking me to visit the wildflower with you?" Lucy asked.

"Only if you want to."

"I don't really, but if it would help you, of course I will."

Annica said, "We—that is I—have been wondering what keeps a spirit tied to earth?"

"Unwillingness to leave it. Gail Redmond was a young woman in college. Her future was snatched away from her. She didn't have time to experience the beauties of our earth."

"But isn't that true of everybody who dies young?" she asked.

"Perhaps some feel more attached to their lives than others," Lucy said.

"We want to help Gail if we can," Annica said.

"Then pray for her."

"That's it?" Annica asked. "Just pray?"

"Let's see what the tea leaves say," Lucy said.

The tea kettle whistled. Lucy rose and poured boiling water in the cups in which she had already sprinkled loose tea leaves. Sky, who had followed her, padded back into the sunroom, her eyes on the box of cookies Lucy carried.

"Maybe there'll be a basket in my cup," Annica said.

"That's asking a lot of a basket...to travel to Dark Gables."

"What's this about a basket?" Lucy asked.

"I brought it home and it disappeared," Annica said.

"Maybe you misplaced it."

"I don't think so."

"This," Lucy said, "is the summer of strange things happening."

~ * ~

Lucy peered into Annica's tea cup. "You couldn't ask for a happier future, Annica," she said. "I see your wish and a ring."

"A diamond?" she asked.

"I can't tell. But here's your basket. It's overflowing with good things, like happiness. It isn't your ghost basket."

My cup was next, and I didn't like the way Lucy paused as she perused it. Or the way she turned the cup around and around. Or her frown. But I didn't say anything. Maybe Lucy was just growing tired.

Then she said, "I see a ring in your cup, too, Jennet. This is odd."

"Not really."

I told her about the ring the poisoner had lost and how we'd left it at Sue's horse ranch for her to find.

"This is puzzling," I said. "Does it mean she'll lose the ring again?"

Lucy smiled. "I just see a ring. And a storm. Not a literal one. Trouble. I always see troubled conditions in your cup."

"We're all determined to catch the woman who's been trying to poison our collies," I said. "Brent has activated the Silverhedge Saviors."

241

"I wish I could help. But there's a limit to my powers, and the tea leaves occasionally like to keep their secrets."

"If you have any premonitions concerning me, be sure and let me know."

She reached over to pat Sky and give her a shortbread cookie.

"I always do," she said.

Forty-eight

The rainbow sherbet lady strolled up the walkway carrying a large square package. Her dress was neon green, and her shoulder bag, a yellow and green straw, hung heavily down to her waist. She hadn't called to inform me that the painting was ready, but what else could be in the package?

The dogs were barking, their voices ferocious enough to give a burglar pause. I shushed them and opened the door.

"It's finished," she announced, holding the package up with a triumphant air. "I was in the neighborhood and took a chance you'd be home. I can't wait for you to see it."

The collies fell back, their eyes on the package, but excitement was low key. It didn't smell of chicken or beef.

"Where should we go?" she asked. "We'll need scissors."

"To the kitchen," I said, leading the way.

Jacelyn set the painting on the oak table, and I cut the strings.

"It turned out well," she said, "and I have copies of the pictures I took for you."

"I'm sure I'll love it," I said as I removed the outer wrap. There was a layer of brown paper underneath.

"It looked like rain this morning," Jacelyn said. "I didn't want it to get wet."

I freed the painting from the last of its protective covering and gasped. It was exactly the pictured I'd envisioned. My two tricolors, Halley and Candy, lay on the porch; blue merle Sky shared the middle step with Misty; and Raven sat beneath them. Star and Gemmy were on the walkway. All of my beautiful collies together, their colors brilliantly captured. Jacelyn had been able to fit the front door with its multi-colored wreath of silk Thumbelina zinnias in the background.

"Do you like it?" she asked.

"Oh, Jacelyn, I *love* it."

"Consider your collies immortalized in color," Jacelyn said. "You'll always have a remembrance of your dogs in this fine summer."

I propped the picture up against the wall behind the counter. "Can you stay for a cup of tea or coffee?" I asked. "I have banana-nut bread."

I was glad I'd decided to bake this morning; otherwise I would have nothing to offer a guest.

"Hot tea would be welcome," she said. "I have a bit of a scratchy throat. Who gets a cold in the summer?"

"Plenty of people." I began to cut one of the loaves in thick slices.

Candy screeched as I backed up and stepped on her foot. She held her paw up in Lassie fashion, hoping my regret for hurting her would translate into her own slice.

I plugged in the electric teakettle. "How long have you been painting, Jacelyn?"

"From the time I opened my first box of crayons. I like to think of myself as an animal artist. What better subjects could I have than these majestic collies?"

"I can't think of any," I said.

As she accepted the dessert plate with a thick slice of banana bread on it, I noticed her hands. Her fingers were long and slender, nails covered with purple polish. She wore a large sapphire ring in a silver setting.

And a stretchy ring that looked like a wedding band on her left hand.

Not just any ring. I stared at it. The one that had been lost on Sue Appleton's farm and left in the same place in the hope that the owner would come back looking for it.

The ring belonging to the Arsenic Hag. It had to be.

"I wanted to go to art school, but I didn't have the money," Jacelyn was saying. "I lived for the day when I could support myself with my art. It hasn't come yet."

I hardly heard her. Could this flamboyant woman possibly be the monster who had drifted in and out of Foxglove Corners leaving poisonous meat for dogs in her wake?

She painted lovely images of collies. It made no sense that at the same time she was trying her best to kill one or more of them.

Stunned at my epiphany, I broke off a piece of banana bread and broke it into smaller pieces. Misunderstanding my intent, Candy whined. The other dogs lay in at the edge of the dining room, not deigning to come closer. Even Misty kept her distance.

"But that day will come," Jacelyn said. "I have plans to market collie greeting cards."

My mind wandered. If by some bizarre chance Jacelyn was the Foxglove Corner poisoner, what should I do? Exercise my right to make a citizen's arrest?

Ill-advised. I had no real proof. I reminded myself that any jewelry store likely carried dozens of rings similar to the one Jacelyn wore. And why would she wear it to my house? Didn't she know Sue and I were friends and I'd be aware of what went on at the horse farm?

Possibly not. She couldn't know the girls had come across the ring and subsequently replaced it as a trap.

You have no proof.

None at all, but a strong suspicion and the collies of Foxglove Corners to protect.

But consider. Jacelyn wore gaudy clothes and eye-catching jewelry. The poisoner wore black.

Of course. She wouldn't want to attract undue attention to her death jaunts.

"I'd like to paint Sparkle, but Minta never takes her anyplace," Jacelyn was saying. "I wonder why."

No proof, but I knew I was right. Call it an intuition. Or a foreboding. Lucy would know, but Lucy wasn't here. Maybe Misty, my psychic collie, sensed the evil in Jacelyn as she kept her distance. Silly Candy only cared about food.

I still didn't know what to do.

"Would you like more tea, Jacelyn?" I asked.

I needed more time to think. Above all, I didn't want Jacelyn to become aware of my suspicion.

But to sit next to a dog killer at my own kitchen table, to eat and drink with the enemy, made me physically ill.

I played a scene in mind that had never taken place: Candy choking on a poisoned meatball that had been tossed on the walkway.

I swallowed a huge lump in my throat. Now, if ever, was the time to utilize my acting skills. First I had to corral my thoughts. Instinct told me the best approach would be to keep Jacelyn from knowing what I was thinking. If she suspected I'd discovered her secret, she might slip a dose of arsenic in my tea while I wasn't looking.

Don't take your eyes off her then.

I fixed my attention on Jacelyn. Her plate was empty, and I intercepted her glance at the rest of the loaf but ignored it. I'd let her finish her tea, write a check for the painting, and get her out of the house. Then I'd call the Silverhedge Saviors together.

Oh, and I'd have to examine the walkway and driveway with great care just in case she left a poisoned tidbit behind.

~ * ~

As soon as I shut the door, even before the white car pulled away, I was on my phone calling Sue.

"I don't think I ever saw her," Sue said.

"You couldn't miss her. She dresses in the most outlandish colors. Except when she's on a murder mission."

"What are we going to do?"

"I'll call Mac Dalby, but I know what he'll say. 'You don't have any proof.' I'm aware of that, but we'll have to proceed without it. Can you call an emergency meeting of the League? I'll call Brent. You contact Ronda."

And Minta? Maybe not Minta. This wasn't her battle, and she lived an hour away.

"I'll try," Sue said. "The girls are here working. Do you want to meet this afternoon?"

"As soon as everyone can come."

"Will we set another trap?" she asked.

"Maybe. We need to brainstorm. I'll be over as soon as I let the dogs out."

And as soon as I examined the path Jacelyn had taken. Deliver a painting...Deliver death. I wouldn't put anything past her.

Forty-nine

The somber atmosphere in Sue's family room underscored the gravity of the situation. Six of us had gathered to plan Jacelyn's undoing. We would have been seven, but Annica had an afternoon class.

"I'll do anything to help," she'd said. "Let me know what you decide."

With Annica, we would be seven against one, which I considered good odds.

As if to cheer us on, the collies were lying close to us. Icy, Bluebell, and Echo, and the Silverhedge dogs Sue had added to her brood considered themselves part of the group. Of the new collies, Scarlet appeared particularly observant. She lay at my feet, front paws crossed, eyes fixed on me. I imagined she knew what we meant to do and wholeheartedly approved.

Brent could hardly control his anger. "Now that we found this poisonous hag, we can't let her get away."

For him, Jacelyn was guilty until proven innocent, and she couldn't possibly be innocent.

I had a moment of doubt. Could I possibly be wrong about her? "I'm pretty sure she's the one."

Ronda said, "We have to trick her into admitting what she's been doing or catch her doing it. Preferably both."

"And why she's doing it," Sue added.

"Because she's crazy," Diane said. "She must be smart to have gotten away with this for so long."

I said, "We'll have to be smarter. We *are* smarter."

"Can we set another trap for her?" Sue asked. "The ring worked."

"I have an idea," I said.

The plan had presented itself to me as I drove the short distance to the meeting. I'd examined it quickly and so far found no flaws in it, but I was anxious to know what the others thought.

"Let's lure her back to the horse farm and see what she does."

Sue gasped. "I don't want that fiend anywhere near my dogs."

"Hear me out. We'll make her think it's safe to make a return visit to your place. The dogs will be in the house the whole time. One of us needs to catch her dropping meat or chocolates or whatever on the property. For that to work, we'll have to contrive to leave her alone for a while."

"We can videotape her," Brent suggested. "I'll take care of the details."

I nodded. "She won't be expecting a trap, so she'll dress like she usually does. Like a rainbow, not in black."

"Or how about this?" Kristie said. "Get her talking. Ask leading questions. If she gives herself away, we'll tape it."

"One of us can be hiding in the barn," I said. "Mac Dalby knows about my suspicions. All he needs to act on them is proof."

"I'll do it," Brent said. "I want to get my hands on that—uh—witch anyway."

I liked the way our plan was coming together. With Brent in command, Jacelyn wouldn't have a chance.

"I know how we can lure her here," I said. "I'll tell her that Sue saw my painting and wants one of her own collies. Jacelyn will make a preliminary trip to meet Sue's dogs and discuss backgrounds. She loves to talk about her art work."

"Wait!" Diane held up her hand. "She didn't drop any poisoned meat on the ground when she visited you."

"We'll take a chance that she makes up for lost time at Sue's place."

"Remember, I refuse to use my dogs as bait," Sue said.

"We won't let them out of our sight."

"We'll have to set a definite time then. Don't forget, I have my riding students."

"And we all want to be here," Ronda added.

"If Jacelyn sees a crowd, she'll be suspicious," I pointed out. "It'll just be Sue and the girls who'd be here anyway and Brent in hiding."

"And you, Jennet," Sue said. "We don't want to do this without you."

"It'll be natural for me to be here. I'm introducing Jacelyn to Sue."

Now all we had to do was work out the details. On the surface, it seemed low risk and likely to work as intended. It depended on Jacelyn taking advantage of a chance to spread her poison in an area where she had a legitimate reason to be. If she was careful, no one would connect her to a poisoned tidbit found later on the premises.

At least that was what I was counting on. Unknown to Jacelyn, we'd have her image on videotape, and this one would be clear.

One way or the other, we were going to throw the net over Jacelyn and put a stop to her lethal activities.

"Does anyone have anything to add?" I asked.

No one spoke.

"Then let's pick a date."

"Tomorrow," Sue said. "And if she can't make it?"

"Then let Jacelyn select the date and time, but it should be as soon as possible," I said.

~ * ~

I stood at the stove, stirring the stew, while Crane opened a bottle of Coke for himself and one for me. "Ingenious," he said. "If it works."

"What could go wrong?" I asked.

"Plenty. She won't bring her poison with her that day."

"I'll bet it's a fixture in her purse. She's not about to let an opportunity pass her by."

"Your crowd might scare her away."

I'd thought of that and discarded it. Diane and Kristie were Sue's hires. It'd be natural for them to be working around the place. Brent would wait in the barn for Jacelyn to make a false move. She'd never see him. Presumably Annica and Ronda would keep out of sight in another room. As for me, I was the one who brought Jacelyn to the horse farm.

I explained all this to Crane. "We plan to give her a chance to be alone outside the house, long enough to leave her poison in an unlikely place. She must be adept at doing this rapidly and stealthily."

"It might work," he conceded.

"And if it doesn't, we'll try again, using another lure, but we'll never have such a good excuse. It makes sense that Sue would see our painting and want one of her own collies."

"What if Jacelyn isn't the poisoner after all? A ring is a pretty flimsy clue."

"Every time there's been an incident, Jacelyn has been in the vicinity," I said.

"Except for the times no one has seen her. How do you explain her changing into a black outfit? I don't think there are any Superman phone booths at Everlasting Park."

Darn. I couldn't think of an answer for that. Brent's men had seen a woman in black and dark gray running from the park.

"Okay," I said. "That was another woman leaving for another reason. Jacelyn stayed behind until almost everybody else had left."

Crane's voice turned stern, his deputy sheriff's voice. "You realize what you're planning is entrapment."

"Yes, but what she's doing is abhorrent."

"If she's the one doing it."

I was tiring of this good cop-bad cop routine. "Don't you want us to succeed?"

"Of course," he said. "As long as none of you gets hurt and Jacelyn doesn't pull out a gun. I'm glad Fowler's a part of this scheme."

"Why?"

"I trust him to protect you."

"For heaven's sake," I said. "We can take care of ourselves, and there is nothing, absolutely nothing, that could possibly go wrong."

I truly believed that.

Fifty

All afternoon I rehearsed what I was going to say to Jacelyn to lure her into our trap. Then I had to leave a message on her voicemail. Shades of frustration. Was she out poisoning more collies or buying meat?

When she didn't return my call, I tried again later—and again, drinking tea to sooth my frazzled nerves. Finally, the next day, she answered her phone. At last!

"Good morning, Jacelyn," I said brightly. "I just wanted to tell you how much my husband and I are enjoying our collie painting."

"I'm so glad. As I told you, you gave me beautiful models."

"My friend, Sue Appleton, loves it too. She wanted to know if you would paint her collie family."

"Collies! I'll make time," she said.

"You may want to meet her and her dogs and arrange a time. Come to my house. I'll take you to her. She lives close by."

"Perfect," she said.

"Could you come today?"

"Not today. I have an appointment. Would tomorrow do?"

"It'll be fine."

So far so good.

We agreed on a time—eleven-thirty—and I ended the call with a hearty 'See you soon,' and pushed back my disappointment at the delay. I should be happy. So far Plan B was going our way. But I'd so wanted to end Jacelyn's demented game today.

If luck were with us, it would be over tomorrow. Every one of the Silverhedge Saviors would be in place with the exception of Annica, who had an early class, then a shift at Clovers.

How to fill the intervening hours?

Misty shoved her cold nose into my hand. Raven stood behind her, wagging her tail.

Walk?

That was one way.

~ * ~

The day of reckoning arrived in a swelter of heat. Heat advisory... High humidity...I filled a pitcher with water and ice cubes and poured fresh water for the dogs. By nine my energy began to dip. I was too nervous to do anything but pace. Naturally the dogs sensed my restiveness. I moved the painting from one place to another and let my thoughts wander.

Should I like the painting less because it was the work of a psychopath?

No. Would I refuse to read a poem because it had been penned by a libertine?

Still, every time I looked at the painting, I would remember this time and the constant fear that death lay in wait in the garden for one of my precious collies.

When I looked at the painting, what I should see was triumph. Justice would prevail. The Arsenic Hag would serve her time. For now, when I admired the beautiful collies so faithfully depicted in oils, all I would think was, "They're mine."

At ten we gathered at Sue's ranch. I intended to drive back home in plenty of time to greet Jacelyn and lead her to her doom.

Brent had brought one of his young employees, Andre, with him, and a supply of snacks and cold drinks, along with a fan, as the barn would be hot. He'd left his car behind the barn and out of sight. "If she makes a false move, we'll have her."

Thank heavens for surveillance video.

Diane, Kristie, and Ronda were inside. All agreed it was too hot for the girls to work with the dogs outside. They elected to practice obedience moves in the house.

I glanced at the clock. "I'd better get home. Girls, keep your eyes on the dogs every single minute."

Jacelyn would hardly take the risk of slipping a lethal morsel to a dog in the house, but I'd promised Sue that her dogs would be one hundred percent safe.

"Don't forget, Sue," I said. "Make this look like what we said it was going to be. Offer Jacelyn iced tea or a soft drink while you discuss business."

"I'd rather strangle her."

It was going to be hard for Sue to disguise her feelings.

"Think of what we're about to do as a play," I said. "We all have our parts. Jacelyn has to believe she has a new commission. Nothing more."

"For the first time, I hope she leaves a nice juicy tainted piece of meat behind," Sue said. "It'll be the last time she ever does it."

"I'll be back with her in half an hour."

If nothing went wrong. I wouldn't let anything go wrong.

Scarlet padded along at my side, her head pressed against my hand, as if to say, 'What can I do to help?'

She was just being a collie, but suddenly I felt like crying.

~ * ~

The woman is like a rainbow, I thought. *Only a rainbow is a lovely thing.*

Jacelyn's raspberry pink sundress was sleeveless and cut low to reveal the beginning of a sunburn. A necklace of large amber beads and gold chains lay heavily on her chest, and she wore a matching ring in an elaborate gold setting. But not the stretchy ring she'd lost before.

She carried the purse with the wide rainbow stripes, large enough to hold small bits of meat.

Not wanting to invite her inside the house, I met her in front. I reminded myself to take my own advice. I was bringing together an artist and a friend who wanted to commission a portrait of her dogs. Mindful of this, I launched a discussion of picture frames and my preference for dark, rich antique styles.

"The Green House of Antiques has a good selection," I said.

In truth it did, and I never passed up an opportunity to visit my favorite store.

"If the frame is too fancy, it'll detract from the collies," Jacelyn said. "You don't want that. Perhaps a thin, simple frame."

I turned right on Squill Lane. "My friend has seven collies and also horses."

But Jacelyn must know this. She'd know the exact location of Sue's ranch as she'd been there before. I imagined she also knew that Sue was the president of the Lakeville Collie Rescue League. Jacelyn knew how to find the people with the most collies.

I was playing my part and doing it well.

The ranch was quiet, baking in the sun. Silhouetted against a burning blue sky, the horses grazed quietly, watching our progress down the driveway. There wasn't a sign of a dog around the place. In fact, it looked deserted. But a lone figure sat on the porch staring at the road.

"There's Sue," I said.

I parked and we walked up to the house, Jacelyn's rainbow purse swinging on her hip.

It was unusual to see Sue with no collies gathered around her. Would she be likely to sit on the porch in the heat of the day?

Maybe.

Sue's smile was friendly. She had managed to bury her loathing for the poisoner deep inside. Poised, the gracious hostess in denim and gingham, she rose, hand extended to greet Jacelyn.

"Welcome to my horse farm," she said.

I introduced them and Sue said, "Let's get out of this killing heat."

"What lovely horses!" Jacelyn said. "Where are the dogs?"

"Inside with the air." Sue held open the door, and we stepped into the vestibule without running into an avalanche of fur. "They must be sleeping. My gallant watchdogs."

Diane and Kristie were inside with Bluebell and Scarlet on leashes. "We're putting them through their obedience paces," Diane said.

On one of the hottest day of the summer? How was that realistic?

Jacelyn didn't appear to notice anything off about the scene. I had my doubts. Suddenly it seemed staged. No one was acting the way they normally did.

Sue led us into her rarely used, formal living room.

"I would love to have a painting of all my collies," she said. "I have seven."

"Where are the others?" Jacelyn asked.

They had arrived, roused from their sleep and subdued. Good grief. Even the dogs weren't acting normally.

"What beauties!" Jacelyn said. "I feel like I'm at a dog show. Are you a breeder?"

"No," Sue said. "I rescue collies."

"Well. Someone has to do it."

"I'd like them painted outside," Sue said. "Either in front of the house or at the corral. Their favorite places," she added.

"It's up to you. If you can get them to stand or sit together, I'll take their picture."

She reached into the rainbow purse. I held my breath. But the dogs had shown no interest in its contents. I hoped that wasn't a bad sign.

"Then I'll immortalize them in oils," she said. "A dog's life is regrettably short, but your portrait will last forever."

Fifty-one

Now came the most important part of the plan—giving Jacelyn the privacy to leave her poison on Sue's property. She appeared to be in a good mood as we walked to my car. And why not? She had a satisfied customer, a new commission, and the friendship and trust of two collie owners in Foxglove Corners. Or so she thought.

I came to an abrupt halt about three yards from the Focus.

"Darn! I forgot something. Sue has a package for me."

Jacelyn switched her rainbow purse to her other shoulder.

"I have to go back to the house," I said. "Wait here. I'll just be a minute."

Her voice was almost a whine. "It's so hot. Can't you unlock the car and turn on the air conditioning?"

A reasonable request, but I pretended I didn't hear it. "I'll be right back."

I hurried to the house and rapped on the door. All according to plan.

Sue opened it immediately. "Did you forget something?" She'd remembered her line. In case Jacelyn was listening.

"The new kibble," I said, and stepped inside. If Jacelyn asked, I'd tell her that Sue had ordered it for me.

Diane peered out the front window. "She's taking something out of her purse."

"Don't let her see you," Sue said.

"A tissue. She's wiping her forehead. Now she's just standing there."

I imagined Brent in the barn, waiting for her to reach in her purse again and drop something to the ground. We were all waiting.

Kristie said, "She's not going to leave anything."

"I'll give her a bit longer." My heart began to race. A few moments had never seemed so long.

"She isn't doing anything," Diane said.

Sue handed me the bag of kibble. "You'd better go, Jennet. It didn't work."

I had to agree with her. Could Jacelyn have suspected a trap? I didn't see how.

"It was a good plan," Diane said. "Maybe we're wrong about her being the Arsenic Hag."

I'd never believe that. "We aren't. I don't know why she didn't take the bait. We'll try something else."

Sue moved away from the window and addressed the girls and Ronda, who had ventured out of a back bedroom. "As soon as they leave, we're going to look over every blade of grass she walked on. She might have dropped a piece of meat when you weren't looking."

I didn't think she had, but let them look. Jacelyn had thrown her tissue to the ground, leaving her trash for someone else to pick up. She was a litterer as well as a poisoner.

~ * ~

Jacelyn was quiet on the short drive back to her car. All she said was, "That went well. Thank you for telling your friend about my work."

"You're welcome," I said. "I'll be looking forward to seeing the painting"

I didn't have the heart to make small talk. At the same time, I couldn't afford to let Jacelyn sense my frustration because we were going to try again. I made a few inane comments about summer heat.

Ordinarily, if Jacelyn had been anyone other than the Arsenic Hag, I would have invited her in for a glass of lemonade.

As it was, I couldn't wait for her to go home.

Once I pulled into my driveway, she didn't linger. Ignoring the barking dogs in the bay window, she said, "I'll be on my way then."

I was still out with the collies when Brent parked his vintage Plymouth in the space vacated by Jacelyn.

"I have excellent footage of you and the lady walking to Sue's house and back," he said as he made his way through the excited dogs. "It was a good idea, but she didn't fall for it."

We all trooped inside. Misty looked confused when she didn't see a bag from Pluto's in Brent's hand, even more so when he sat at the kitchen table instead of going on to the living room.

He petted her absently as I poured him a glass of lemonade.

"We have to come up with another plan," I said. "Crane didn't think much of this one."

"Looks like we're back to waiting for her to strike again."

I slammed my fist down on the table. "No. If we did that, we'd be putting other collies at risk."

"Are you sure you're right about her?" he asked.

"Yes, and not just because of the ring. It's everything I know about her. I've been putting it together."

Every odd thing she'd ever said or done. Her interest in knowing why Minta wasn't showing Sparkle, for instance. Her presence every time a collie met with misfortune. Her habit of wearing bright clothing and flashy rings. So no one would link her with a figure in black?

"I don't understand what she has against collies," Brent said.

"Who knows? She has a collie herself, Valentine. She brought her to a show..."

I stopped. I didn't like what I was thinking. "How do I know Valentine was even her dog?"

"You don't. Maybe she was using it as a cover."

All the unknown aspects of the Jacelyn Connection rose up to taunt me. In the end, I had to admit that my certainty of her guilt was built on a shaky foundation. Nothing more substantial than a strong feeling.

"This mystery is defeating me," I said. "My foolproof plan didn't work, and I can't think of another way to trap her."

I paused to think, and my gaze fell on the counter and the lone piece of orange chiffon cake safe in its stand. "I hope she didn't realize what we were doing," I said.

Because if she had, she'd be alerted. Forewarned is forearmed. That was *my* motto. It was unacceptable that my enemy shared it.

"You'll think of something," Brent said. "I'm going to take off. What's for dinner tonight?"

"Steak and baked potatoes. I could bake a pie, I guess. I need something to take my mind off my failure."

"Don't say that. It's just a little setback. We'll get her next time."

"We have to."

"See you later," he said. "By the way, if you bake a pie, could you make it lemon meringue?"

~ * ~

The day or, more likely the heat, stole my ambition. My one achievement was the lemon meringue pie in the cake stand. I'd eaten the last slice of cake, hoping it would restore my energy and optimism. The collies were lethargic, most of them asleep.

Except for Misty and Raven, who kept me company on the porch as I tried to read a Gothic novel that should have been a page turner. They both sprang to life when Minta's car came up the driveway.

Company again. The house was becoming Grand Central Station. She swung out onto the grass, crisp and sprightly. Raven and Misty dashed down to escort her onto the porch.

I closed my book, leaving heroine Annabel wandering perilously close to quicksand, and prepared myself for yet another problem.

"Hi, Jennet," she said. "I came to visit with your collies. I miss my Sparkle so much."

In the house she sought Sky, who was about to retreat to her safe place under the dining room table.

"My precious blue," she murmured. To Sky she posed a question: "Who's the fairest of them all?"

Sky stared blankly back at her as Misty made a bid for attention. Surprisingly, Sky followed Minta to the sofa and lay at her feet.

"Did you have any word about Sparkle yet?" I asked.

"None. That ransom note was a fake. Somebody wants to torment me."

She leaned forward and stroked Sky. "Why do some people do that?"

"It gives them pleasure, I suppose. How's your separation from Gavin going?"

"Not well," she said.

"Is he bothering you?"

"In a way. He sends me flowers every day, and every day I throw them out."

"He wants you back," I said.

"That isn't going to happen. I still think he has Sparkle. He's deliberately keeping her from me."

"Well..."

An idea came to me, perhaps an unlikely one, but I had to voice it. "I think if Gavin had taken Sparkle, he'd have made his move by now. Whatever that is."

"It's been too long," Minta said. "I think...I'm afraid...Do you think he killed her?"

That beautiful blue merle. The thought of that sparkle winking out made me ill. How could anyone kill a collie?

How, indeed? Case in point, the Arsenic Hag.

"Maybe he dumped her out in the country," Minta said. "Or he put her somewhere in a garage or barn and left her there to starve." Her voice trailed off. "Sparkle loved to eat."

How easily Minta slipped into morbidity. In her position, I'd do the same. She needed to be around people who cared and, yes, around collies.

"Stay for dinner," I said. "Brent's coming over. Maybe together we can come up with some new ideas."

Fifty-two

I glanced out the kitchen window into an unrelenting wall of white.

Fog had moved in during the night. It lay heavily on the earth, wrapping the yellow Victorian across the lane in floating white strands. At least I assumed the house was still there. I couldn't see it.

Crane had left for his shift, well-fortified by the hearty bacon-and-eggs breakfast I'd cooked for him. But what would his day be like? Uneventful, I hoped. Safe.

Reckless country drivers often failed to slow down in poor weather conditions, assuming they had the road to themselves. They ended up colliding with wandering wildlife or, worse, with other vehicles. Fog could be magical, turning the world into an eerie fairyland and providing atmosphere for poems and Gothic novels. In real life it was a menace. Even deadly.

A dense fog advisory is in effect for all of Lapeer County until nine o'clock...

I turned the radio off. Looking at a fog-enshrouded landscape never failed to set my nerves on edge. It was all too easy to imagine that I was alone in a silent, white world, cut off from the other inhabitants of Foxglove Corners, my seven collies and me. In other words, on a morning like this, it was easy to let my imagination take me to dangerous places.

Misty padded into the kitchen, carrying her white goat in her mouth. She dropped it at my feet and stood watching me, seemingly fascinated by the dishtowel I was folding.

"Do you want to play?" I asked.

Returning the towel to the oven handle, I tossed the goat into the dining room, expecting her to scamper after it.

She sat and whimpered. The goat had landed under the dining room table, Sky's territory. Apparently content to leave it there, Misty whined—and went on whining. Curious to see what bothered her, Candy peered into the kitchen. Then Star joined us.

"You want out," I said.

The dogs had been outside once, and it had been a harrowing experience for me as I'd tried in vain to keep track of them. They'd dashed out the door and promptly melted into the fog. On the way in, I counted noses.

I might as well take them out. The fog wouldn't burn off for a couple of hours, and they'd all need a bathroom break before then. Afterward, I'd give the downstairs a perfunctory cleaning, as good a way as any to wile away a foggy morning.

Calling them together, I opened the door. "Beware of the fog monster," I told them. "Hurry!"

And I stepped after them into a world gone white. Immediately the unease came back as I watched my babies disappeared into the fog. I should have taken them out, one by one, on leashes.

Nonsense. They never wandered far from the house, not even Raven, who had once lived outside. It was just that I couldn't see them. I liked to be able to know what was in front of me.

I gave them five minutes, which should be ample time to take care of any business. Then, "Inside, girls," I said.

Misty fell behind, but I grabbed her collar and gave her a shove into the kitchen. Her sharp yip held a hint of anger. How unlike her. But *I* was the mistress here.

A noise broke through the silence.

Something had landed on the walkway with a muted but discernable plop.

A downed bird? A broken branch weakened by the fog's heavy hand? A stone? What would fly through the air like a missile?

If only I could see.

Inside, one of the dogs howled. Misty?

I took a few steps forward into the tiny bit of visibility and saw a splatter of gushy red glistening on the pale stones. Meat! Loosely formed, coming apart as though it had been hastily formed into meatballs without a thickening agent to hold them together.

The howl turned to a screech. Trapped inside, the collies began to bark.

The meat hadn't fallen from the sky, and I hadn't heard the hum of an engine which meant...She had come on foot and couldn't have gone far. I could catch her. The Arsenic Hag. Jacelyn.

I pushed on the door to make sure it was securely closed, my collies safe. Now...

Which way? Up or down the lane? I couldn't waste time trying to decide. The wrong choice, and I'd be moving away from her.

Left, I decided. Up the lane. Where there were no houses.

As I half-jogged, I kept my eyes fixed on the ground. Jonquil Lane had several uneven areas which were easy to see in daylight. But in fog?

Don't break a leg!

An intense silence had come with the fog. It was unnatural. Where were the birds? The tiny woodland creatures scampering across the forest floor? Snapping twigs?

Worse, how could the Arsenic Hag run without making a sound? And why wouldn't she have driven?

Where was she going?

I could make out the abandoned construction, its edge littered with branches and building parts blown down from the unfinished mansion closest to the lane.

Could she have taken refuge in this savage place? At least one house was more or less intact. But nothing would lure me into its dark depths, even if the fog suddenly gave way to brilliant sunshine.

I ran on. The Squill Lane road sign rose out of the fog. Would she head for Sue's horse ranch to unload more of her poisoned meatballs? Let her. Sue and her collie pack would help me subdue her.

The other way, something told me, and I listened. It was as strong a premonition as I'd ever had. *The cottage at Lane's End.* I turned left.

Squill Lane dead ended at a cornfield and a charming yellow cottage that was vacant more often than not. Its owner kept it as a kind of memorial. The last time I'd visited the little house...

Don't think about that.

It had been traumatic. But I remembered the gaudy scarecrow that watched over the field. Collies hated it. So did crows.

My legs grew tired, and sharp pains knifed through my thighs, but I couldn't stop. Not until I confronted her.

'I saw what you just did,' I'd say. 'It's over, Jacelyn.'

Saw what you just did. Saw what you just did. Saw what you did.

The phrase echoed as I ran, like a tune that lodges itself in your mind and refuses to end.

I should be getting close to Lane's End and the cottage.

A dog's bark punctured the silence. For a moment, I thought one of my collies, probably Misty, had followed me, run ahead of me, but no. They were all back at the house. Safe.

The small yellow house materialized in the moving fog, and there was the scarecrow. The barking originated inside. A pinprick of light told me I had trapped the Arsenic Hag in her den.

What now?

I should have brought my gun. In case she was armed. But I hadn't thought beyond catching up to her, confronting her.

No. No gun. She might be armed.

I needed time to plan what I would do and say. Time was a luxury I didn't have.

Knock on the door.

A hand landed on my arm. She'd come up behind me. I turned to face her.

Wait! Don't accuse her. Yet.

"I was just in the neighborhood," I said.

She wore black jeans and a tight black top. Nestled in the V of her neck was a pendant on a silver chain.

Wait for what?

"I saw what you did," I said. "Back there at my house. With the meatballs."

"That?" She smiled. "Oh, I was leaving food for the birds."

"Meat?"

"They have bread crumbs in them."

"In my yard?"

"I leave food all over. Birds are everywhere, you know."

The dog in the cottage kept barking. It was a frantic sound, as frantic as the scratching of nails on the door.

"Is that Valentine?" I asked.

"Valentine?"

"Your collie?"

"Won't you come in?" she asked.

Walk into my parlor... I'd heard that line before.

Well, why not? That was the reason I'd followed her.

"We'll have coffee, and you can see Sue's painting," she said. "It's finished."

She pulled open the door and said, "Back!" in a sharp, unfriendly tone to the barker who seemed about to spring out onto the porch.

I had a quick glimpse of a blue merle collie whose eyes held not even a trace of a collie's merriment and sparkle.

She wasn't Valentine.

Fifty-three

"Sparkle?" I said.

The collie laid her ears flat against her the sides of her head. She knew me.

Jacelyn closed the door. "Her name is Blueberry Muffin. Muffin for short."

"You stole Minta's collie. You had her all along."

Sparkle continued to scratch at the door. Jacelyn ordered her to stop, and Sparkle lay down, her face turned away from us.

I looked quickly around the living room. I hadn't been in the cottage at Lane's End for years. After it burned, the owner had furnished it minimally, but it didn't looked lived in. Nothing personal hung on the walls or sat on an end table. Nothing of Jacelyn was here. No neon green or glaring orange.

It must be my imagination, but I thought a smell of smoke still lingered in the air.

One end of the room whose wall boasted the largest window and drew the best light served as a studio. Oil paints, brushes and other artists' supplies vied for space on a card table, and canvases leaned on the wall. A tall easel held another canvas covered with a white cloth.

"You don't understand, Jennet," Jacelyn said. "I'm not a thief."

"You're a thief and a loathsome poisoner of dogs. Why did you do it? You're right. I don't understand."

"I never poisoned any dogs," she said.

"No, you just left poisoned meat where they'd find it."

Her expression changed subtly; her stance grew rigid.

"You don't have any proof," she said. "That's slander."

"We do," I said. "We have you on videotape."

Why had I said this?

She took a step toward me.

"That is, I don't have it, but a friend of mine does," I said. "The police know all about you. Lieutenant Dalby is a dog lover. Tell me, what do you have against collies?"

"It's a long story," she said. "All I can say is that collies ruined my life. Let's forget all this unpleasantness and have that cup of coffee."

As she slipped into the kitchen, Sparkle rose and stretched, pointing her nose toward the door.

I felt as if I were drifting in space, my objective moving constantly away from me. One minute it seemed as if I were confronting a criminal. The next my antagonist was a woman who couldn't comprehend the gravity of the charge I'd levied against her. Or appeared not to.

She was a good actress. Or delusional.

I wondered how long she had been living and working in the cottage, a stone's throw from Sue's horse farm and my own house. No wonder we were her favorite targets.

I wished I'd brought my gun.

"Did you buy the Lane's End cottage?" I asked.

"I'm renting it for the summer. It's a nice place to paint, nice and quiet. All that country atmosphere, you know. I don't have anything to go with the coffee. Sorry."

Of course I didn't intend to drink anything Jacelyn served me. Not even water.

She returned to the living room and offered me a seat.

"I'll stand," I said. "How could you do this to Minta? She's devastated by the loss of Sparkle."

"She'll get over it. Everybody loses dogs."

Sparkle moved closer to me, keeping well away from Jacelyn. So many questions remained, and this might be my only opportunity to ask them.

The warning messages, for example. Jacelyn must have written them. But why? More important, how could she know the amount of money Nessa Whitman had left for Sparkle's care? Did she plan to return Sparkle to Minta once she had the ransom?

Unlikely. It was never about money.

"Why did you want to hurt her?" I asked. "Because that's what you're doing. Through her dog."

Jacelyn shrugged. "Because Minta has everything. Why should she be happy and not me?"

"Minta isn't happy."

"She should be. She has Jeff, a career, a future. She has youth, beauty..."

Minta had Jeff? Where had Jacelyn gotten that idea? And why was I still here, hoping to draw rational answers from a lunatic? She didn't appear to be violent; she hadn't threatened me She'd just flung my accusation back in my face.

In a way, she was right. I didn't have any proof to give Mac, and without it, his hands were tied. Jacelyn was virtually unrecognizable on the videotape, reduced to a fleeting figure in black. She would babble on about feeding meatballs made with breadcrumbs to the birds, and people would write her off as delusional. Not guilty by reason of insanity. To my knowledge she hadn't killed a dog. Only tried to; only made two of them sick.

Let Karma have her.

"One more question," I said. "Where's Valentine?"

"Oh, she died."

"You can't continue to scatter your so-called bird food around the countryside," I said. "Lieutenant Dalby knows what you're really up to. He'll be watching you."

Maybe. *I* certainly would be.

"Okay," she said. "I won't."

She brought the coffee into the living room and set it on a dusty side table. One cup, laced with only heaven knows what. "Come see the painting," she said. "It's finished."

She swept the cloth aside, revealing Sue's seven collies lying alongside the corral. In the background, a horse's head made a shapely dark splash against an impossibly blue sky. The collies lay on their side, their coats dull and lifeless, their eyes staring at a world they could no longer see.

"All the pretty little collies," Jacelyn said.

"You monster!"

I felt sick, was certain I was going to throw up.

What a fool I was for taunting her. I had to get away.

"You haven't touched your coffee," she said.

Inspiration struck. "I can't drink it black. Do you have cream or even milk?"

"Mmm. Should have."

As soon as she stepped out of the room, I rushed to the door, keeping my rising nausea and panic in check. Inasmuch as I could.

When I opened the door, Sparkle streaked past me into the fog, into freedom.

I couldn't lose her now!

I called her, and she bounded back to me, a spring in her step, the sparkle back in her eyes. The fog, still heavy, had a welcome freshness about it. I was sure Sparkle felt it too.

She stayed by my side all the way to Jonquil Lane. All the way home.

~ * ~

While Sparkle reacquainted herself with my brood, I gathered the meatballs in a trash bag, never doubting that Jacelyn had poisoned them. The first person I called was Minta.

"I have Sparkle," I said. "She's fine. Come and get her anytime."

"But where...? Jeff had her, didn't he?"

"No, but it was someone you know. Jacelyn Holloway We'll talk when I see you."

"Jacelyn from the shows? I'll be right there. I'm leaving now."

Mac was out of the office. I left him a brief message and pressed Sue's number.

It took Sue a few minutes to absorb the gist of what I was telling her.

"All this time," she said. "That creature was practically my neighbor. I don't want her living so close to me."

"I don't know what we can do. She must have signed a lease."

I tried to remember what I knew about the cottage's owner. He lived out of state and rented the place when he could find a tenant. Somebody must know his name.

"Can't the owner evict her?" Sue asked.

"On what grounds? She'd deny everything. Claim we were harassing her. She's crazy, but crazy people can be cunning."

"I don't want to see her painting," Sue said.

I'd tried to erase it from my mind, that horrible depiction of Sue's beloved collies lying dead. It didn't work. I thought I would see it to my dying day. I wasn't going to describe it to Sue. Ever.

"We can't leave it like this, Jennet," she said.

"We have to—for now. She didn't exactly confess, but she doesn't have to. I know the truth. She'll say she was just feeding the birds. People will think she's either stupid or insane. But neither one is a crime. Maybe Mac will detain her."

"I'm going to talk to her. I want to hear this story about how collies ruined her life."

"Don't go alone," I said quickly. "I'll go with you, and I'll bet Brent will want to come with us."

"Can we do it now?"

I was suddenly aware of the enormity of what I'd done. Of what might have happened. "Let's wait. I want to talk to Crane."

"Call Brent," Sue said. "First thing tomorrow we'll be on her doorstep."

~ * ~

Crane gave me my traditional home-from-work kiss. I made it last a little longer than usual, loath to let him go until Candy moved her body between us.

"How was your day?" I asked.

"Once the fog burned off, okay. Nothing unusual. What did you do today?"

"I found the Arsenic Hag and intimidated her, I hope, then I got Sparkle back for Minta."

Clearly he hadn't expected that. "I thought I saw an extra collie at the door."

He locked his gun in its special cabinet, which was a signal that our evening had begun. Instead of going upstairs to shower, he opened two bottles of ginger ale and handed one to me.

"Best of all, I lived to tell the tale," I said.

"I see."

"And I wasn't in a bit of danger."

"Sit down and tell me all about it."

I told my story again with every detail, starting with the meat that came flying out of the fog.

When I was finished, he said, "You didn't figure you were in danger confronting a crazy woman?"

"I didn't have time to think about it."

I concluded my story with a sight that still burned in my memory: Sue's beautiful collies lying dead at the corral, immortalized in oils.

"She's still in the cottage," I said. "Sue is freaked out. What can we do about it?"

"Mac can take Jacelyn in as a person of interest in the poisonings. She's obviously unbalanced. There's bound to be something."

"I'll admit this only to you. I'm afraid of her, still afraid for our dogs."

They'd dispersed throughout the house. Only Candy remained in the kitchen where I was cooking ground beef for chili.

"Our dogs," Crane said. "I'm going to give them so much extra attention they won't know what hit them."

"I've been hugging them all day."

"And I'm going to do the same to my wife."

I liked the sound of that. "All's well that ends well then."

Still, it wasn't quite ended. As long as Jacelyn lived in the cottage at Lane's End.

Fifty-four

I finally had a chance to talk to Mac on the phone. He promised to investigate the matter. I hoped he'd place Jacelyn Holloway high on his priority list.

In the morning, Brent picked me up in his vintage Plymouth, then we stopped for Sue and drove to Squill Lane. Brent's rage threatened to boil over as I repeated key parts of my conversation with Jacelyn.

"I won't let her get away with it," he vowed. "There's no hiding behind a 'crazy' screen."

"Your vigilante justice isn't an option," Sue pointed out. "We don't want to lose you, Brent."

"Then Mac had better do his job."

"Mac will do what he can," I said.

All the way to Sue's horse ranch, I had been thinking about that horrible painting I didn't want Sue to see. I hoped Jacelyn had replaced the cover, hoped she wouldn't present it to Sue and expect payment.

She wouldn't dare? Would she?

The day was warm and bright, but a darkness pressed on the cottage. Jacelyn's white car was gone, which caused my heart to skip a beat. Was she out roaming the roads and by-roads of Foxglove

Corners, tossing meatballs to the unwary? Had Mac interrogated her yet?

The scarecrow in the cornfield seemed to beckon to us. It didn't look particularly scary in plaid and denim with a straw hat decked in daisies, but it seemed to have moved a bit closer to the cottage.

Sue peered in the front window. "It doesn't look like she's home."

"Let's knock on the door anyway," I said.

Brent pounded on the door while I looked again at the scarecrow. No, it was where it'd always been, broomstick arms held out as if in supplication.

"Open up," Brent shouted. "We know you're in there."

On an impulse, I turned the doorknob. To my surprise the door opened. The cottage was empty. It had a look of abandonment about it. The folded card table leaned against the wall, the paints and brushes were gone. Most significant, I didn't see the easel that supported Jacelyn's demented picture.

Now Sue would never have to see it.

"Devil take it," Brent said. "She got away."

"I want to check on something," I said.

In the kitchen, I opened the refrigerator door and recoiled at the sight that greeted me—and the smell. The shelves were crammed with meat. Steaks and chops still in plastic wrap, opened packages of ground beef and turkey, an aluminum bowl filled with loose meat of some kind. Mystery meat. The 'Sell by' dates were long past, and the odor that drifted into the air was vile.

The freezer compartment was likewise filled. She had left all of this expensive food to rot.

Sue came up behind me. "Does this mean she gave up her wicked ways?"

"It means she couldn't take it all with her."

Brent's voice boomed out from the back of the cottage. "She's not here." He joined us, frowning as he examined the crowded shelves. "Where did she keep the poison?"

"She must have taken it with her," I said. "It wouldn't take up much room."

Jacelyn could have vacated the cottage as early as yesterday, as soon as I'd left with Sparkle.

"Who's going to ditch all this meat?" Brent asked.

"Not us. We shouldn't even be here."

Sue opened one of the cupboards. "It's empty. She didn't have any kitchen staples or food. Just this." She took out a jar of instant coffee.

"Let's get out of here," Brent said.

Sue closed the cupboard door. "I wanted her gone, but I wish I knew where she went."

"Just so she stays the hell out of Foxglove Corners," Brent said.

I didn't think she'd return. She'd go on to some other place, to make a fresh start. I imagined her putting on one of her rainbow bright dresses and going out to find new victims.

God help them.

~ * ~

The next day, at the end of her shift, Annica and I sat together at Clovers, drinking lime coolers. The menace of the Arsenic Hag had ended with her unceremonious departure from Foxglove Corners. Minta and Sparkle were reunited. We were looking forward to the premier of Lucy's movie, *Devilwish*, and the elaborate celebration Brent was hosting at the Hunt Club Inn.

"The last piece of the Jacelyn puzzle may have fallen into place," I said. "The reason she targeted collies."

Annica set her drink down and pushed back a flyaway curl. Her earrings tinkled faintly. They were tiny silver fairies or angels. It was hard to tell.

"Why?"

"Minta and Jeff had a long talk. He told her that Jacelyn was married to a man who bred collies. He had a successful kennel in the south, but Jacelyn wasn't happy with him. She thought he loved the dogs more than he loved her. He spent more time with them and showered them with affection.

"Did she leave him?" Annica asked.

"Jeff said he left her. He died."

Annica's lit up. "He died or she poisoned him?"

"I'm sure she didn't confide in Jeff to that extent," I said.

"It makes you wonder, though, doesn't it?"

"She *did* say that collies ruined her life."

"I'm just glad she moved out of town. Now, if only you could solve *my* mystery."

I'd thought we had. We had identified the ghost in the wildflower field and said a prayer for her soul to pass on to the other side. That, Lucy had assured us, was the best we could do for Gail Redmond.

It wasn't enough.

"There's the basket that vanished," she said. "The flowers that died before their time. The fact that I can't stop thinking about Gail and wondering if she's still there, gathering flowers. I took her basket," she added. "Or maybe Angel chewed it. We'll never know."

"Why don't we drive out to the field now and say another prayer for her?" I said.

"And light a candle?

"Heavens no. Do you want to start a forest fire?"

She brightened considerably. "Do you have time?"

I was taking dinner home, Clovers' pork chops and homemade apple sauce, and best of all, a strawberry pie. We hadn't yet commemorated the end of Jacelyn Holloway's reign of terror. We'd do it tonight.

"There's no time like the present," I said.

We finished our drinks and drove to the wildflower field. Sagramore Beach was crowded with sun worshippers, but Huron Court was, as usual, quiet and atmospheric—and ominous. But we reached the wildflower field without incident and stood in the sun, watching the colorful floral display wave in the wind.

There couldn't possibly be a quieter, more peaceful place in Foxglove Corners.

"I'd like to have a bouquet of bachelor buttons," Annica said, "and some of those purple daisies, or whatever they are."

"Go ahead. There was nothing wrong with the last flowers you picked."

"I'd better leave well enough alone."

If we were hoping for some sign that Gail Redmond was at rest—I know I was—it didn't come. But the tranquility of the place reached out to me, placed a reassuring hand on my heart.

The spirits of Huron Court were at peace, the current haunting had reached its end, and the future looked promising. For Annica, for Crane and me, for Minta, for us all. And it was time I went home and walked the dogs.

I glanced at my wrist and saw that I'd worn the weird watch from the field, the one whose hands ran backward. It wasn't going to give me the right time.

I looked again. The hands had stopped.

Meet Dorothy Bodoin

Dorothy Bodoin lives in Royal Oak, Michigan, with her blue merle collie, Layla. Dorothy worked as a secretary for Chrysler Missile Corporation for six years, two of which were spent in Italy. On returning to the states, she attended Oakland University, earning Bachelor's and Master's degrees in English literature. For several years she taught English in a Michigan high school before leaving education to write full-time. She is the author of the Foxglove Corners Cozy Mystery series, six novels of romantic suspense, and one Gothic romance.

Other Works From The Pen Of
Dorothy Bodoin

Treasure at Trail's End (Gothic romance) - The House at Trail's End seemed to beckon to Mara Marsden, promising the happy future she longed for. But could she discover its secret without forfeiting her life?

Ghost across the Water (romantic suspense) - Water falling from an invisible force and a ghostly man who appears across Spearmint Lake draw Joanna Larne into a haunting twenty-year-old mystery.

Darkness at Foxglove Corners - Foxglove Corners offers tornado survivor Jennet Greenway country peace and romance, but the secret of the yellow Victorian house across the lane holds a threat to her new life. (#1)

Winter's Tale - On her first winter in Foxglove Corners Jennet Greenway battles dognappers, investigates the murder of the town's beloved veterinarian, and tries to outwit a dangerous enemy. (#3)

A Shortcut through the Shadows - Jennet Greenway's search for the missing owner of her rescue collie, Winter, sets her on a collision course with an unknown killer. (#4)

Cry for the Fox - In Foxglove Corners, the fox runs from the hunters, the animal activists target the Hunt Club, and a killer stalks human prey on the fox trail. (#2)

The Witches of Foxglove Corners - With a haunting in the library, a demented prankster who invades her home, and a murder in Foxglove Corners, Halloween turns deadly for Jennet Greenway. (#5)

The Snow Dogs of Lost Lake - A ghostly white collie and a lost locket lead Jennet Greenway to a body in the woods and a dangerous new mystery. (#6)

The Collie Connection - As Jennet Greenway's wedding to Crane Ferguson approaches, her happiness is shattered when a Good Samaritan deed leaves her without her beloved black collie, Halley, and ultimately in grave danger. (#7)

A Time of Storms - When a stranger threatens her collie and she hears a cry for help in a vacant house, Jennet Ferguson suspects that her first summer as a wife may be tumultuous. (#8)

The Dog from the Sky - Jennet's life takes a dangerous turn when she rescues an abused collie. Soon afterward, a girl vanishes without a trace. Ironically she had also rescued an abused collie. Is there a connection between the two incidents? (#9)

Spirit of the Season - Mystery mixes with holiday cheer as a phantom ice skater returns to the lake where she died, and a collie is accused of plotting her owner's fatal accident. (#10)

Another Part of the Forest - Danger rides the air when a kidnapper whisks his victims away in a hot air balloon, and a false friend puts a curses on a collie breeder's first litter. (#11)

Where Have All the Dogs Gone? - An animal activist frees the shelter dogs in and around Foxglove Corners to save them from being destroyed. Running wild in the countryside, they face an equally distressing fate and post a risk to those who come in contact with them. (#12)

The Secret Room of Eidt House - A rabid dog that should have died months ago from the dread disease runs free in the woods of Foxglove Corners, and the library's long-kept secret unleashes a series of other strange events. (#13)

Follow a Shadow - A shadowy intruder haunts Jennet's woods by night, and a woman who can't accept the death of her collie asks Jennet to help her find Rainbow Bridge where she believes her dog waits for her. (#14)

The Snow Queen's Collie - A white collie puppy appears on the porch of the Ferguson farmhouse during a Christmas Eve snowstorm. In another part of Foxglove Corners a collie breeder's show prospect disappears. Meanwhile, the painting Jennet's sister gave her for Christmas begins to exhibit strange qualities. (#15)

The Door in the Fog - A wounded dog disappears in the fog. A blue door on the side of a barn vanishes. Strange wildflowers and a sound of weeping haunt a meadow. The woods keep their secret, and a curse refuses to die. (#16)

Dreams and Bones - At Brent Fowler's newly purchased Spirit Lamp Inn, a renovation turns up human bones buried in the inn's backyard, rekindling interest in the case of a young woman who disappeared from the inn several decades ago. As Jennet tries to solve this mystery, she doesn't realize it may be her last. (#17)

A Ghost of Gunfire - Months after gunfire erupted in her classroom at Marston High School, leaving one student dead and one seriously wounded, Jennet begins to hear a sound of gunshots inaudible to anyone else. Meanwhile, she resolves to find the demented person who is tying dogs to trees and leaving them to die. (#18)

The Silver Sleigh - Rosalyn Everett was missing and presumed dead. Her collies had been rescued, and her house was abandoned. But a blue merle collie haunts her woods and a figure in bridal white traverses the property. (#19)

The Stone Collie - Jennet's discovery of a collie puppy chained in the yard of a vacant house sets her on a search for a man whose activities may threaten Foxglove Corners' security. Meanwhile, horror story novelist Lucy Hazen is mystified when scenes from her work-in-progress are duplicated in real life. (#20)

The Mists of Huron Court - The house was beautiful, a vintage pink Victorian in a picturesque but lonely country setting, and the girl playing ball with her dog in the yard was friendly, suggesting that she and Jennet walk their dogs together some time. Jennet thinks she has made a new friend until she returns to the house and finds a tumbling down ruin where the Victorian once stood and no sign that the girl and dog have ever been there. ((#21)

Down a Dark Path - What hold does the pink Victorian on Huron Court have on Brent Fowler who is determined to re-create the home of long-dead Violet Randall? When he disappears, could he have been cast adrift in time? (#22)

Shadow of the Ghost Dog - An invisible dog grieves inside the house chosen as a setting for a movie based on Lucy Hazen's book, *Devilwish,* and a landscaper unearths a human skeleton in the backyard while planting shrubs. (#23)

The Dark Beyond the Bridge - The discovery of a secret ghost town in a densely rural area of Michigan's lower peninsula leads to mystery and danger for Jennet Ferguson and her friends. (#24)

The Deadly Fields of Autumn - An antique television set that airs an obscure Western at random times, and a woman who disappears with her newly adopted rescue collie draw Jennet into a puzzling mystery. (#25)

The Lost Collies of Silverhedge - Jennet Ferguson vows to find eight prize show collies who disappeared from their kennel after the suspicious death of their breeder, Madselin Rivard. (#26)

Letter to Our Readers

Enjoy this book?

You can make a difference

As an independent publisher, Wings ePress, Inc. does not have the financial clout of the large New York Publishers. We can't afford large magazine spreads or subway posters to tell people about our quality books.

But, we do have something much more effective and powerful than ads. We have a large base of loyal readers.

Honest Reviews help bring the attention of new readers to our books.

If you enjoyed this book, we would appreciate it if you would spend a few minutes posting a review on the site where you purchased this book or on the Wings ePress, Inc. webpages at: https://wingsepress.com/